COPPER MAGIC

COPPER MAGIC

JULIA MARY GIBSON

STARSCAPE

A TOM DOHERTY ASSOCIATES BOOK
NEW YORK

COPPER MAGIC

Copyright © 2014 by Julia Mary Gibson

Map by Jennifer Hanover

A Starscape Book
Published by Tom Doherty Associates, LLC
175 Fifth Avenue
New York, NY 10010

www.tor-forge.com

The Library of Congress Cataloging-in-Publication Data
is available upon request.

ISBN 978-0-7653-3211-0 (hardcover)
ISBN 978-1-4299-5593-5 (e-book)

Starscape books may be purchased for educational, business, or promotional use. For information on bulk purchases, please contact Macmillan Corporate and Premium Sales Department at 1-800-221-7945, extension 5442, or write specialmarkets@macmillan.com.

First Edition: July 2014

0 9 8 7 6 5 4 3 2 1

for

JOSEPHINE MANDAMIN,
who walks the walk

PIGEON HARBOR

1. Depot
2. Peterssen's Store
3. Jail
4. Butcher
5. Hat Lady
6. Mill
7. Church

WOODS

DUNES

BIG LAKE

Big Tent

Town Road

Front Street

Hotel

Gypsies

7.

BLUE LAKE

Preacher
Camp

Ratroot

SWAMP

Deer
Path

Treehouse

Cherry
Trees

Blake
Farm

7.

7.

5.

6.

River Road

Mrs.
Agosa

RIVER

BAY

COPPER MAGIC

1
RAGS

There wasn't one soul who knew how I made up things. I did it just for the doing of it too not just lying when you're cornered like anybody will. I used to ponder over my lies and polish them up. It was hard work and I'm not sorry. When it came to the Hand, the lies were the saving grace, and good thing I'd had practice.

I found the Hand the third hot summer day. The spring had hung on too long, but when it left, it was gone for good. The first warm day made my wool dress itch me. That night I went into the wardrobe in my room and took out the dresses from the summer before. Only two of them would let me move my arms when they were buttoned up, and only one had any kind of hem to let out. When I ripped the hem to give it some length, I did it too fast and made a tear where the stitching was.

It was my mother's fault. If she'd been there, she'd have spent the spring fixing up the ones that could be fixed, and making me new ones of goods we chose together. She always asked what I thought, and didn't make me wear anything I considered to be ugly, and didn't tell me it wasn't when it was.

"You're growing too fast," she'd told me at the depot. "When I get back, you'll be as tall as I am." She held me hard against her. Then they had to board, and my little brother's eyes were big and scared. The train was loud, and he'd never been on one. Nor had I, but nobody invited me.

The champion of the liars, is what I thought of her. She wasn't coming back and never had intended to, and she could have left me with something to wear if she cared anything about me. But certainly she didn't, and that was how it was.

The next day was hotter than ever. The skirt of the hastily unhemmed dress caught on a nail when I was helping my father patch the roof. The long uneven rent would have come out a lumpy travesty if I'd tried to fix it. A blotch of tar punctuated the devastation. My father didn't notice, and wouldn't have cared if he had. My mother would have been able to salvage something from the dress, an apron or a shirt for my little brother, but I tore it into dustrags when I went in to start supper. Now I was down to a single dress that barely covered my knees.

I put on water to boil for potatoes and considered appealing to my aunt Phyllis, who had money for dresses galore. But had I done so, she'd have embarked on one of her railings at my father—how I'd certainly turn out just like my mother if I wasn't taken in hand, and how did he think he could possibly raise me on his own?

While the potatoes cooked I went into their room, thinking to purloin a pair of his trousers. I took up a pair that lay crumpled in the shambles. Snaky thin as he was, I'd have fit into them twice, and it was more than I knew how to do to take them in. When Aunt Phyllis saw me in them, I'd surely be snatched away and made to live with her and Uncle Fowler in their stuffy house next to the jailhouse right in the bustle of Pigeon Harbor, with no forest and no Blue Lake right nearby. The town did have the big lake at the end of Front Street, but the big lake was vast and crowded with fishing boats and freighters and steamers and ferries and tugs going in and out of the harbor. Blue Lake was quiet but for the bustlings of ducks and raccoons, and we didn't have to see anyone we didn't want to see, except for Aunt Phyllis, who came by whenever she was in the mood to make trouble.

I hadn't been inside their room in a long while. The floor was crusted with mud he'd tracked in. A crumbled leaf lay dead on his pillow. My mother would have taken one look at the mildew on the windowsills from the rain leaking in and all his things strewn across the filthy floor, and she'd have turned around and left again without a word to anyone.

Anyhow, she wouldn't be returning, I told myself. She had a new man, no doubt, who liked to dance and owned a big house that she didn't have to clean because he had a fleet of maids to do it. She wouldn't ever tell him that she herself had been one. Maybe that's why she hadn't taken me, so I wouldn't spill the truth by mistake. My brother was too little to know things that he shouldn't say.

Kicking a boot aside, I went over to the trunk by the window where she'd always kept her scraps and remnants to make over. The trunk was the little one she'd had when she ran away from school and met my father, who swept her off her feet because he was so handsome and so funny and so serious with his wide green eyes with the dark eyelashes, the exact same as my brother's. Soon after she met him, she put everything she had in that trunk and came to live by Pigeon Harbor, the town she wound up hating, with a man who left her there all winter. Once the cherry trees began to bear, he always told her, he wouldn't have to cook for loggers. He was the best camp cook in the state, and got good pay, and his cherries would taste like wine and honey. But so far there weren't any.

She was always mad when he left, but when they were together she was mad at him anyway for things he did or didn't do. It was peaceful without their snipings, but without my brother's prattle it was too quiet. I missed him all the time, even with all the work he made, the little brother I called Fry, little fish. His name was Francis really. I couldn't imagine he was happy a minute without me. When I thought of him calling out "Tister" in the night, my insides knotted up. He couldn't say "sister."

I yanked on the latches of the trunk. One came open, but the other latch was twisted and bent and hurt my hand. I heard my father come in from outside. I made a quick retreat, closing the door to the bedroom softly so he wouldn't hear, and went into the kitchen.

"Glue for supper?" He prodded the potatoes with the tip of a knife. "You have to keep an eye on the stove, Violet, I keep telling you." He yanked the pot from the stove. "It's too damn hot for cooking, anyway." He drained the water off, sent me to the ice house for milk and butter and to the garden for corn, which he cut from the cob and added in. "Potahhge," he pronounced it, pretending it was fancy.

We ate it on the back porch. Blue Lake was asleep and there wasn't any breeze, so it was just as hot outside as in. "Those summer people won't like this heat," he said. The summer people were preachers from Chicago who'd bought up the strip of woods between us and Blue Lake. Even Aunt Phyllis didn't know when they were expected.

"Are they here?" I said.

"You'll know when they're here," he said. "Quacking their hymns day and night. Building cathedrals all along the beach. Teaching Bible verses to the heathen raccoons."

He wasn't in favor of churches. Churches made a mockery of God, he said. And he hated summer people, because they all were rich. He hated Chicago and St. Louis and Cincinnati and anywhere that had factories that made the working man a piece of a machine and not a man, and he hated the big new hotel in Pigeon Harbor, where the owners of the factories came to get away from the blazing city summers that the workers had to sweat through.

Sleep didn't come easily that night. It was hot and still,

and I had no dress to wear, and I wasn't one for sewing like my mother was. My sewing always came apart, since I always did it with the speedy needle to get it over with, and I'd get stabbed for my haste, and whatever I was making always came out askew and blood-spotted.

Like it or not, I had sewing to do the next day. My father went out early with a naked biscuit to ponder his trees. It was the year they were supposed to bear, but they hardly had leaves, and the cherries were small and dark and hard and rattled in the wind.

Once he was out, I went into his room and raised the top of the trunk, letting the clutter on top of it fall in a heap on the floor by the window. A musty smell came at me. Everything inside was all scrambled up and haphazard. She wouldn't have left her things that way even if she didn't intend to wear them anymore. She liked everything smoothed and folded, stacked and put where it should go.

I propped the trunk lid against the warped and swollen windowsill. In the tangle inside the trunk I saw a blue I recognized. I reached inside and drew out the radium silk dress with the tucks in the front she'd stitched and picked out and stitched again until they fell just the way she wanted when she had it on. It was the color of the big lake in a storm, and the white trim was like froth on the breakers. The dress was twisted up with a flannel petticoat, a white shirtwaist, green ribbons from a hat. It looked as if he'd taken out her things to cry over them or curse them, then threw them back like a string of skinny perch.

I held up the blue radium silk. Mildew streaked it. The

cloth was rotted through in places. Why had she left this dress behind, one she'd worked so hard on, to molder in an old trunk by a leaky window?

I thought of how she'd gotten Mr. Peterssen to order the cloth. She'd sent away for samples from an advertisement in McCall's, and brought them to him when she knew Mrs. Peterssen would be upstairs with baby Clara. "It won't sell," he said. "Too fancy."

But she tilted her head at him. "I'll take a good piece," she said, "and if you haven't sold it all by summer, you can triple the price and one of those ladies from the city will call it a bargain. Don't you think this one's just the shade for me? Or do you like this one?" She held the samples to her throat. He blushed like a girl.

She made the dress that winter, and on Easter she wore it to the First Congregational in Pigeon Harbor. My father didn't like her taking us, but Fry and I liked the singing. They left not long after, when the ice was off the tracks and the trains were running, and she said she'd be back for my birthday—my twelfth, on the sixth of June, nineteen aught-six.

The day arrived and then the evening. The last train pulled in, and they were nowhere in sight. My father's green eyes looked sad, but he pretended not to be. "They missed their connection, that's all," he said. "The tracks up north are always getting clogged up with fallen branches and polar bears and such."

He made a cake for me, but left it plain. My mother would have slathered it with icing even if she had to go without tea for months to get the sugar for it. The ache in my throat made it hard to get the cake down.

It wasn't until the fifteenth that a letter came. She was visiting her sister, she said, and her sister had a new baby who wasn't well and she was helping to take care of him, so the visit was taking longer than she'd planned on, and she would bring a present for me when she came home, but she didn't say when that would be. Then there was another letter that came on the twenty-first, a short one written in a hurry, and then no more word, and weeks went by, and there was no reason not to believe that she hadn't done what Aunt Phyllis said she'd done. There were plenty of rich men in the world, and my mother was beautiful enough to get one.

The radium silk dress sprawled on the floor, twisted like someone strangled. Even if it hadn't been streaked and stained, the fabric was too swank for a dress to feed the chickens in. A celery green skirt huddled in the trunk, musty and rumpled worse than the blue silk. Why had she left these things if she was going to stay away forever? And if she'd gone to be with a rich man, why had she worn her work dress on the train and left her best clothes behind?

There was no way around it. Georgia Blake had surely departed the earth. She wouldn't have left the radium silk if she hadn't intended on coming back, or the wine-colored jacket, or the white shirtwaist she put on to please my father, who liked how dark it made her skin, eyes, hair. As for Fry, she'd said how much he liked my mother's sisters and the children who were all related to us once or twice removed. Most likely he'd forgotten me. There was somebody else he called to in the night.

The white shirtwaist had mostly escaped the damp. I slipped it on and buttoned it up. It was too long and bagged on me. I snatched the sewing box and stamped up to my room, where I sliced off the length with the help of the wardrobe mirror, snipped away the cuffs to make wide, short baggy sleeves, and used the chopped-down hem as a sash. There wasn't any need to sew the cut edges. Let them fray. Nobody would notice or care.

There was no use keeping the other sodden, crumbling garments. She'd never make the green skirt over for me or scrub the ribbon pretty again.

I had to be rid of her things. I thought of burning them, but they would have made a stink and my father would want to know what I was up to. I could have thrown them in Blue Lake, but our skiff had a hole in it, and without a boat I wouldn't be able to get out to any kind of depth, and if I sometime found a scrap of faded radium silk on the beach it would be too awful.

So I tied everything together in a bundle with the green ribbons from the hat and went to the shed and got the shovel. I carried everything out beyond the garden and into the cool green strip of woods between our farm and Blue Lake's shore. I knew just the place.

The sound of water rushing over stones led me to the spot. White birches loomed before me. Stones glistened in the stream. There was the rat root my mother often gathered, more of it than I remembered.

I found a mossy patch bare of rat root and ferns. Thrusting the shovel's blade beneath the moss, I lifted it away, intending to put it back over the spot when I was done so it could keep on growing there.

Everything was quiet—no wind in the birches, no birds calling to each other, no stream rushing along. I couldn't hear the waves of Blue Lake. My heart thundered. Sometimes it gets more quiet when a ghost is on the prowl. If it was my mother's ghost, it was fitting that she'd come to visit this very place, and maybe she would tell me something, as ghosts sometimes will if you don't shoo them off.

But she didn't come. Nothing did. I jabbed the shovel again and shoved it down with one bare foot. The metal edge hurt, but the blade went deep. Soon there was a hole, crisscrossed with roots. I knelt to clear them away. The dirt smelled like everything that could be important was in it, nourishment and blossomings and ancient seasons. My fingers dug around the roots to loosen them, and met with something flat and hard.

Treasure, I thought. Money. Maybe a lot of it. I began to work out what to buy—dresses I'd seen in McCall's, books with colored pictures, chocolates from the Greek's. I scrabbled with both hands, almost falling in the hole, and took out a flat bit of something, nothing more than a rusty old tool, I thought. Another disappointment, of course, like always.

But it wasn't. I took it out and in the dim dappled light I could see it was a hand—a hand with narrow, tapered fingers and a thumb curving outward like a moon. I rubbed at the dirt caked on it and glimpsed something maybe written on its palm. If I could rinse it clean, I could see what it was.

I waded along the shady stream until it gave out into Blue Lake. The lake was smooth and clear and cold, but not colder than it usually was in the middle of July. Holding the Hand by the tip of the curved thumb, I dunked it in. Dirt came off and made a cloud. I could see that it was copper now, ruddy and rich. Where I held it, the copper chilled. Cold jolted along my arm and took my breath.

I was in winter. Snow covered the beach and road, white all around but for the dark trunks of trees and the blue water that was freezing me but wasn't frozen itself. So it wasn't deep winter then. From the corner of my eye I thought I saw someone. I turned to look, and saw a wrinkled lady with long white braids in a cape of white swan feathers waving in wind. She wasn't ghostly. She looked like she was really there. But then she wasn't. She'd only been a flicker, like a bird on a branch that's gone in a blink without you seeing it fly off.

Maybe a glint off the lake had blinded me. Or I'd mistaken the white bark of a birch tree for white hair and feathers. The smell of cold and the white of snow were gone, and the road was the road and the trees weren't bare, and winter was like a dream that soars behind the eyes before you recognize it, and the harder you try to bring it back, the more you can't.

I was well acquainted with my grandmother's ghostly

lingerings, but what I'd seen wasn't like that. And the lake was often tricky, bloating my foot to make it look like a dead man's, making waves when there was no wind. Sometimes I saw and heard things—the dart of a fox when there wasn't one, someone talking in an empty room, a glowing light in the woods where nobody lived. Whenever I told my mother, she'd say I should stop making up nonsense.

But the feather lady had been no trick of wind or light. I'd seen the white braids, the white swan feathered cape, the red designs sewn on the white skin dress, the spirals tattooed on her wrinkled chin. Hadn't she held the copper hand between her palms with rays of metal peeking between her fingers? Hadn't her hands been held to the snowy sky?

Somehow I'd let go of the metal thumb. The Hand was sinking. Patterns were etched in copper, but with the water moving over the Hand and the Hand moving on top of the rocks and the clouds reflecting on the water, I couldn't make out the design. The water began to stir, as the lake will do when it just becomes restless for no reason you can see. The Hand drifted. I reached to seize it and it twisted away, as if to escape.

But I caught it. Now it was warm, and light as a moth. Fearing that the wind would take it, I put it flat on my hand with the thumb over my thumb and the fingers on my fingers, and put my other hand on top so it was trapped between, just the way the feather lady had done.

Loneliness stabbed me. Without a mother, I had nothing. I was a fallen, dried-up leaf drifting between the endless blues of lake and sky. But as I pressed the copper hand between my palms, the sadness melted. I wasn't alone in the slightest. Everything seemed—not noisier, but packed with understandings. A watery glint can be an invisible someone. Dirt can remember what happened on it. *Someone's coming*, a crow seemed to cry as she flew over.

"Hello!" someone called.

When you think you know what birds or ghostly presences are telling you, you hear them inside your mind. They're not out in the world for just anyone to hear. But this was a voice as you would know a voice to be, and sounded real.

And so I suspected. It might be magic, this copper hand I'd found.

2

THE HAND

A girl came toward me, carrying two pails. There were no girls living nearby, and girls from Pigeon Harbor didn't usually come to Blue Lake. She didn't look in the least magical, but with magic you don't always get what you expect.

The copper hand lay in my palm, not warm, not cold. Quickly I slid it between my dress and the shift I wore beneath it, and tied my sash extra tight to hold the Hand in place.

The girl began to trudge across the sand. She was wearing shoes, which made her progression awkward. The pails didn't help. She was a stubby girl with pale, waxy skin and bug eyes and dull brown hair held back by a wilted bow. "I was told there wouldn't be any other girls," she called. "When did you arrive?"

I thought it wouldn't be wise to be rude to someone who magic might have summoned. "I live here," I said.

"Lucky! I wish I could live here all the time. I'm from Chicago. It's vile there."

What could be vile? In Chicago they had it all—stores with everything from everywhere, music halls with orchestras, buildings half a mile high, even the big lake. The copper hand seemed to slither around my ribs. I pressed on it gently with an elbow. I had the feeling it didn't like being hidden back in the dark again after being in water and light.

"We just arrived this very minute," the girl said. "My mother told me to get water from the stream, but I couldn't find it. We won't have a well until my father digs one. Getting water's going to be my job. The boys get to cut wood."

Magic hadn't brought her. She was one of the preacher summer people. Already they were taking over Blue Lake. The beach would never again be mine alone.

"I wouldn't drink out of that stream," I said. "Cows are always slopping around in it."

This wasn't true. I just wanted to keep anybody from seeing the hole I'd made and finding anything else in it, magic or otherwise.

"Revolting," she said.

"Also you'd be trespassing," I said. At one time that would have been so. My aunt was always going on about how we'd all be rich if my grandfather hadn't had so many bad winters in a row and got hounded into selling this acre and that. "Plus," I added, "the stream's haunted."

"I don't mind ghosts," the girl said. "They don't hurt you if you're polite to them."

"How do you know?" I said.

"There used to be a ghost in our house," she said. "I'm the only one who believed in it, even though my brother heard it too. He said it was our clanky old stove. What kind of ghost does the stream have?"

"A mean one," I said. "Are you living here or visiting?"

"We're going to live here every summer," she said. "We'll be here from now until the fifteenth of August. Five weeks. And it's practically a miracle I met you, especially the exact instant I arrived. Ever since I found out we were coming here, I've been hoping and wishing every minute for a girl to do things with. I'm so sick of boys I could scream. My brothers are hideous barbarians. They incessantly plot things and spy around and are nefarious and never get caught. My big brother thinks he's the emperor of everything, and my little brother's his devoted minion."

I didn't mind this girl somehow. She didn't squirm at the mention of ghosts like Ingie Peterssen would have. And I didn't like boys either, except for Fry.

"What's your name?" She tossed her hair away from her face and smiled. Her teeth were too big for her, like a beaver's.

"Violet."

"Violet! Sublime. What's the rest?"

"Blake."

"Violet Blake. Is there a middle?"

It occurred to me to lie, just because I'd get away with it, and I liked to stay in practice. But I liked my names, and I liked her. She couldn't help being a summer girl.

"Marie," I said.

She balanced on one foot to pull off a shoe, hopping a little to keep from teetering. "Violet Marie Blake. Now *that's* a name. You can be somebody with that name. I can't stand being called Mercy Jerusha Rankin. It sounds like somebody's been sneezing. Where do you live?" She thrust her toes into the sand and smiled at me.

"Past the woods."

"On a farm?" She strode into the lake and didn't exclaim that it was cold, but drank from her cupped hand and splashed her face with water.

"We've got an orchard," I said.

"An orchard," she breathed, as if I'd said a palace.

"Yes," I said. "In the spring the white flowers float in the air. It looks like snow and it smells like honey." This wasn't entirely a fabrication. The trees had budded, and the buds opened a mere crack and let a thin line of ruffle through.

"I'd better get back," Mercy said, coming out of the lake. "My mother's always saying how long I take to do everything. But first show me where you live." She squatted down and smoothed a patch of sand. "That way I could come and call. You'll let me, won't you?"

She kept smoothing the sand, making a large flat area. I saw that she really was a beaver, fastidious and exacting, in every aspect. It wasn't just the teeth. With her finger she made a long liver-shaped oval in the sand.

"Here's Lake Michigan. Blue Lake is here. This is Pigeon Harbor. Here's the road we took to get here from town. And this is us." Blue Lake was a small circle. We were two dots.

"Chicago's way down here," Mercy said, "and we crossed

like this." Chicago was a square on the low end of the oval that was the big lake, and the crossing was a wavy line.

"Did you ever go to Marshall Field's?" I said before I could stop myself.

"My mother can't abide that place. She says it's for ladies with nothing better to do but spend money." She smiled up at me. "But I think it's glorious." She turned back to her sand picture. "Here's where our tents are. Show where you live."

I liked her mapmaking. Places had routes between them that sailors or railroads or thirsty deer could make, and if you pointed yourself in the right direction like a weather-vane, you'd get from here to somewhere. But I didn't want her coming by. My father would most likely snarl at her and put her to work patching the roof or plowing a field or something.

"My father's got a fever," I told her. "You don't want to get it. Plus we're not that close to here. But I could come and see you." It wouldn't be bad to have someone to pick berries and go swimming with.

"I wish I could live in the country," Mercy said. "When I have children I won't make them move every two years and live where it's dark and dirty and there are too many people crowded all together so all they ever do is argue. Every time I make a friend, my father goes to work at a different church, because he always has to go where people are really poor, and then at the new school everybody's always best friends with somebody since they were infants. And they always think I'll be a prissy little goody-goody just because my father's a preacher, and I'm not like that. Do you have a lot of friends?"

"Not really. Everybody at school likes to giggle about boys all day, except Ingie Peterssen, and she's scared of everything and her mother's mean." Mrs. Peterssen sniffed and glared at you unless you came into her store with a lot to spend. She was always shooting the stink eye at my mother, who was too pretty and could only afford a bargain.

"Mercy!" someone called.

She hurried to fetch her pails. "I was supposed to come right back with the water," she said. "Stay just a minute, so I can introduce you. Otherwise she'll think I was wandering around looking for fairies." She tipped the pails into the lake, scraping them against the bottom.

"Your water's getting sand in it," I said.

"Mercy!" someone called again.

"Here I am, Mother," Mercy cried, struggling to lift the pails, which were heavy with wet sand and pebbles.

"Let me," I said, and took them. I waded out to past my knees and was rinsing out the sand when a skinny woman in a straw boater came bustling through the beach grass.

"Here you are," she said. "I knew I should never have sent you by yourself." She saw me then, and threw me a narrow smile.

"That's Violet Blake," Mercy said. "She lives here all the time."

"I see. We've been waiting for the water, Mercy. Why must the simplest thing take you so long?"

The mother looked me up and down, from the braid I

hadn't combed out that day to the dress that was for someone much bigger.

"Violet," she said, "has your mother given you permission to go in the water? We wouldn't want you to get in trouble because Mercy didn't follow instructions. She was to get water from the stream, you see."

"The lake water's better," I said. "So we came here to get it, and then I started asking her all about Chicago, and she kept saying she had to go, but I kept her. We don't get to see too many people out this way." Mercy gave me a grateful look.

"That's just what we like about it here," Mrs. Rankin said. "The fellowship with nature. Take the pails, Mercy. Don't let Violet do everything for you, for pity's sake."

As I handed Mercy the pails, the copper hand shifted inside my dress. I put one hand behind me to keep it from falling out.

"Could Violet come and visit sometime?" Mercy said.

"When we're settled." Mrs. Rankin flapped her hands at Mercy to get a move on. "Your mother must keep you busy, Violet, I imagine. Won't she be expecting you?"

Already she wasn't going to let us be friends. Someone in town had warned her. The father's white, the mother's Indian. Yet they think they're better than everybody, and the girl's a strange one.

"My mother's dead," I burst out. My breath caught. The Hand went cold against me.

Mrs. Rankin pulled me to her. "You poor sweet lamb. You come and see us anytime."

Mercy slipped her sandy feet into her shoes and hurried after her mother. They turned onto the road. Mercy waved and was gone around the bend.

I hurried across the road to where I'd left the hole uncovered. It gaped like a dark mouth. The bundle of my mother's things lay beside it. Maybe there was something else in there to dig up. Maybe the copper hand was a mere bauble, and true splendor was yet to be unearthed.

But it didn't pay to be greedy like the fisherman's wife in the story, who wasn't satisfied with her castle or even with being pope, and ended up with nothing in the end. I had the copper hand, and it seemed to have magic to it, and with magic you couldn't be too careful. That much I knew.

"Vii-let! You've got a caller! Viii-let!" I could tell my aunt's high, breathy voice, even braided into the sound of the waves getting stirred up by the wind. I considered hiding there among the birches until she went away, but that would have been purely fruitless. She'd never leave until I was found, and then she'd upbraid me for half an hour for being missing, and *then* would come the harangue over whatever she'd come the two dusty miles to say in the first place.

I reached inside my dress and drew out the copper hand. The designs seemed to waver, as if in rippling water, but then they were still again, just etchings in metal.

My aunt called again. I couldn't leave it behind, but what if she found it and I never had another chance? I pressed the copper hand between my palms.

"I wish," I whispered, and said what first came to my mind. "I wish for a new dress."

Then I hid the copper hand inside my raggy torn-down shirtwaist and ran for home with the shovel. I ran my fastest too because Aunt Phyllis was easily exasperated, and even magic would have a time to put things right if she was in a mood.

Greenstone had plenty of food for the journey. The dead wouldn't be eating much dried whitefish or golden sturgeon roe. The burning rash had arrived during the sturgeon run. Few would be nourished by the bounty of that catch.

She left as soon as the last apprentice was no longer breathing, slipped away unseen by the loved ones who would bathe the dead and do what could be done for those who bubbled and burned. Nobody needed another farewell.

She was Greenstone, the dreamer and singer and seer, well-traveled on the earth world and other worlds too. The canoe she chose was heavy enough for the swells of the big lake, small enough for a woman who was alone and not so young.

The river gave out into the big lake that stretched all the way west to the invisible opposite shore. Underwater beings granted her safe passage. She was properly humble and lavish with her gifts. Water was her responsibility, her charge.

She was worn to the bone with grief, but being on the water lifted the bleakness.

She headed south. She was the keeper of the sacred copper hand, made in her grandmother's grandmother's time from copper hammered flat. It had been passed along from one woman of learning to the next. Greenstone had been entrusted with its teachings long before. She sought the next keeper.

She knew of a shrine where an icy creek emptied into a lake famed for its beauty and power. It was up to the wind and the water whether she would get there in time. People of knowledge gathered there in autumn, which would soon give way to winter.

Even one woman would be someone. Even a girl.

She had never been to the clear blue lake, but she could see it in her mind, a graceful oval of blue. When she passed the great dunes she knew to look for a certain point of land. She beached the canoe there and set off into the dark pine forest. Soon the lake was shining between the trees.

She touched the water, soft as baby skin. How could it be so blue and so clear at the same time? She walked along the shore and found the icy stream. Nobody had put up a single lodge. Nobody was gathering wood for the fires. A crayfish scuttered in the clear ripples. She splashed her face and dried it on a sleeve, then sat on the cold sand, made her offerings, made her appeals. She broke off a piece of rat root from the length she carried, began to work it with her worn old teeth. It was hard untying the bundle with her chilled stiff fingers.

She saw what she'd seen before, what others had seen and

mulled over. The forest would be flattened. The big lake would go sour. Every clan and nation would be orphaned. She saw the gnarled hands offering, her own young hands receiving. The bundle passed between them. New trees came up, fed by the rotting stumps of the old. The blue lake shone, still and clear.

The moon was up and the sky still had color in it. Her ears were cold, and the tips of her fingers, and her nose. Breath misted out of her. The aftertaste of rat root hovered in her mouth, a fiber of it lodged between two back teeth. Her tongue worked it. The copper was ruddy in the dull light.

There is nobody, she felt it tell her. Not now.

It was clear to her then. What had been passed to her she couldn't pass on, not in the way she'd received it. The song, if someone's heart could hear it, had been hammered into the copper, fashioned into its fingers, inscribed in its palm. The song wouldn't run away. The copper would hold it. Just because she wouldn't sing it to the next bearer didn't mean the song was lost. She bundled the Hand back up.

She stood. Her legs were stiff. She unwrapped her cloak, left her dress on. She'd be colder that way, with the deerskin wet against her. She waded in, submerged herself, stayed in the icy water until her bones were brittle. The dress was heavy and stuck to her legs. When she got to shore she was out of breath. She laid her white cloak over her shoulders, not for warmth, but to keep it with her on her final journey. The copper bundle went back around her neck, next to her chilled skin.

In the woods, she found a shallow gully near a rotting birch log. She held the copper hand to the sky and called for snow to cover her. The sky darkened. Snow came fluttering from above, collecting on the earth. She lay herself down and willed the shivering to stop. Her cold hand went over the bundle, one last protection.

Clouds were coming from the opposite shore. She smelled the frost making its way. Thank you, she told the north wind. Greenstone rose above herself, above the lake. The rocks shimmered beneath the clear blue.

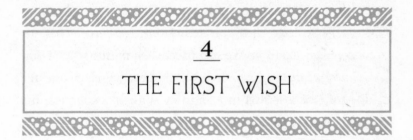

4

THE FIRST WISH

At the edge of the woods by the pasture, I stopped to listen. The wind was in my favor and I could exactly hear Aunt Phyllis. "This garden's a disgrace," she was saying. "I don't understand you, Henry. Why bother to plant just to let the weeds take over?"

She wasn't wrong. But if she'd stopped by when we were planting, even she would have approved of the methodology—unless she considered we made too much of the planning and preparation, and should have just poked the seeds in without the fuss. My father had plowed the plot not once but twice, so that the ground was airy. Then together we worked out a diagram, and I planted exactly to its measure, pinching out the seeds from the brown paper packets my mother had labeled the year before in her fine, small hand.

That was when we thought she'd be returning.

Now the cornstalks were spindly from wrestling the horsetails, and the cabbages were smothered and small. But there were still peas, and the bean plants were collapsing with beans so long they spiraled. I only gathered what we needed a meal at a time. We still had a shelf of dusty jars from last year I couldn't bear to look at, because each one reminded me of Fry: his mouth juicy with blackberries, his plump hands tearing cabbage into scraps, his grin when our mother told him to plunge those hands in the bowl of skinned tomatoes to squeeze them fine.

I came out from the woods behind the shed and hid behind a crooked wall. "Falling apart," my aunt said. "Just hire somebody for a week or two, Henry. Papa always had help in the summer."

"I don't need anybody," he said.

"There's no future in a small farm these days. You could get something for the place if you don't keep running it down. I don't know why you don't let Fowler give you a job."

"I don't want a job."

"I don't understand you, Henry. Isn't cooking for fifty godless, foul-mouthed lumberjacks a job?"

"It's a winter job," he said. "I don't mind a winter job."

"Don't be smart with me, Henry Fryman Blake. You're still Mama's spoiled baby boy. You do whatever suits you and never think about anybody else. *Violet!* Where *is* that girl? This is my point exactly, Henry. You don't even keep track of her. She could be drowned in the lake for all you know. Far be it from me to tell you what to do, but we weren't raised to run off whenever we took the fancy."

"I know your platform, Phyllis, and I already said I'd

think about it. If that's what you came to talk about, I'm not done thinking."

"It's not a *platform*," she snapped. "It's the only reasonable course, and you know it."

She didn't have any children of her own to snip at, and with my mother gone she was itchier than ever to install me in her stuffy spare room, drape me in flounces, sit me down at her piano, for which I hadn't a grain of knack, and switch the backs of my knees when she didn't like how my eyebrows were angled.

"Well, Henry. I didn't come to talk to you anyhow," said my aunt. "I have a perfectly lovely surprise for your daughter, but I certainly don't have all afternoon to wait for her."

I slipped over to the far side of the shed so it would seem I was coming straight from the woods. Aunt Phyllis was bent over a row of carrots, yanking weeds and tossing them in a pile. My father stared at the carrot tops as if they reminded him of something.

I thrust the shovel in the shed. It fell over in a clatter. Aunt Phyllis looked over. "Finally!" she remarked. She wore a frock of yellow and light orange plaid. People called my aunt a beauty, with her curly hair and curly mouth and bright blue eyes, but her mouth pinched and her eyes bored into you and everything she put on had too many tucks and flowers and feathers and bows. She'd have looked better if she dressed more like my mother, plainer, and in colors that suited, and if she wasn't always flicking her gaze around looking at what everybody else had that she didn't.

"Good afternoon, Aunt Phyllis," I said sweetly. "How nice of you to visit us."

"Yes," she said. "I had more than enough to do today without coming all the way out here, and I've got the Poetry Club tonight. If anyone had bothered to ask me, I could have told them that Ingie Peterssen couldn't possibly be qualified to work for someone like Miss Nadia Zalzman."

I quailed. Some crony of my aunt's was in the market for a nursemaid, and I would be charged with the care of a slobbery squaller for the rest of the summer.

"Don't get your hopes up, Violet," Aunt Phyllis went on. "Nothing's written in stone. She might not even like you. And I have no idea what she's paying, but it's the opportunity that matters, not the few extra pennies you would make."

"But there's so much to do at home here," I said piously. "Father can't do it all himself."

"Oh, he'll get by." She shot him a look. "He wouldn't deny you the chance to be exposed to a little culture and refinement. Miss Zalzman is a photographer of great renown. She made a portrait of the mayor of Chicago!"

"Well, la-di-da," my father said. "The mayor! Anybody who takes *his* picture should make it a mug shot."

"Oh, Henry, don't be ignorant," admonished my aunt. "You don't know a single thing about the man."

"Read the papers, Phyllis. He's a hundred percent capitalist stooge."

"I read what's written by responsible journalists, which is more than I can say for some people who supposedly *got* a good education. Come with me, Violet. Hurry, now."

Aunt Phyllis took up her plaid skirts and swept herself up the steps. My father stood by the peas, pressing the back of his neck with one gray thumb. Most likely he was working on another strategy to get the cherries to plump and redden. But there would be no crop, and he'd have to work all winter, and Aunt Phyllis would keep me forever.

"Miss Zalzman arrived on Monday with Mrs. Guy Dell, the railroad man's wife," Aunt Phyllis chattered in her usual imperious manner. "*He* was a farm boy who made something of himself. Miss Zalzman is a discovery of Mrs. Dell's. She needs a girl to run errands and hand her things and whatnot—nothing amazingly complicated, but certainly above Ingie's head. None of those Peterssens have a grain of intelligence. Ingie didn't last an hour."

As she related this chronicle, Aunt Phyllis bustled through the kitchen, waving off the flies that hovered over the unwashed dishes, and ascended to my room, where she flung open the wardrobe and snatched my one good dress off its peg. It was a pretty dress, the last one my mother had made me, a spring green with leaves and curlicues and billowy sleeves. Aunt Phyllis held the dress up beneath my chin. It wouldn't have covered my knees.

"Your appointment with Miss Zalzman is at three," said my aunt. "And I see you have nothing to wear. He's got you in rags. Rags! All right. I'll have to take you to Fairchild's and pick you out a dress."

A new dress. I'd wished for that very thing with the copper hand!

Aunt Phyllis held the leafy dress against me. "This isn't

fit for more than an apron, is it?" I felt the copper hand shift beneath my sash and turned so it would be as far as it could get from my aunt's sharp eyes and nose.

"Stop scratching and fiddling!" she snapped, yanking at my elbow. "Can't you stand still for one minute? Where are the scissors? No, don't go fetch them. You'll take forever with your dawdling and dreaming. Just tell me where they are."

"The table by the fireplace," I lied, hoping for the chance to take the copper hand out from under my dress and away from the clutches of Aunt Phyllis. But she spotted the scissors on top of the dresser, where I'd left them after cutting down my mother's shirtwaist.

"You scatterbrain!" my aunt exclaimed. "Don't you ever put anything away? Now put your arms out straight, like so. Don't move or I might stab you by mistake."

With that, she tossed the dress on the bed and clacked the scissors along the seams, savaging skirt from bodice. I tried not to care as the folds of the skirt melted away into a length of cloth. It was only a silly dress that I'd hardly ever worn, but my mother's tiny stitches had formed it. Aunt Phyllis shook out the cloth. Threads flew about like so many windblown caterpillars. As she wound the cloth around me I couldn't keep from twitching and pulling to distract her fingers from finding the copper hand. She couldn't have it. Nobody could. It was mine. It would bring me more bounty, more than just one dress.

"Be still!" she cried, slapping my arm. "I don't have all day. Why is your skirt soaking wet?"

"I was scrubbing the pantry shelves," I lied. "They were sticky."

"They wouldn't be if you'd remember to wipe off your jars before you put them away," said my aunt. "I thought so. Not enough cloth here. Why your mother didn't allow for some extra length, I can't fathom, and with all these tucks, it's no good for anything but scraps."

She folded the cloth in half, in half again. My arm stung where she had slapped me.

"We'll get you looking decent," she pronounced. "One frock ready-made, and two more run up. That should hold you awhile." She took hold of my chin and tilted my face. "You've got your mother's bones. You're bound to be pretty someday. Shoes! Quickly! We barely have enough time."

The top half of the dress lay forlornly on the bed as she trotted downstairs, taking the leafy cloth with her. She would have scurried me into her buggy, copper hand and all, but I couldn't have her finding it. I had a magic amulet—a talisman—a charm. I would hide it and keep it safe and it would grant me my heart's desire.

I told Aunt Phyllis I had to visit the privy. There couldn't have been a more unbeseeming place to hide the copper hand, but nobody would pry around in there. I held the door closed with my foot and regarded my talisman. In Fairchild's window I had seen a dress as blue as a hot summer sky, with no sash tying in a silly bow, but a pair of buttons fastening at the low waist.

"A *nice* dress," I whispered, clasping the copper hand between my own. "One I like. Please."

And then, of course, all the many other things I wanted flooded through my mind. A stateroom on a ship to Paris. Pie I didn't have to make myself. My little brother's return. I would have them all, surely. I reached up and put the copper hand on the highest ledge, where it couldn't be seen except by the wise, patient spiders, and told it I'd find a more fitting hiding place for it as soon as I got back.

Little was said on the ride to town. Aunt Phyllis pulled up in front of the brand-new herringbone brick house that she was so proud of, with the jailhouse right slap in back of it, and directed me to the washroom with a brush for scrubbing my fingernails.

"Do what you can with these," she ordered the hired girl, thrusting my shoes at her. The hired girl was Ingie's cousin whose name I always forgot. When I emerged with cleaner extremities, Aunt Phyllis gave me a pair of black stockings to wear, redid my braid so tight it gave me a headache, and steered me out the door. She grasped my elbow all the way to Fairchild's store, as if I was a convict who might make a sudden break for freedom.

Each step was a misery. It wasn't just that my shoes squeezed my toes and the black stockings scratched my legs as bad as briars. All I could think was that the sunny clear blue morning would be spent acquiring new garments I would despise, and then there would be the dreary encounter with this Miss Zalzman, whoever she was, whatever it was she did. If I had to work for her, the summer would fly away. There would be no swimming in Blue Lake or fishing from the skiff.

When we got to Fairchild's, the very dress I'd been

thinking of was still in the window. Aunt Phyllis wanted me to get one that was downright ghastly, but when I tried it on it was too tight in the arms. Only two dresses in the entire store fit me perfectly, the blue one with the low buttoned waist, and a cream-colored one that wasn't altogether bad, and Aunt Phyllis said I could have both.

The copper hand had done it. I would have wishes now. I could have anything.

Then it was time to head over to the hotel. The new blue dress was soft and I had room to move my arms, and I had new shoes, soft with three straps, and feathery light white stockings instead of the itchy black ones, because Mr. Fairchild said all the girls from Chicago had white this season, and Aunt Phyllis always had to be up on things.

At the end of the street we turned the corner and there was the rollicking big lake with its wide expanse of smooth sand, and the Voyageur Hotel perched like a gull at the edge of the bay. The lake stretched so wide that you couldn't see the opposite shore. You could sail across it to Chicago and other places too, and from there you were practically in St. Louis or Cincinnati or New York.

One of the big schooners was heading out of the harbor. I couldn't help but run to see. Aunt Phyllis clucked at me to walk like a lady, but I flew like a deer on the toes of my supple new shoes to the end of the street, almost to the depot that brought the summer people right to the big hotel's front door, and turned around and skipped back to my aunt's side as the schooner billowed away, heading south with wood to build up cities.

"Thank you for the dress, Aunt Phyllis," I panted.

"You're wrinkling it, running like a wild beast," she sniffed. But the waves on the big lake leaped and pranced, and I had two dresses that even my mother would have considered in good taste, and I was sure Miss Zalzman was going to like me.

I would have some money. And I would get my little brother back. The Hand would see to all of it.

I dared—I did—to hope it could be so.

5
MISS NADIA

All I'd ever seen of the Voyageur Hotel was the back gate, where my brother and I used to wait for my mother to be done with work when she was a maid there. My father called the hotel a monstrosity with its two hundred rooms, but my mother said it had every modern convenience, like telephones everywhere and a bowling alley and everything electrified, and the beds were as soft as clouds.

Some people said the hotel was cursed, because it had to be built twice. The roof collapsed under the weight of snow and they had to postpone opening a whole year to make the place sturdier. And when they did open, the slot machines came dented and had to go back to Chicago and new ones shipped in.

A man opened the big front door for us and held it as we entered the lobby, a room an enchanted bear prince might have had for entertaining. Chairs and tables made of swirls and burls of wood surrounded a massive fireplace made of the smooth round stones thrown up by the big lake's waves. The open windows gave onto the veranda, with women in white dresses lounging, and the pale beach and the wide wild lake beyond.

My aunt directed me to a high counter, behind which stood a cheerful tow-headed young man. "Mrs. Fowler Wilmot to see Miss Nadia Zalzman," Aunt Phyllis said.

The man picked up a telephone receiver and spoke into it, then listened. "You are Miss Blake?" he said to me.

"She is," my aunt affirmed.

The man hung up the telephone and gave my aunt a stiff smile. "Miss Zalzman says that Mrs. Wilmot needn't bother to come up," he said. "She says Miss Blake won't be long."

"I don't understand," said my aunt. "I am escorting my niece. It isn't any bother."

"Of course," the man said. "Room two twenty-five. The elevator is to your right."

"We'd prefer the stairs," my aunt said.

"As you wish." The man inclined his head at me. "Miss Blake."

I was Miss Blake. I lifted my chin and straightened my spine and conducted myself up the staircase with haughtiness unnoticed by my aunt, or she would have instructed me to stop it.

I had thought Miss Zalzman would be a drab sparrow of a woman, but she was more in the line of mink, slight of figure, with round, assessing hazel eyes sliced with green. On opening the door to two twenty-five, she reached for my aunt's hand and enclosed it in both of her small ones.

"Thank you, Mrs. Wilmot," she said. "You've saved my life."

"Why, Miss Zalzman," my aunt said. "It is you who must be thanked—for breathing life into this dull little town."

"I find it anything but dull so far. I have fallen in love already with this place." Miss Zalzman wore a linen smock the color of new leaves, unadorned but for a stair-stepped band of dark brown around the square neck and hem, and a plain white blouse beneath. The hoops in her ears were silver, and on her right middle finger she had a wide silver ring with a blue stone. Beside her, my aunt looked overdressed and fussy.

Miss Zalzman extended a hand toward me. Her fingers were stained brown. A leaky pen, I thought it must have been.

"Miss Blake," she said. Her eyes, probing as they were, had pouches beneath, but they seemed kind, and I thought I would like Miss Zalzman. I wondered what language she had grown up speaking. Her consonants were hard and throaty, while she drew the vowels wide, putting me in mind of a land of rocky crags and expanses of ice, and a small Miss Nadia with a fur hood and rounder, pinker cheeks.

"Your presence here has already created quite a stir," Aunt Phyllis was saying. "I hear that Alice Dell had to arrange a bigger room for your lecture, there's been such a groundswell of interest."

"Mrs. Dell is wonderful at publicity," Miss Zalzman said. "Now, Mrs. Wilmot, I beg you, please leave us. If you are here, I will want to engage you in conversation and find out all about your fascinating life, and the afternoon will be spent too pleasantly."

"Oh, I don't mind," my aunt said.

The edges of Miss Zalzman's mouth tipped up in a smile, but I had the feeling that she wanted to take my aunt by the shoulders and shake her.

"Don't tempt me," she said. "I am already behind in my work. We won't be long in our discussion, Miss Blake and I. Please have a cup of tea on the porch and watch the colors of the water change from one to the other and relax yourself. Twenty minutes. No longer." She held her hand out, my aunt took it, and then somehow Aunt Phyllis was in the hallway and I was inside Miss Zalzman's parlor.

At first all I could notice was the big lake out the window and the sky above the lake, both of them blue in their different ways, and what the wind was up to, blustering the clouds, but I tore away from the sight and sat where Miss Zalzman showed me, at a round table that had papers strewn willy-nilly across it. A row of boxes stood against the wall, leather with buckled straps.

"So," Miss Zalzman said. "I know already some things about Miss Violet Blake. She is twelve years old. She lives a mile or two out from town on a farm. Yes?"

"Yes, ma'am."

"She is smart, they say. True?"

I didn't like to boast, but I knew she was after someone quicker than Ingie Peterssen, and to exhibit that wouldn't be terribly immodest. "I mostly get one hundreds in school," I said.

"That's good. And how else do you use your mind?"

There was something about Miss Zalzman that made me want to tell her things somehow, and I was curious to know what was inside the black leather boxes with their brass fittings, and what kind of pictures Miss Zalzman liked to take, and where she had ever been. She had surely sailed the ocean, and taken trains through mountain passes.

"My aunt says the books I read are too old for me," I said.

"I see," said Miss Zalzman, smiling. "And for example?"

"Well, she doesn't approve of novels unless they're the uplifting kind. And I had a book called *Kidnapped,* and when Aunt Phyllis opened it up she saw some bloody parts. So she said it was a book for boys, and she told the lady at the lending library not to give me a single book anymore, so now my father has to get them for me. But he hardly ever goes to town, and when he does he forgets, so I mostly just read what we have already."

"That is a sad story," Miss Zalzman said. "But there can be something in reading again what you've read before. Now. Are you as strong as you are quick?"

I didn't know what to answer. Hefty Ingie Peterssen was certainly much stronger than I would ever be. But Miss Zalzman didn't seem to expect a reply. "Bring me one of those, if you wouldn't mind," she said, indicating the row of black cases with her narrow minkish chin. "It doesn't make any difference which. But please be gentle. My livelihood is in them."

This was to trip me up, surely. If I tried the biggest one and it proved too burdensome for delicacy in handling, I would have to tackle another, and I didn't wish to appear irresolute. I lifted the big case. It was awkward by virtue of its size, but not too heavy, and I made my way over to Miss Zalzman slowly, step by step. I put it down as easily as I could manage, but it thudded, meeting the floor, and a wave of hotness went all through me. What if I'd broken whatever was inside?

If Miss Zalzman was concerned, she said nothing about it. She leaned over the case, unfastened the buckles, and took up the lid to reveal another black box inside, nestled in padding, which she drew out and placed on the table in front of her.

"This is my new fancy camera I got for this job." With a click and a snap, the box on the table extruded tubes and levers. "Have you used a camera before?"

"My aunt has one, but I'm not allowed to touch it."

"Mine you would be touching," she said. "But only where and when I tell you. I want someone to help with the carrying, and to keep the dust and sand away. Every speck is an enemy. You must be careful with everything and do just what I say to do precisely that way and no other way. Is that possible for you?"

"Yes, Miss Zalzman," I said.

"And would you like to work with me, or is it your aunt's idea?"

"It was her idea, but I want to."

"Then good. I would like you to. I am here until the twentieth of July, another week and a little. Are you free until then?"

"Yes, Miss Zalzman." I liked to say her name, with all the buzzes in it.

"Excellent. And you will call me Miss Nadia, please. At the end of a day I tell you what time to come the next day and that is when you get here. Not before and not after. I pay five cents an hour, and the hotel will feed us both. Payday is Saturday at the end of work. All right?"

I nodded, afraid my voice was out of operation. I was figuring how much I'd get in a week, and too bad it wasn't for the whole rest of the summer. She told me to arrive the next day at exactly seven o'clock, and I was outside in the hall. I found my aunt out on the veranda, where she was chattering away at a city lady in the kind of fluttery frock my aunt was always oohing over in the magazines.

"This must be your little niece," the lady said. "Did she win Miss Zalzman over?"

"I start tomorrow," I said.

"I was just telling your aunt," the lady said. "Miss Zalzman's terribly artistic, but she does have the Russian temperament. I hope you'll do what she says to the letter, so she doesn't bite your head off."

"There will be no call for any of that," Aunt Phyllis declared. "Violet is a most capable young lady. I expect her to do an impeccable job."

"Of course she will," said the lady. I was surprised at Aunt Phyllis. She'd never called me capable before, or anything but a dawdler and a shirker.

"Violet, you may stop by the house and pick up your new things," my aunt told me. "Hurry home so your father won't be worried. And don't scuff your new shoes on the road."

6

BRANCHES

He was in the orchard, perched on the splintery ladder, sawing at a branch. The hard dark cherries rattled. The branch came away and fell. "Start loading the cart," he said. His saw pointed to the edge of the woods, where Bonny the horse nibbled at ferns.

"I have to change," I said. "Aunt Phyllis got me a new dress."

"Get right back," was all he said. I watched his bad foot search for the missing rung until his leg stretched down to the next solid place. The cut trees looked lopsided and wary, as if they'd been punished. Both feet met ground. He yanked the ladder and headed for the next tree.

In the privy, I reached up to the ledge and thought for a gasp that the Hand was gone. Maybe a mouse had carried it away. Or had the Hand taken itself into someone else's realm? Had I used up a valuable wish on a silly dress?

My fingers pinched it. I pulled it to me, dragging dust

and a cemetery of flies. Wants jumbled in me, and questions. I didn't doubt the Hand's capabilities. The dress had me convinced. But what were the particulars? Sometimes you got three wishes, sometimes as many as you could dream up. But still, it would be best not to waste wishes, however many I may or may not have already had.

The Hand lay on my palm, no hotter or cooler than my own skin. I traced its etchings with a finger. *Bring Fry back.* Wasn't that the only important thing?

Make us all happy. How was that? No. Ingie Peterssen's uncle was a halfwit full-grown man who chortled and crowed like a baby. *He* was happy. Careful, I told myself. Magic is tricky. Didn't the man who wished for sausage end up with one growing on the tip of his nose? I would have to think about the wishes before asking for anything else. I tucked the Hand in my new blue dress and headed inside to hide it in my room.

Where to keep it? The top of the wardrobe was too exposed, I decided, but this drawer was subject to my aunt's pryings, this shelf too musty, this gap between the beams precarious. I fussed about, tucking it into my grandmother's linens in the bottom drawer, closing up the dresser and staring at it, throwing doors open, kicking them shut, scraping a chair across the floor so as to reach the inaccessible, and thus came across an old bedwarmer. The Hand fit inside with room to spare. I padded the interior with a clean napkin embroidered with someone's initials, and slid the whole business beneath my bed.

The new dress looked a bit gray from my efforts. I

changed into my shabby shirtwaist and hurried back to the orchard. The heat had blown away and clouds crossed the sun. Bonny was hitched to the cart. I stroked her between the eyes. Branches with crusty black boils lay scattered on the ground. The wood wasn't heavy, but I got tired from the bending and throwing into the cart in the sunny heat.

He finished before I did and came over with the empty pail. "When that's all loaded, take it to the beach. I'll go burn it when I've got the rest."

"Shouldn't I start supper?" I said. "I could take the cart over when the potatoes are cooking." I was hungry from my aunt's watery soup.

"Those branches have disease on them. They can't be sitting. The spores'll fly around and reinfect the trees."

My face must have told him something, though usually I was good at keeping my insides hidden. "Say!" he said. "You get the job?"

I could only nod, because I felt like I might cry for no good reason. I never cried.

"Good," he said. "You tell me about it later. I've got to give those trees more medicine. You had to eat daffodil soufflé flambé over there, didn't you?" He made me laugh sometimes with his funny way of saying things. I swallowed down the sting in my throat. He looked a lot better when he was smiling. His eyes didn't droop as much, but there wasn't much light in them either.

"Take an apple with you," he said. "Scrub your hands first. I don't want *you* getting the black knot." He went into the shed to stir something up. I finished loading. My hands were sticky and streaked black. I scrubbed them hard at the sink and threw the dark water out by the shed and washed out the basin with soap.

Bonny didn't want to go on the main road. My eyes were dry and dusty. I was going blind from the spores, I figured. I wondered if I'd grow black warts and would I die if they weren't cut off, and how disfigured I might become. Then Fry would be afraid of me, if I ever saw him again. I tugged at Bonny and she shook her head. I fed her part of my apple. She still wouldn't make the turn. I had to use the stick on her. She was mad.

We trundled toward the lake. The tents of the preacher people hulked in the maples. Someone, maybe Mrs. Rankin, poked at a tidy fire. Two ladies sat at a long table, busy with sewing or some such close and peering work. We passed them by and made the turn onto the beach road. The lake was restless. I stopped the cart by the widest stretch of sand, where the grass was sparse and there weren't any birches to catch in the wind. The wind had rain in it. More rain was probably bad for the cherry trees, unless it helped their new wounds.

I unhooked the tailgate and pulled at the slashed branches in their spiky heap. Afraid I might pull the pile down on top of myself and be imbued with the blight, I climbed up and over the seat onto the cart bed and pushed. A branch lodged in a corner, the green wood bending, then snapping like a switch. I wrestled the pile until it slid out, tumbling onto the road, leaving dark flakes and grit on the floor of the cart. Then I saw two boys at the edge of the water, kicking and stomping at the waves. The bigger slammed into the smaller one and sent him staggering. The small one almost fell, but recovered himself. He saw me and pointed.

I started dragging my pile across the sand. "Hey!" someone called out. "You can't do that." I turned to look. The smaller boy was throwing rocks into the lake as if he wanted to bruise the water. I hoped Fry wouldn't turn into a boy like that, instead of the kind who talked to stones and gave them names and gathered blossoms to give the stones to make them happy.

The bigger boy was running at me. "You can't!" I heard him say. I turned away and swept my pile through a stand of beach grass. The tiny hard cherries clacked like beads.

I heard the boy come up behind me. "You can't dump your trash here," he said. "This is a private beach."

"No, it isn't."

"It is. And you can't be on it unless you're an Association member. It's a regulation."

"According to who?" I said.

"Common knowledge." The boy had big ears that stuck out and bony ankles and big feet. Lake water dripped from his rolled-up trouser legs. He had a hard, thin mouth. "I'd take all that out of here if I were you."

"I've got special permission," I said. I was almost back to Bonny and the cart.

"Permission from who?" The loudmouthed boy was right beside me with his big ears.

"The railroad. I'm related to the owner."

"And who's that?"

"My uncle."

"What's his name?"

"I don't believe that's any of your business, young man," I said. One of the big white clouds slid over the sun. The breeze chilled.

"You don't know what you're talking about," the boy said. "Mr. Dell's not your uncle. He doesn't even live around here. He lives in Chicago."

"Do tell. My other uncle's the sheriff. Fowler Wilmot. Ask anybody." This was true. The other wasn't.

"Sure he is," the boy sneered. "*My* uncle's Theodore Roosevelt."

I strode back to the cart. The small boy had noticed that he'd been left behind, and was running for us with his stick. I took up a piece of tree, weaving my fingers and the wood together. "If you were a gentleman, you'd help me," I said. "But then, gentlemen don't start bossing people when they haven't even been introduced."

"Well, Miss Madame, I *would*, but I'm otherwise engaged. You call this a horse?" He slid his fist along Bonny's harness and yanked on the rein. "It's a nag, is what it is. A nag."

Bonny twitched and sighed. I wished she'd kick this jug-eared boy, but she was a gentle horse, and I took the wish back in case the Hand was listening. I yanked branches from the cart. My hands had dark dust on them.

"I guess I'll have to report you," the boy said.

"Go right ahead," I said. "Give my uncle a good laugh."

Mercy was coming along the road, walking fast. I was

surrounded. I wanted all the summer people to go away and conduct their prayer meetings and rule-making summits elsewhere. Except Miss Nadia. As long as she didn't bite my head off, she could stay.

"Willis!" Mercy called. "You'd better get back right this minute. Emmet too."

"Who says?"

"Father." This Willis was Mercy's brother then, poor girl.

"What do I have to do?" the little boy said. He was at the cart too, reaching for Bonny's mane. I dragged my branches over to the pile.

"Father's unhappy with you two," Mercy said. "The tent you put up fell down and just about suffocated Miss Stebbins. Father said if you'd taken the time to do it right, it never would have happened, and you were supposed to have him look at it before you went running off. He said he told you to interrupt him even if he was working on his sermon."

"Did Miss Stebbins have to have a doctor?" the little boy Emmet asked.

"Not so far," Mercy said. "I can't believe you didn't hear her screaming. She was having the biggest hysterics you've ever seen. Mother had to practically throw water on her. They ripped the tent getting her out too. Father says you two had better figure out how to fix it. I'd hurry if I were you. He's getting madder by the second."

I'd finished piling up my branches. I put up the tailgate and nudged sand over the places where the ground was spotted with crusty fragments of black. It didn't seem good for it to blow around. Emmet followed Willis across the road.

Mercy's hand cupped my elbow. "Listen," she whispered. "I've got something to tell you."

"I've got work," I said. I didn't want to talk to anyone. I was sticky and dusty and hungry and annoyed. I hoisted myself onto the seat of the cart.

Mercy pulled herself up to join me. "It isn't far. It won't take any time at all. You'll want to see it. Go that way." She pointed down the road.

Bonny started off, happy to be leaving. "I guess those are your brothers," I said.

"Aren't they abominable? Willis especially. He's a disgusting horrible sneak and liar. All Emmet does is follow him around. He'll be just like him one of these days. I wish I had a sister more than anything in the world, but not a baby one. I hope we don't get any more babies in my family. I'd have to take care of it every minute and babies are exhausting. Do you have any sisters?"

I shook my head.

"You can stop right there," she said, and scrambled down.

She can't have found my hole, I thought. I covered it all up. But she was headed exactly to the rat root place.

"This is all my fault," she whispered. "Say you'll be my friend still."

"I don't know what you did," I said. "Maybe it's something terrible."

"Well, that's what I don't know," she said. "Maybe it's

not very bad. Let's make a pact. I'll tell you everything if you tell me everything."

"Sure," I said.

"Promise?" she said.

"Promise," I said, but of course I intended to tell her exactly nothing.

7
PIE

"So listen," Mercy said. "Yesterday when I was looking for the stream I saw you digging, and I thought maybe you were burying a dead kitten and wouldn't want to be disturbed. And when you went to the beach, I waited a little and then I went there too. And I would have told you before, except my mother came. Now it's your turn. What were you digging up?"

She was a canny beaver girl. Beavers plan things out, what log to use to patch the broken house, where to direct the water to float supplies.

"I didn't dig up anything," I said. "I was burying some moldy old rags. I'm tired of this game. I should have been home already. My father's going to skin me."

"So you're not mad?"

She was blocking the path. To get around her, I'd have had to wade through poison ivy. I felt like pushing her into it, but I wanted her to finish telling me what she wanted me to know. "Of course I'm not mad," I managed to say.

"That's good. My father says it's always best to be honest, but sometimes it isn't, because you could get in trouble when you wouldn't have. And even if God knows everything bad you do, I don't think he cares about some little shady thing that doesn't hurt anybody, when there's people doing much worse things, like making children work in mines."

She moved forward. I followed her through the ferns. My guts felt unsettled.

"I wanted to see if I could follow your tracks and find out where you live," she said. "Because you never did say, and I was afraid I wouldn't run into you again. And I thought if I showed my mother your house, she might ask your father if you might come visit, and then you'd have to, because it would be all arranged. In case you might be shy. I used to be shy myself, but I'm not anymore. So I came back here, because I thought maybe I'd find a path to your house, and I saw the hole all covered up. So I poked around with a stick. And I saw something that wasn't dirt or leaves, and it was a bone."

I remembered then: slash of white in the dirt. Severed root, I'd thought.

Where the ferns weren't trampled flat, they were covered by green canvas weighted down with stones. Papers impaled by sticks read: DIG IN PROGRESS. DO NOT DISTURB SITE.

"A big long curved bone," she went on. "And I just knew it was a rib bone of a person. There wasn't anything else it could be. So I screamed. I couldn't help it. And Willis and

Emmet heard, because they're always spying around, and they found some beads and a knife, and there might be a whole entire Indian graveyard right—"

The tattooed feather lady! "This is *our stream*!" I cried. "You don't just go around *digging*!"

"*I'm* not doing it! I think it's morbid. But Father—"

"It's breaking the *law* to tear up peoples' land! It's ours all the way to Thomas Road."

I didn't really know if it was. Aunt Phyllis was always moaning about the pieces my grandfather had sold. For all I knew, we barely owned our own house.

"I'm not saying it's right," Mercy said. "But the laws are different if it has to do with history. The bones might be a famous chief. Or there could have been a murder. My father says the authorities have to be notified."

"*What* authorities?"

"The land people, I guess. And maybe archaeologists. My brother's dream come true. He says the copper knife could be an important find."

"My father won't allow it. He hates unjust laws that aren't fair. *Slavery* used to be a law."

"Well, I hope he puts a stop to it. Dead people should stay buried, even if they're worth studying. The grave could have a curse on it, for all anybody knows."

Is that why the feather lady had the Hand between her palms—to curse the ground?

"What were you sneaking around following me for!" I kicked at the makeshift sign and toppled one of its sticks. "People can't just dig wherever they feel like it!"

"Well, nobody's done any actual digging," Mercy said. "The bone was just sticking out. And if it's your land, maybe you'll get to keep the beads. They're really mysterious and old looking. You would have found them yourself, except you didn't see them. They were lying right in the dirt. Willis and Emmet didn't see them either, they were so fascinated about the bones."

"Oh! So *you're* the one who went poking around."

"I didn't mean to! And I'm really really sorry I followed you, but it was just to make friends, and I already said so. And you don't have to be so mean about it. And just so you know, the tent didn't fall down because the boys didn't put it up right. I pulled out the pegs so I could talk to you alone *and* Willis would be out of the way *and* he'd get in trouble. And if he hadn't been skulking about, I would have stuck that bone back in the ground and I wouldn't have said a thing about it."

We looked each other over. She was someone with a lot of ideas, a straight talker, not snooty or a giggler.

"Did the lady the tent fell on have to see a doctor?" I said.

She shrugged. "Not even close. She thought it was kind of funny. I just said she had hysterics to get my brothers' blood going. And don't think I'm some screechy sissy because of that bone. I didn't really scream. I gasped. But loud enough for them to hear. But I'd better go now. *Please* come and see me, won't you?"

"I've got a job, so I don't know when I can," I said. "But I will."

A cool wind had come up and we were both due elsewhere. I went first down the path and she followed. We didn't speak, in case of lurking spies. She waved. So did I. She went her way along the deer path into the woods. I got into the cart and clicked at Bonny to hurry home.

From inside the house there was a thumping, as if someone was throwing boots at a wall. My father was at the counter wielding a cleaver. A plucked chicken sprawled beneath his hand. Bone shattered as the cleaver thunked down. "What took you so long?" he said, flinging the meat into a pot.

"I found something out. Those preacher people—"

"I told you! Stay away from them. When a preacher's not telling working people it's noble to be poor, he's drinking the governor's brandy or pawing at some war widow who came to see about milk for the baby. Stew this up and make a chicken pie." He clattered on the pot lid to keep the flies away and wiped his hands on the bloody towel.

"But over by the stream, that's our—"

"Is the wood on the beach?"

"Right where you said. But I've never made chicken pie before. What do I—"

But he was out the door and flinging more trash for burning into the cart. I wanted to hurl the pot of chicken parts at the wall. It wouldn't be my fault if the pie came out stringy and gummy and bland. He never explained anything or listened or cared about anything except the doomed cherries.

I watched flies gather on the cleaver until I heard Bonny and the cart clanking and creaking away, then went upstairs, crouched by the bed, and pulled out the bedwarmer.

The Hand hadn't gone anywhere. I unwrapped it and put it between my palms and felt it get warm, and then I was no longer weary and empty. I was strong and smart and had a good job. I would make the best chicken pie anybody ever had, and my father would make them stop the digging and nobody would disrupt the magic of the Hand or ever find out about it, and I would have everything I deserved in life.

Figuring out the pie, I realized that things you can eat will talk to you. The meat didn't like it when the water boiled too hard, so I let it barely bubble. The sauce wanted parsley and all the cream we had. The crust wanted to be leaf shapes in an overlapping spiral. He got back before the top got brown, but by the time he watered Bonny and fiddled around in the shed and washed up, the pie was exactly done. His eyes were red and he smelled of smoke from the sick green wood. After the second bite he almost smiled. I waited until his plate was half empty.

"You know the stream where it goes into the lake?" I began. "Whose land is that?"

"Probably ours," he said.

"You mean it might not be?"

"Pieces got bought and sold," he said. "Who wants to know?" He speared a single creamy pea with his fork.

"Well, some of the summer people kids were playing around, because they thought over there it was their land. And they found a skeleton and an ancient copper knife and beads and things. Their father says if you find something old, you're supposed to report it to the authorities, so he's going to. But if it's our land, he shouldn't do that, should he?"

"Oh, ho! That's the church for you. Why do you think the Indians lost everything they had? The damn gold-mongering missionaries! They've thieved away all the godliness from the world!"

"So you'll stop them, right?"

"What, the grave robbers? Too late! They got their loot."

"But you could talk to them! It's probably just a misunderstanding. It won't be dark for a long time. You could go right now."

His chair scraped back. "Later, maybe. Too much to do."

"But what if these copper things are rare and valuable? They *took* them! They could just go ahead and sell it all, and we'd never get a dime. And they're saying it's *their* land!"

"Well. It might be. The property lines are screwy."

"Well, how do we find out? Aren't there papers that prove it? I could look for them."

"Deed office. Sure, go ahead. Traipse on up there, wait for seventy hours for the dusty old coot to shuffle papers, then oh surprise, back taxes someone miscalculated a hundred years ago. That's how they get you. I *said* I'd look into it when I've got a spare couple of minutes. Get the water going, would you? I'll need a bath when I come in, get the black knot off me." He clattered out.

Black knot on *me* was of no consequence. I heated water and hauled more and filled the tub for him and did the dishes and he wasn't back, but if I bathed first he'd surely arrive in the middle of it and tramp around and glower, so I took a basin outside and washed my face and neck and feet and hair. I was drying it by the stove when he came in.

"I have to be at work at seven," I said.

"Your aunt says she's a big shot, this boss of yours."

"She doesn't act like it," I said. "She's nice. I get to hold her cameras. They're much bigger than the one Aunt Phyllis has."

"Don't put up with any guff," he said. "She yells at you or anything, you just walk off that job, you hear me? No job's worth being treated like a dog. Just feed the chickens before you go. I'll get my own breakfast—the rest of that pie. I couldn't have made it better."

I left him to his bath. He was the emperor of guff. He gave my mother so much guff she ran away. He was always telling her how to do things she could already do and then he'd try to make up when she was already mad and it was too late.

Upstairs, I slid out the bedwarmer from beneath the bed and unwrapped the Hand. It was dull in the fading day, and it didn't seem very magical now. I traced the curves and lines with a finger in the air, not touching. Touch seemed to chill it. The jolts of cold—maybe they were the feather lady cursing me, mad about her bones.

As far as wishes went, there was really only one. But if my mother was indeed dead and I wished for her to come home, would I be visited by a specter? Or if I wished that she wasn't really dead, was that something the Hand could arrange somehow, and would my soul be taken in return?

The Hand was still. I covered it back up, shoved it back into the dusty dark beneath the bed, and let the lapping waves of Blue Lake hush me to sleep.

8
THE SITTING

The next morning I got to the hotel at ten to seven by the lobby clock. I took the stairs up and stood by room two twenty-five until my breath slowed down. Then I knocked.

Miss Nadia was wearing a blue-green dress with black appliqued loops at the sleeves. She waved me into the room. "First thing, we have a sitting. I hope it won't be too dull, but we'll do our best to spice it."

"Yes, Miss Zalzman," I said.

"Miss Nadia, I prefer." She closed the door. "Remember?"

I nodded. I'd gulp like a fish if I tried to speak. My heart resounded in my ears. I wanted to do everything right.

Miss Nadia was looking out the window at the lake dancing in the sun.

"The light maybe won't be too bad," she said. "I don't like to do a sitting in the morning. Afternoon light is better for faces. But this child has her sleeping time that the mother refuses to disarrange, much as I pleaded with her."

She turned away from the window and saw me standing in the middle of the room. She motioned to a table, set with a gold-rimmed plate and silverware and a small dish with slices of strawberry in it and another dish with a silver dome Aunt Phyllis would have coveted.

"Sit," she said. "There is your breakfast. I hope it's all right for you. I have some things to do while you eat it and then we'll go down."

"Oh, I'm not hungry, thank you," I said.

"You didn't understand me? I said that I would feed you. What did you eat this morning then?"

"Bread and tea," I said, but really I'd had nothing.

"That isn't breakfast. Later you can see the menu and decide about tomorrow. If I forget before you go, you'll please remind me. You will often be reminding me of things, and you mustn't be shy about it. Now eat for your mind and eyes to be strong. We're going to the sand, a bad place for cameras."

A bell rang. "Already you're working," Miss Nadia said. "Answer please, and take a message. I am not here. Not for anybody." The bell rang again. It was the telephone. "Quickly!" She thrust a paper and pencil at me.

I had never spoken into a telephone receiver before. When Aunt Phyllis's telephone rang, she always pounced on it eagerly, and it was never for me. I lifted the instrument. "Hello. This is Miss Zalzman's room," I said, hoping it was the right thing.

"Put her on," said a voice. "It's Alice Dell."

I faltered. Surely Miss Nadia would want to talk to the

wife of the boss. But Miss Nadia had disappeared. I saw then that there was an open door leading to another room. She had two rooms, then. "Miss Nadia is out at the moment," I said.

"Out where?"

"She'll be right back," I said. I didn't want Miss Nadia to be in trouble with Mrs. Dell, but maybe Mrs. Dell would expect a call back soon, and what if Miss Nadia didn't want to?

"Well, tell her to go ahead with the little girl on the beach this morning. I have some things to do. I'll call her later. Can you remember that?" She clicked away.

I looked at the paper Miss Nadia had given me to write on. *Mrs. Dell*, I put down, then wondered if that was sufficient. Because I was hungry, I decided that it was. Besides, Miss Nadia had said I had to eat.

Under the dome was a mound of scrambled eggs, with toast cut into triangles and a cluster of tiny purple grapes that were like fairy cordial when burst. Miss Nadia came through the door and stood at the window holding up a photograph and then another one to the light.

"Who called?" she finally said.

"Mrs. Dell. She said you shouldn't wait for her."

"A godsend," Miss Nadia said. She tossed the stack of pictures on the table, flipped one onto its back, and wrote something on it.

The eggs were good, but I couldn't finish them, or all the little buttery toasts either. I covered the rest with the dome and finished the tea Miss Nadia had poured for me. The last of it was extra sweet from sugar that hadn't gotten stirred.

Miss Nadia told me which cases to pick up. We went out

into the hall. There wasn't much to the carrying. The boxes she had me take were heavy for their size, but not so difficult, and she took a canvas bag and a long rolled-up umbrella and another long contraption of wood. We jostled ourselves into the elevator. The two gentlemen who were already in it pressed themselves to the back. They were holding tennis rackets. Everything they wore was white.

The elevator man pulled at the lever that closed us in. Miss Nadia's hand swept over her head. "My hat," she exclaimed. "You didn't tell me!" She gave me a look of accusation. "Out, please," she told the elevator man.

The elevator man made the door open. "Thank you so much," Miss Nadia told him. "Violet, meet me in the lobby." She thrust the bag and umbrella and wooden contraption at me. I had to put my two boxes down to take them. Miss Nadia stepped from the elevator to the solid floor. The elevator lurched and sank. Should I have noticed that she had no hat? Already I wasn't measuring up. I would have to pay attention and move fast or I'd be on the wrong side of this darting mink of an employer. But how could I do things I didn't know I was supposed to do? I didn't even know what anything was called.

The elevator doors slid open and the elevator man helped me take everything out. The two gentlemen slid past me as I attempted to load myself with everything at once. After a couple of tries, I managed to do so, and trudged myself over to a chair, out of the way of the people coursing through the lobby. The train had recently arrived, and the room was loud with greetings and children's chatter.

I watched the elevator. She didn't come out the first time the doors came open, or the second either. I began to think I'd misunderstood her. Maybe she'd taken the stairs down and was outside wondering why I couldn't follow a simple instruction. I couldn't very well wander about looking. I couldn't carry everything easily, and her things couldn't be left alone.

"Need a hand, Miss?" One of the young men who hoisted luggage stopped by my chair.

"Oh, no," I said. "I'm just waiting." Then I saw Miss Nadia behind him, coming from the stairway. I waved, but she had seen me already. She had on a nicely shaped hat with a cream-colored band, and was carrying a small case she must have left behind the first time.

"Mr. Duvall!" she exclaimed to the young man. "How are you today?"

"I'm well, Miss Zalzman," he replied.

She put a hand on my shoulder. "Isaac Duvall, I'd like you to meet Miss Violet Blake. Miss Blake and I are taking all this business to the beach. We would be most gratified if you could help us. We're in a hurry. Mrs. Peterssen might be thinking we forgot her."

"Yes, ma'am," Isaac Duvall said, loading himself up. Miss Nadia handed me her small case and hoisted the wooden contraption over her shoulder like a rifle. We followed her out the big doors, down the steps, along the boardwalk that stretched over the sand.

There were few people on the beach, as it was still early. If I was staying at such a place, I thought, and no work to do, I'd be outdoors as soon as it was light, letting my feet cool in wet sand, diving under the waves. Unless it was raining, in which case I'd have a stack of books to choose from, and a bowl of those grapes.

Before I drifted into reverie, I did my best to harness my mind. I'd already caused Miss Nadia to be annoyed about the hat. Though she seemed to not be dwelling on it, she might be keeping count of my negligences, and I liked this job so far.

Miss Nadia stopped at the end of the boardwalk and pointed at a driftwood log near the edge of the water. "I want to use that. The little girl can sit or climb it. So if the two of you could put these things let's say twenty feet this side." We did so.

Miss Nadia thanked Isaac Duvall and told him that we would manage now without him. He went back to the boardwalk, stepping off it to let Mrs. Peterssen by. She carried a small squirming girl and sailed past him, not looking his way.

"There's Mrs. Peterssen and Clara," I told Miss Nadia. Mrs. Peterssen put Clara down on a bench to retie the little girl's bonnet. Clara kicked at the seat.

"Ah. So you know them." Miss Nadia said.

"Just because of the store," I said. I didn't want her thinking I was friendly with dreamy, squinty Ingie.

"Certainly. Small-town life, yes? Go meet them, please, and bring them over." She bent over one of the cases, unlatching it.

As I stepped across the sugary sand, I was glad I'd been

the one to land the job that Ingie wasn't fit for. Mrs. Peterssen was one of those who didn't like my mother. She never did anything to show it, was always polite in her tight-lipped way, but I could tell. I wouldn't have liked my mother either if I looked like Mrs. Peterssen, with her chapped, peeling cheeks and watery eyes.

"Good morning, Mrs. Peterssen," I said, cheerful as the day.

Mrs. Peterssen was blowing her nose in a rumpled handkerchief and couldn't reply. Clara had found two stones and was clacking them together.

"Miss Zalzman is down the beach," I said. "I can show you."

"Where?" Mrs. Peterssen said suspiciously, as if I might be leading her and Clara to a den of baby stealers. She tucked the damp handkerchief into her sleeve and squinted. "All the way down there?" she croaked, and coughed into her fist.

"Do you have a cold, Mrs. Peterssen?" I said sweetly. I knew it was nothing that simple. Mrs. Peterssen was a chronic sneezer and sprainer, a collector of ailments.

"I'll be all right." Mrs. Peterssen bent down to pick up Clara.

"Don't want to," Clara said, kicking.

Mrs. Peterssen took a step back. "We're going to see the nice lady," she said. "Come on, now. Don't be fussing."

"No! Don't want to," Clara said, clutching for rocks in the sand.

"Clara," I said, crouching down so my face was by hers. I put my hands lightly on her loaded fists in case she decided to flail out. "See the water? There's so many rocks there, a thousand million, all different colors. You want to get some?"

She thought about it and took off, scuttling for the shimmering lake. Her legs were short, but she was fast.

"Get her!" Mrs. Peterssen cried. I caught Clara up and lifted her in a twirl to make her laugh.

"Well!" Miss Nadia exclaimed. "Clara is with us." She eyed the approaching Mrs. Peterssen and dropped her voice so I had to strain to hear. "The poor child has too many garments. Get her shoes off, and whatever else is keeping her from enjoying the beauty of this day. Before the mother comes. Quick." She went back to unfurling her big umbrella.

Everyone who saw Clara always declared she was an angel, but there was nothing angelic about her, kicking at me with her hard heels as I tried to undo her shoe buttons.

"Rocks!" she exclaimed, waving at the shoreline. The big lake shied out a wondrous array of stones, some of them embedded with fragments of ancient creatures. When Fry and I used to wait on the beach for our mother to buy soup bones and buttons, he always filled his pockets with them. Then on the way home when his legs wore out, I'd have to tell him to hide them by the side of the road or I wouldn't carry him. I always let him keep just one.

One of Clara's shoes was off, and Mrs. Peterssen was hurrying at us. "No, no, no!" she cried. "She'll catch something!"

Miss Nadia thrust the umbrella at Mrs. Peterssen. "Will you hold this for me, please?" she said. "I don't have enough hands. Thank you. Oh, we must have Clara barefoot for this picture. This is the child of the woods and lakes, free from the city life. You see?" Miss Nadia had fastened a camera on top of the wooden spider contraption. She darted beneath the camera cloth. Clara was sitting in the sand, picking up stones. The camera clicked.

"Let's get the bonnet off, Miss Blake." Miss Nadia came out from under the cloth. "Mrs. Peterssen, one step to your right with the umbrella."

"But her curls!" Mrs. Peterssen cried. "I had such a time with them!"

"We must see them then!" declared Miss Nadia. "The curls must be kissed by the sun. Miss Blake, when I tell you, the hat comes off, but not until I'm ready. Be waiting right by her to pounce when I say so, like a cat. Mrs. Peterssen, you can take yourself a walk if you like. We will be half an hour. No more." She strode around with her camera.

"Look at the lady, Clara," Mrs. Peterssen offered.

Miss Nadia, now crouching, waved at her impatiently, as if Mrs. Peterssen were a bee. "Thank you, but I will be the one to say where Clara looks. All right. Now, Miss Blake."

It was like being in a show. Now smooth the hair. Now give her this cookie, but have her sit on the driftwood first. Now tell her a story about something in the sky, so that she looks out at the water like she was doing when the camera was being loaded. Hold the umbrella right exactly here. Make the sand flat so all those footprints are gone. I did everything exactly like a cat, every move deliberate, and held stock still in between.

"All done!" Miss Nadia exclaimed. "Thank you, Clara. You are a most cooperative model. Mrs. Peterssen, thank you for your patience." She reached into the canvas bag and emerged with an envelope, which she handed to Mrs. Peterssen. "For Clara's services."

Mrs. Peterssen opened the envelope. All seemed to be in order inside. She tucked it in her bag. "Well, that didn't take long, anyway," she said. Miss Nadia knelt, closing up the camera cases.

"You can't carry all that," Mrs. Peterssen said.

"Certainly we can." Miss Nadia pulled at a strap.

"The hotel's got those boys," Mrs. Peterssen said.

"We'll manage," Miss Nadia said.

"I don't blame you," Mrs. Peterssen said. "I wouldn't let one of them touch my things. The colored steal."

"Do they?" Miss Nadia raised herself. "And you know this how?"

"Everybody knows it."

"Who's this everybody? I know many Negro people, and none of them are criminals."

"Lots of them are," Mrs. Peterssen insisted, stuffing Clara back into her bonnet.

"I think not," Miss Nadia said, not unkindly. "There might be young men in your town who want the jobs at the hotel—bellboy, waiter. Instead the hotel brings in people from hundreds of miles away."

"Yes, when my son is strong and needs work."

"I see. But not the workers' fault. They work hard for low pay, and many have experience in hotels. A management decision. Where did your people come from? Sweden, maybe?"

"Norway." Mrs. Peterssen sniffed.

"Norway. It's beautiful there, I understand. You remember it?"

"Not much. I wasn't so much bigger than Clara when I came."

"A long way, yes? I made almost that same journey, fourteen years old. Long and hard. For you too, it must have been."

"I'll never forget that boat," Mrs. Peterssen said. "My mother almost died. I had to help take care of her."

"Too much for too little a girl," Miss Nadia said, putting the blanket in the canvas bag. "You and I, we had the hard trip over. But those bellboys, their people came here on much worse boats. As captives, yes?"

"That doesn't give them the right to steal."

Miss Nadia stood straight. "That's ignorance you're speaking," she snapped. "Every one of those waiters and bellboys are in college. The young man who was just helping us, Isaac Duvall, is studying to be a doctor like his father. I don't worry about stealing."

"Well, you should," Mrs. Peterssen said. "Clara! We're going home now." Clara was busy creeping up on the waves, backing away when the water came too close. I felt bad for her. The Peterssens lived a quarter-mile from the beach and never came to watch the sky or bury each other in the sand. She'd grow up to be like Ingie, dull and slow.

"Sad story, that woman," Miss Nadia said. "Sick with fear." She hoisted the canvas bag, the umbrella, and the folded wooden spider.

So this is what the lady on the veranda meant about Miss

Nadia biting peoples' heads off, I thought. Well, she's somebody who doesn't just simper around and let people say bad things about people they don't even know. And even if Miss Nadia did bite Mrs. Peterssen's head off, she felt sorry for her too.

That would be worse, I thought. Better for Miss Nadia to bite my head off than feel sorry for the motherless mite. But I didn't want either one, so I hurried after her and made sure I didn't drag anything in the sand as we made our way back to the hotel.

9
QUILLS

Upstairs, Miss Nadia presented me with a menu and said to choose what I liked for lunch. I didn't like to ask her what a Halibut a la Delmonico was, or Poulet Parisienne. I said I'd have Floating Island, liking how it sounded.

She looked up and smiled. "That's a sweet, did you know? How about something more substantial beforehand? Soup, maybe? Now watch and listen. Next time you will do it." She showed me how ordering was done, what numbers to dial and what to tell the kitchen.

While we waited for lunch, Miss Nadia showed me the darkroom. Really it was the washroom in the room she called her studio. The darkroom was all set up so Miss Nadia could make pictures in there. The window was covered with black velvet, and there was a curtain that went over the closed door. If even a speck of light entered, the pictures would be ruined. In case she had to see, there was a red electric bulb that didn't hurt anything if it was on.

The soup was fish in a tasty but thin red broth, and Floating Island was an airy bubble of nothing, but I wasn't hungry anyway, and the phone kept ringing with people Miss Nadia didn't want to speak with, and I had to write down who they were.

Then for a good part of the afternoon we dragged ourselves all over the hotel, from kitchen to ballroom to casino and other rooms whose purpose I didn't know. Miss Nadia only took a few pictures in each of the rooms we went into, but she wrote a lot down in a thin black leather notebook, narrowing her eyes as she looked at windows, frowning as she tugged at curtains to let more light in.

Finally she looked at her watch. "Ten to the hour. We'll call it five o'clock. That's ten hours you worked today. Too many. I'll wear you out before we're even started."

"I'm not tired, Miss Nadia."

"We keep track so nobody forgets," she said, writing in her notebook. "Eight o'clock tomorrow. Not seven like today. You'll remember, yes?"

"Yes," I said. "But you can't carry all these things by yourself, Miss Nadia. I can take them for you before I go."

She was looking out the window. "The light's good now," she said. "Maybe I can get a shot of the hotel outside. Then you'll leave me. And then I'd better think about what to say at this talk I'm giving tonight, or I'll be standing like a fish with my mouth open and nothing coming out." She smiled her quick minkish smile.

We went to her room and left everything there but one

camera and the wooden spider that she stood it on. She was in a rush to get outside, so we took the stairs down. The lobby had hardly anybody in it, just a man with a gray pointed goat beard sitting in one of the chairs. A bellboy opened the door for us.

Outside, people were starting to gather at the depot for the next train to take them to the bigger station in the next town, where you could get the train to Chicago. Two Indian ladies sat by the depot on a mat woven from rushes, with decorated bark boxes spread out in front of them. One of the ladies was old, with a white braid down her back. Some of the people waiting for the train were picking up the boxes and turning them over and opening their lids. Every box had a different design—a hummingbird, a trillium, a woven pattern of colored lines.

"Two dollars," the old lady said.

"I'll give you one-fifty," a man said.

"Two dollars." The old lady held out her hand for the man's money.

Miss Nadia headed their way and I followed with the camera in its case. Even with the wooden spider over her shoulder, Miss Nadia moved like lightning.

"These are beautiful," she said to the old Indian lady. "Birchbark, yes?"

Black reeds or stalks jutted from the old lady's mouth. She pulled one between her teeth, flattening it. "That's right," she said, giving me a flit of a glance, too quick to be a glare, but not a friendly look. She had probing eyes and a wide face. The younger lady was making a woodpecker with a red head on a round piece of bark.

"Where I'm from, we have birch boxes too." Miss Nadia steadied the wooden spider on the sand and squatted by the boxes. "Not embroidered like yours. Carved and painted. The people there make everything from birch—houses, boats, medicine. Traditional people, I mean. Not in the cities."

"Where's that?" the old lady said.

"Russia. You know Russia? A big country, but not enough room for everybody. Many of us went elsewhere to find a better life. What's that you're using for the designs?"

"Quills," the old lady said. "Porcupine."

"It must be difficult to do well," Miss Nadia said. "Years of practice."

"It depends." The old lady stabbed a quill through a hole that was already made for it to go into. "My granddaughter here, she's only just learning, but hers all sell out. She's not fast, though. I can do them fast."

The granddaughter had finished the woodpecker's red head. "Aren't you Georgia Blake's girl?" she said to me.

My throat went thick to hear the name. I could only nod.

"I wasn't sure I recognized you," the granddaughter said. "You've grown a lot. You came to our house one time, you and your little brother, with Georgia. On the river road."

It came to me then. My mother had taken Fry and me to a house that had stalks and leaves drying from every rafter. Fry hadn't liked it there.

The evening train blew its whistle from the other side of

the harbor. It would come over the bridge by the river road, loaded with more city people. The old lady pulled a quill between her teeth. She wasn't making a picture of anything, just black lines and red ones.

"My husband caught a big sucker fish that day," the granddaughter said. She was working on the bird's eye in tiny stitches with a white quill. "Your brother was afraid of it."

"Maybe she doesn't remember," the old lady said. She had a sour face. "It was awhile back now."

I did remember. Fry hadn't been afraid of the sucker fish, but of her. She'd darted looks at him as if he was a cornered mouse that might run at you. He'd hidden behind my mother until she made him come out.

"It's good to meet you both," Miss Nadia said. "I'm Nadia Zalzman. It seems you know Miss Violet Blake."

"I'm Lucy Thornwood," the granddaughter said, shaking Miss Nadia's outstretched hand. "That's my grandmother, Angeline Agosa."

Angeline Agosa lifted her chin at Miss Nadia. The train hooted again, coming around the narrow end of the harbor.

"Mrs. Agosa. A pleasure," Miss Nadia said. "I'd like to talk more another time. Maybe you'll tell me how you get the porcupines. But before the train comes, I wonder if you'd let me take a picture of the two of you. Not posing. Just do what you would do if nobody was here. May I?"

"A quarter," Mrs. Agosa said.

"That's fair," Miss Nadia said.

"Each," Mrs. Agosa said.

Miss Nadia opened the camera case. Clouds gathered

around the sun. "It might be too dark," she said. "The light can't decide what it's doing." But as soon as she got the camera ready, the sun came through. The camera snapped. She held her hand out for another plate. I gave it to her. "Don't look at me," she told the ladies, and clicked.

She came out from beneath the cloth. The train had passed the mill and was coming along Front Street. "I'll be off now," she said. "You too, Violet. Oh! Breakfast. You didn't remind me. Write it down or I won't remember." She handed me the black leather notebook and the little pencil it came with. *Asparagus omelette*, I wrote on a clean page.

My mother had always picked the wild asparagus when it first came up, until the spring she left, when she'd been sad the whole winter and didn't leave the house much. So Fry and I had picked it and brought it home and she looked at it like she'd never seen asparagus before. Fry went into the scrap bag and cut strips of red and yellow and green to tie around her wrists and waist and feet and in her hair.

"Now you can be Christmas all the time," he said. She laughed then, and kissed us both, and cooked the asparagus and tossed butter over it to melt. When Fry ate it, he burst into a smile. "I'm green all over!" he said. That made her laugh again, and she was better for a few days.

I gave Miss Nadia her notebook back. The camera was in its case, the wooden spider folded, and Miss Nadia had her eye on the stripes of clouds over the lake.

"I look forward to meeting you again, Mrs. Agosa, Mrs. Thornwood," she was saying. "I don't want to be in the way of the people coming off the train. Let's hope they buy everything you have." She hoisted the wooden spider and gave me a smile. "Thank you for all you did today, Violet," she said, picking up the camera case. She strode into the sand.

I pretended to be admiring the birch boxes. The day we visited, Fry and I were left with Lucy Thornwood while my mother and Mrs. Agosa went elsewhere. After a time, my mother came back to the kitchen alone. On the walk home, she told me not to tell our father where we'd been. It would worry him, she said. I'd only been ten then, so I didn't disbelieve her.

Lucy Thornwood looked up from her sewing. "Tell your mother I said hello. We haven't seen her in a long time," she said.

"She's been gone since the fourth of May," I said. My throat stung.

"May," Lucy Thornwood said. "That's awhile ago. Where did she go?"

"Up north."

"Georgia went up north," Lucy Thornwood said to her grandmother, but Mrs. Agosa had her eye on a lady who was gathering up boxes and stacking them on the blanket and didn't even nod to say she'd heard.

"I want all these," the lady said. "Let me see that one over there with the white bird." She looked like a white bird herself, dripping with lace from the elbows down. She was wearing a pearl ring as big as a grape.

"Georgia's got all those relatives up there," Lucy Thornwood said to me. "It might take time to visit them all."

All what relatives? All I'd ever heard about was the sister my mother hadn't seen for twenty years. Why did she have to spend good money on a ticket to go see people she hardly even knew?

"Did she tell you where they all are—these people?" I ventured.

Lucy Thornwood shook her head. "I don't know that area up there, so the names didn't stick with me. One place she talked about was an island. Maybe my grandmother would remember, but she's busy now." And she was packing up the stack of boxes for the lacy lady and telling another lady the prices and ignoring me.

What was my mother doing telling everybody all about these relatives and their islands—everybody but her own and only daughter? I flung myself into the crowd, not caring if I stepped on the fancy shoes of the people coming off the train as I passed them by. I hoped to cripple them, or at least leave dark marks on their shoes that would never scrub off. They were rich, and could buy tickets to anywhere, and have asparagus any day of the year. I hated my mother for her secrets and for taking Fry and leaving me. I hated all grown people. They never had a spare minute for anybody. All they cared about was money and keeping children in the dark.

But as I climbed the hill away from town, I remembered that I had a copper hand. My luck was on the rise: white stockings, a brave friend, money from a job. I turned in at our road. The sun was right on top of the trees so they seemed to be on fire. I heard singing. My father hadn't sung in months and months, and he was belting out a wordless tune, rousing and hearty.

The cherry trees, I thought. They're already better, and he's happy again. If that's not magic, what is?

10
BAUBLES

But it wasn't my father who was singing. A man was ambling along our road, a thick-necked man in suspenders, swinging a bulging paper sack, his fishy mouth gaping wide. He waved when he saw me, grinned, and increased his volume.

"The byoo-taful, byoo-taful rii-ver!" he bellowed. "Good day, young lady! You look as if you could be the girl they call Violet. I've been given to understand she lives around here."

"I'm Violet," I said.

He offered me the sack. "Some of my wife's baking. I believe you've made the acquaintance of my daughter, Mercy. I hope the two of you become fast friends. Is your father about?"

Of course. He was Mercy's preacher father, wanting to unravel ownership of the Indian relics his boys had found, thanks to being sneaky.

"My father's in the orchard, I expect," I said, and led him out back, leaving the sack on the steps. As we proceeded, he told me how lucky I was, growing up away from the degradation and despair found in such abundance where too many people live too near each other. He himself had been raised a city boy, but there was nothing like nature to renew the spirit. "God's country!" he proclaimed with the sweep of an arm.

I'd grown up close to godless, to the dismay of Aunt Phyllis, but his statement seemed almost a slap at God. It wasn't God's fault that cities were dirty and crowded, and if God made the earth, wasn't everywhere his country?

"Mr. Blake!" the preacher called out. "Quite a place!" He held out a square white hand. "Reverend Wesley Rankin, sir. One of the newcomers down over by the lake there, banging and sawing away."

My father was knee-deep in raspberry brambles, fashioning a lattice for them. He drew off a glove and took the preacher's offered hand, gauging the strength of the other man's arms and back, resolve and volition. I'd heard him say he could tell if a man was honest by his grasp, but there's a lot of ways to fool someone into believing you, as I well knew.

"Thought I'd stop over and put a face to who's making all the racket down in the woods there," Reverend Rankin said. Their hands parted.

"Go finish the milking," my father told me.

"I was just saying to your girl what pretty country you've got up here. We came out day before yesterday from Chicago on the steamer. Ever been down that way, sir? Chicago? Hotter than the devil's front porch this time of year. What do you grow, sir?"

"This and that." My father had no use for preachers or priests. They were about keeping working people ignorant, he said.

I went as slowly toward the barn as I could get away with. It wasn't my father I was trying to fool. If I didn't milk, he most likely wouldn't notice. It was the magic I hoped to impress. Magic won't do a thing for you if you're not humble and virtuous all the livelong day and share your stale crust with the scabby beggar.

The conversation dimmed away once I was in the barn. He hadn't started the milking at all and maybe hadn't done it in the morning either. I felt bad that I'd left it to him. Moony was our only cow and was lonely, apart from her kind. I milked her enough to ease her, then slipped out of the barn and around the side. Shielded by a broken plow and a tangle of scrap, I was able to hear.

They stood several paces apart. The reverend's hands were clasped behind him. "If you've got a moment, we can go and take a look," he said.

"Don't need to. By the stream it's all mine up to the road," my father said. He spoke with certainty, though he'd told me the boundaries were screwy. I hadn't been aware he was a liar too. So it was in my blood then.

The reverend nodded slowly. "Well. Let me ask you this. If the land's yours, what would you say to allowing my old-est boy Willis to play archaeologist? He reads everything he can get his hands on and knows the tricks—the brushes and such. He's already made a diagram showing where each item was found. And if it happens that you're in a position to sell whatever we find down there, Willis knows the publications."

No, I almost said aloud. Not hideous Willis.

"What all did he find already, this boy of yours?" my father said.

"Not much so far," said the reverend. "A few baubles. As I say, he and some of the other young people came across a bone lying on the ground, partly covered by leaves. It may be the grave was shallow and it's been eroded away by time and weather. When the bone was picked up, their eyes were drawn to the other things. I'll tell you the truth, Mr. Blake. You'd be doing us a favor, keeping our boys occupied. You know boys, I expect. They get wild if they're not put to work. I know I did, when I was one. You have any boys?"

My father didn't even nod. I hoped he was hating himself for letting Fry be taken. "Robbing graves," he said. "What does the Bible have to say about that? Is it on the sin list?"

The reverend let out a burst of air, half a laugh. "Why, Mr. Blake!"

"I'd think it would be frowned on," my father said. "But I'm no churchgoer. I'm ignorant of the particulars. That's why I'm asking."

"I wouldn't call the study of an ancient burial grave robbing," said the reverend.

My father looked up at the tall maple, where a crow lit. "Maybe I didn't understand you right. Didn't you just say you could help me find a buyer for a dead woman's jewelry? She didn't leave it to me in her will, as far as I'm aware. And in my way of thinking, if someone's belongings get dispensed without their knowledge, that would constitute robbery. So, no. I'm not authorizing any digging up of the dead. Not on *my* land. Your boys want work, they can put all they found back in the ground where it was. Whoever's buried there deserves their rest. I want everything buried back up. My land, my say so."

I shuddered. The feather lady—was the Hand's icy coldness her displeasure at the disruption of her bones? Would she blame *me*?

"Well, Mr. Blake," the reverend said. "The matter of ownership has yet to be resolved. My colleagues and I believe that the site in question is contained in the parcel recently purchased by our little group. But perhaps we're misreading the survey. How about you bring your papers and we bring our papers and we pace it out together?"

"Papers!" my father cried. "I don't have the time to go around chasing down papers! All I know is, my father cleared and dug the stumps out of that land, and it's been certified, notarized, and authorized as such."

"As I say, Mr. Blake, I invite you to examine the deed. Ours clearly indicates a transfer of property, the eastern boundary of which is several hundred yards east of the stream. If you have records that contradict that, let's put them side by side."

My father yanked at the raspberry stake. It held fast.

"You bought your piece of forest from Guy Dell, didn't you?" he said.

"That's right."

"Well, no wonder there's confusion."

"Why is that, sir?"

"He's the swindler type."

"That's a serious accusation. Has he swindled you?"

"He's swindled his way across the whole country! Pays off the folks up top. Get next to Guy Dell, you get your pocket picked."

"I hope you're mistaken, Mr. Blake. Our dealings with Mr. Dell were absolutely uncomplicated. His price was reasonable, and so was he."

"Buying his way into heaven," my father said.

"Mr. Blake, I only wish to be neighborly."

"Wish away," my father said. He turned to his trellis.

"We intend to continue the dig," the reverend said. "I give you my word that all artifacts will be kept in a safe and responsible manner." Reverend Rankin stood and watched my father whack a stake into the earth, then gave a stiff nod and set off down our road. His white trousers gleamed in the dusk. A crow crawked. *Clear out,* it seemed to say.

If my mother had been the one to talk to the reverend, she'd have sweet-talked him into putting everything back in the hole and covering it back up and he would have thought it was his own idea. My father had made everything worse.

He kept me doing this and that for him until past eight. He worked me and worked me and then he wanted his supper on the table right that minute and sent me inside while he washed at the pump. The reverend's sack was still on the steps. I opened the sack and slid a hard knobby loaf out onto my palm. It smelled all right. I had a time breaking off a piece, but it was soft inside.

While the milk was heating, I sliced the bread. I felt like I hadn't eaten for days, though Miss Nadia had given me more than I was used to. I ate two pieces of bread, a stuffed mouthful each, the crusts pulled off and hidden in the cupboard for the chickens later.

My father came in. I filled our bowls with bread. He was limping, the bad leg stiff.

"Where's that from?" he said, letting himself into his chair.

"That preacher brought it." The bread floated at first, then sank in the warm milk. I poured maple syrup in each bowl, brown spirals like the spirals on the copper hand. Everything reminded me of it. I gave him a spoon and myself one and sat down.

"This is it?" he said. "Isn't there some fruit?"

I went to the cupboard and took the first jar my fingers touched. He tapped the edge of the lid on the table and wrung it open, sniffed the redness inside. Last year's raspberries, a basketful packed in glass, velvet rubies. A day long past came back inside me, the smell of the tiny fruit, the scratches on my hands soothed by the wetness of the leaves. The berries were dark and soft. You eased them with your thumb and they dropped into your palm. Fry had resisted eating them, knowing we couldn't go swimming until our baskets were full.

My father dug out a scoop of the smashed soupy fruit and put it in my bowl. "No, thank you," I said. "I don't want any."

"Why not? It's good." He stuck the spoon back in the jar for more.

"I don't like raspberries," I said. "The seeds get in my teeth."

That wasn't it. I didn't want a soup-pot sweetened version of the fragile downy berries. The real ones would be ripe soon. I ate them one at a time and Fry did too. A gentle press of the tongue and it disintegrated. Each had its own measure of flavors: meadow, shadow, dew. In the jar the berries were all broken and combined into mush.

My father ate what I didn't, hunched over his elbows in a turtle curve. "What did you and the preacher talk about?" I said.

"Land's not ours where they're digging, he says."

"But that's a lie, right? We can prove it!"

He made a face almost like Fry's when he was trying not to cry. "Your grandfather's papers—mostly chomped up by mice. Leases, mortgages—big tangle. But he always used to say he'd never sell the land by the stream. Lake access. It was always our beach. Take the boat out and fish. Swim. Good watercress and crayfish in the stream. Maybe he let it go by mistake, or forgot. Never told anyone—couldn't admit it. It doesn't matter. A few rotten old beads, not enough to pay the court fee to fight it. Whoever's got the money wins."

"Couldn't Uncle Fowler help?" I said. "He's all about keeping to the law."

"Fowler! Always itchy to stick his nose in my business! Don't you breathe a *syllable* of this to him—or anybody!" He clanked his spoon, suddenly fierce the way a raccoon who's been calm and friendly will snarl and hiss out of the blue.

"But we can't just let them get away with it!"

He glared at his empty bowl. "What do you care?" he said. "Go down there any time you want. Make them serve you a summons so you can't pick watercress. So they're messing with a grave. Maybe they'll get a ghost in their tent."

I went cold. The feather lady—even if everything else got put back and buried, mightn't she be mad that the Hand wasn't? You don't want to be on the wrong side of someone with a tattooed chin.

I'd have to do everything myself, as usual. I would search the house for the mouse-eaten papers or walk the ten miles to the deed office and use my money from Miss Nadia to pay the court, and I'd prove that the rat root place didn't belong to the preachers. Uncle Fowler would make hideous Willis dig in the dirt until his fingernails fell off, and the feather lady's bones would get put back nice and tidy, and she wouldn't go around haunting or cursing anybody, and then the Hand would be in exactly the right mood to make everything perfect for the rest of my life. And Fry's, of course.

The bedwarmer scraped across the floor as I pulled it out

from beneath the bed. The Hand lay quietly in my palm. Beneath the trees, flickered with shifting shadows, or by the lake, patterned by watery reflections, it had seemed mysterious and lively. In the dismal indoors, it didn't look like much. It didn't give off any heat or cold. Maybe it was out of steam after just the one wish. I tried being stern with myself. A girl who's twelve, who makes her own money and keeps her father's house—she doesn't spin fancies. An ornament doesn't bring you presents. Birds don't signal girls. You keep it up and you'll believe in all sorts of invisibilities. Just like the grandmother, people will start to say.

Most days until the morning she didn't wake up, Grandmother Blake would swat unseen hands away that rumpled her hair. Ghosts of her long-gone sisters hid her shawls. Demons skulked inside the rest of us. My grandfather would remind her of our names, explain and explain that her sisters rested peacefully beneath engraved stones. My mother, though, would open windows, shoo the ghosts and put stones on the sills as discouragement.

"They'll find a way in," Grandmother would say, her head wagging like a tail. She knew them.

I knew them too, a little. I'd seen two girls running in the meadow once that were Grandmother's sisters, and Grandmother herself had come around from time to time after her body was taken to the cemetery. I hadn't seen her in a while, but hadn't ever really minded her. She was more peaceful as a ghost, never speaking, just lingering by the fireplace or on a stair. But I'd never run across an angry ghost, and didn't want to.

I wrapped the Hand carefully and hid it back beneath the bed. Did my mother really believe that stones kept ghosts away, or was it just to calm my grandmother down?

Just in case, I lined up my rock collection on the sills and left the lamp burning. I would get up in plenty of time to care for Moony and scrub the kitchen and every other possible chore. I was industrious and obedient and polite, the kind of girl who gets emeralds and pearls, not snakes and toads like her selfish stepsister. The magic would have no reason in the world not to reward me.

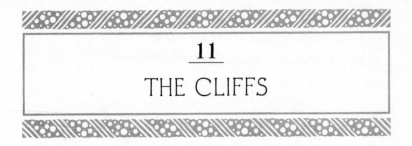

Even as a small child, Greenstone traveled the realms. When her family was about to go hungry, deer came to her dreams. Wolves told her when traders would arrive. Birds spoke to her of the ancestors. She was only eight when she was chosen to study with Crooked Woman, the famed seer and starwatcher, the most knowledgeable of all the wisdom keepers of that time.

Crooked Woman had many other apprentices. Some stayed with her for a season, others for years. Greenstone lived with Crooked Woman while she was growing up and went with her where Crooked Woman was needed, where understanding was needed, where water and sky were disgruntled, where healing was needed.

Crooked Woman was the keeper of a certain bundle that was brought out from time to time to coax certain powers. Of all her many apprentices, she chose four to receive the copper hand's teachings. One of these four was Greenstone.

When it was time for Crooked Woman to rest from her responsibilities, she called the four apprentices together. One of them would be the next keeper of the bundle, the thirty-fourth in line.

The first apprentice made entreaties to sky beings with the copper hand. Rain came and soaked the dry ground that became green with rat root and moss. The rain lasted for nights and days. The rivers filled and swelled. The lake became so strong that the fishermen got blistered hands from fighting the waves. The rain had been needed, but it was time to ask for it to stop.

The second apprentice did so. The rain went elsewhere. The fishermen's blisters healed, and the sunflower fields weren't washed away. But because of all the rain, the lake was excited and restless, and sometimes underwater beings are known to become arrogant when they get too much excitement. The underwaters belted out insults to their ancient enemies of the sky. The winds took sides. Lightning split trees in two.

The third apprentice did her best, but the skies and waters were so loud that they didn't listen to her entreaties and didn't accept her gifts. Winds fought each other. Half the forest was in splinters.

Greenstone was the last apprentice to show Crooked Woman her abilities. The rivers were flooding, the sturgeon had fled, her new grandbaby had never had a sunny day.

Greenstone brought Crooked Woman and the other three apprentices to the sacred cliffs. To get there, they had to cross a choppy channel that was tricky to maneuver at the best of times. Bolts of lightning sizzled all around them as they pitched in the wild waves. Finally they landed on the beach below the cliffs. Greenstone led the way up the slippery rocks. Hail pelted their faces. Thunder crashed on every side. It took all night to get to the cliff's peak.

The five women stood at the edge of the highest crag, far above the rocks that spiked up from the hurling slamming waves. Ropes of dark cloud spiraled and twisted, spinning down to meet the roiling water. Greenstone made her appeals and held the copper hand to the sky.

She was heard. Waterspouts spun their ropes so thin that they disappeared. The winds raced each other away. The lightning followed and was gone.

The sun was about to come up. Everyone agreed that Greenstone would be the thirty-fourth keeper of the copper bundle. There were no hard feelings. She'd won the privilege. She'd bear the sacred burden.

The women sang and danced their way down the slope to the canoe on the beach. The canoe headed back south as the sun rose on calm water. The spirals on the copper hand danced in the new day.

12

KIDNAPPED

I woke up ten minutes earlier than I had to. Out the window it wasn't altogether dark. I was thinking about the feather lady. What was she doing, lurking by her grave like that, holding the Hand as far above as she could reach? Maybe the Hand got its magic from the sky. No wonder it wasn't acting magical anymore. I needed sky myself. A day of school was too long to be without clouds and ever-changing color. I remembered days of deathly boredom and stupid boys who called my mother a squaw and wanting to scratch their faces off, and as soon as school was over and I was alone with the sky, I only pitied them. Their mothers weren't pretty and didn't read books.

I opened the bedwarmer, took out the Hand in its cloth, twisted it up in the folds of my nightgown, and situated it under my arm, hidden enough not to be noticed by someone who didn't notice anything. My father never slept much. He could well have been up.

To remind the Hand that I was the kind of sweet-tempered industrious girl that magic enjoys rewarding, I fed the kitchen stove and blew on the coals and got the fire going, all with utmost silence and stealth. My father could get his coffee faster, thanks to me.

Being out in the world that early was magic in itself. Crimson streaked between silver clouds and dark ones. Birds trilled their announcements. Rain wasn't far away. All the Hand needed was a whiff of blue and silver to give it back its strength before going back into hiding.

But the Hand and I couldn't just be out in the open, where someone in a preacher tent or someone in the garden or fields or orchard could see. Everybody else in the world had their secrets, and the Hand was mine. Gray clouds came ever closer, covering most of the sky. By the stream, a sliver of sun would be cresting the hills and the lake would be fiery. I huddled in the shadow of the barn by a ragged sumac bush.

It was about to rain, maybe for the whole day, maybe for a minute, or maybe the gray clouds would pass us by. I placed the Hand between my palms like the feather lady, with the copper fingers peeking through my own to make rays of flesh and metal. Nothing burned or froze or twitched or fluttered or rippled or shone, but something came into me the way a sip of soup on a cold night soothes a tight chest and a tired soul.

Everything sounded different—not noisier, but packed with understandings. Or there were voices in the wind and trees, but not voices you could exactly hear, but ever after you would listen for them. Or I made it up, because it was all in a bare moment, and while I was wondering what I'd heard, if anything, I heard something else—the clopping of hooves on our road, coming closer.

I tumbled the Hand into its cloth before turning around to see who it might be. Nobody ever visited except Aunt Phyllis, and there she was indeed, perched high on the seat of her shiny new buggy, driving with one hand and holding an umbrella above her head with the other. Rain was sprinkling down as if she'd brought it with her. She looked straight in my direction. I stood stock still, glad of the barn shadow and sprawling sumac. She didn't wave or shout, but that didn't mean she hadn't seen me.

Of course she was bringing bad news. Why else would she show up at dawn? Maybe there was a telegram. Telegrams came when people died. Where to put the Hand? My fingers shook as I tied it in its cloth to my leg right above the knee and knotted it tightly. My toes went numb. My foot would probably have to be chopped off. I had to get inside or I'd never know what was going on. Rain swept down. I ran.

"Goodness!" Aunt Phyllis exclaimed as I went in. "She's *not* upstairs asleep, Henry. You never seem to know where the girl is at any given moment. She's out getting the chores done, bless her, while you're still in bed. Where's the milk, then, Violet? I'll take some in my tea. Heavens! You didn't go out in your nightdress!" She glowered at my bare feet and took the kettle off the stove. "Henry, I mean it," she said. "Simply untenable. Don't be surprised if she comes down with something."

"It's the dead of summer, Phyllis." He was at the kitchen

table drinking his coffee, which he took straight. It didn't matter to him if there was milk in the morning or not.

"A person can catch pneumonia any time of year. Violet, the milk. How many times do I have to ask you?"

"The milking's not done, Aunt Phyllis," I said. "I was just about to, but then I heard you arrive, and you don't usually come so early." It was all completely true. Normally I'd have claimed a twisted ankle or a snake in the barn, just to stay in practice, but I didn't want the Hand getting the wrong impression. "Is everything all right, Aunt Phyllis?" I said.

"Why wouldn't it be? Hurry and get dressed, never mind the milk. I'm giving you a ride to town. Your father can't spare the time to take you, and we don't want you ruining your new shoes in all this mud, do we? We need to leave in ten minutes. You're due to arrive at Miss Zalzman's at eight sharp."

"It's faster to walk," my father said. I was already on the stairs. I crept up one stair at a time in case anybody had anything interesting to say.

"Don't aggravate me, Henry. I'm so exhausted, I can't tell you. Miss Zalzman's lecture last night wasn't over until past eleven. If you have any milk in the ice house, I would be most grateful if you would fetch me a sixteenth of a cupful."

"There isn't any," my father said. "Drink the damn tea, Phyllis, or toss it out the door."

Silence fell between them. My father had to nurse his coffee in the morning. He let it get cold and sipped it like whiskey. He wasn't ready for anything, least of all conversation, until the pot was empty. You'd think his own sister would have known that.

"You won't take two steps out of your way," I heard my aunt say. "Even for a lady. No wonder she left you. Not that she was a *lady*."

"Get off your high horse, Phyllis," he growled. "You act like you were born in Paris, France, instead of on this mud-hole piece of swamp. You want a waiter, go get a suite at the fat-cat emporium you think so much of."

Everybody's always fighting in this house, I thought. My grandmother and her ghosts, relations with each other, strangers and landowners. Bonny was often a disagreeable horse, and Moony the cow was mean-eyed and full of kick. Even the crows were bossy once they came inside our screwy boundaries. Fry and I were the only ones that got along.

The leak in my room had wet most of the floor, as if our place being a mudhole was coming true. I untied the copper hand from my leg and unwrapped the wet cloth. The swirls in its palm seemed to move, as if the Hand was coming alive, like a rolled-up caterpillar will slowly unfurl after it's done being scared.

Water, I thought. Water wakes it up. I remembered washing it off in the lake and how I felt the winter upon me and saw the lady with the tattooed chin in the white feather cape. And so I threw the edge of the quilt over the copper hand to shield it from my eyes and to dry it off, if water was making it move or speak or whatever it would do, but then I thought it might be rude to toss something over it as if it were a fire to be put out, and so I patted it gently with the quilt as if I had its well-being in mind, because magic isn't something you want to offend.

"Enemies are about," I whispered to it. "I have to keep you hidden." And then of course I told myself I'd only seen a glint of morning sun on a drop of water or some such trick of light, and the swirls in the palm hadn't been moving at all.

I heard the unmistakable tread of Aunt Phyllis on the stairs. I opened the top drawer of my dresser and slid the Hand beneath the stockings and shifts and closed it quick.

"Violet," she began. "I think it will be nice for you to stay with us while you're working for Miss Zalzman. I won't have to come over and get you every time there's any weather, and you won't have that long walk. Let's gather up your things. You have so little, we might as well bring everything, shall we?" She opened the very drawer the Hand was in.

"Oh, but Aunt Phyllis," I said. "Father didn't want to tell you because you know how you worry, but he isn't well. If I'm not here there's nobody to give him his medicine at night."

She picked up a shift from the drawer and held it to the light, looking for holes. "Whatever happened to that lovely old portmanteau of your grandmother's? Do you know the one? Brown leather?"

"Yes," I said. "It's downstairs, I think, on top of the wardrobe." I knew it wasn't. My mother had taken it.

"Why on earth would anyone keep it up there to get buried in the dust? So many of my mother's pretty things aren't being properly cared for." She put the folded shift on top of the dresser and reached for another. Soon the copper hand would be in her grasp.

"You can't make me go with you," I said. "I won't." I stamped my bare foot.

She did just what I'd actually hoped, whirled to me and took me by the shoulders and shook me hard. "Don't dare to speak to me in that fashion," she said through her teeth. Then she slapped my face and pushed me away. "Your father is letting himself go to ruin. There's nothing to be done about that. But I will not allow a niece of mine to be turned into a wild, willful, common girl." Her nostrils flared. My cheek burned. The drawer was forgotten.

"Do I have to dress you like a baby?" she hissed. "You be ready by the time I come back up here. And I'd better not see any pouting. What's *this* doing in the middle of the floor?"

She swept out with the bedwarmer beneath her arm. I dove for the open drawer. One copper finger peeked out from beneath the muddle of underthings.

I couldn't leave it. I might not ever be back. For all I knew, she was sending me to a workhouse or the orphanage. But if I took it with me, surely she would nab it, as she was always rummaging in every cabinet. My father never poked into anything. I could have left the Hand in the middle of the floor and he wouldn't ever find it.

I slid the Hand beneath the mattress. "I'll rescue you as soon as I can," I told it. My aunt came in with a dusty carpet bag and jammed my clothes in, ordering me to hand her this and that. I did what she said.

She left him a note on the table. He was with his trees. "How on earth did you already ruin your new dress?" she said. "I should have known better than to get you anything expensive. Carelessness seems to be in your blood."

On the ride to town she sat straight and kept out of the ruts. She let me off in front of the hotel and said she'd expect me no later than five-thirty. "Miss Zalzman works until dark," I told her. "Sometimes later. And she gives me supper."

"As well she should if she keeps you so long." She was relieved. She wouldn't have to worry about me chipping one of her ugly fancy plates with my carelessness. Besides, she had a new bedwarmer to polish up.

I hurried to Miss Nadia's room, knowing I was late. The door was open a crack, but I knocked anyway. "Hold on," I heard her say. "Somebody's here."

I went in. She was on the telephone. She motioned me to sit at the table, where breakfast was laid out. "It's Violet. I thought it might be Alice Dell with another bright idea. Arrange your friends for another day, I told her. She's beside herself. Mrs. So-and-so is leaving tomorrow. Mrs. Thus-and-such has no other day this week. I can't help it, I said to her. This is no day for a picture on this famous veranda. I had to explain to her about the light, the wet windows not to mention, the beach all wet. Nobody swimming. Well, if your husband wants to advertise a gloomy place, we will do it, I told her. Is this what he wants people to expect, their beautiful vacation time inside? The picture we're after is the ladies with the summer light on their faces and people in the water!"

The omelette was tasty, the tea strong, the big lake in a frenzy. I spread soft butter on toast. Miss Nadia hung up the phone and came and sat with me at the table and looked at me as if to see what I was made of. "Today we play hooky," she said. "And we don't want to be found out. We will need to be stealthy, like spies in wartime. Do you know this kind of game?"

Clouds hovered over the lake, water meeting water. It would rain again soon. I hoped the game took place indoors, but I'd have gone anywhere with Miss Nadia.

"Yes, Miss Nadia," I said, ready to begin.

"One thing," she said, craning her neck forward to catch my eyes with hers. "I can't have you being late again. Rain or not. Do you understand?"

I didn't look away. "I'm sorry," I said. I really was, even though it was all because of Aunt Phyllis. Usually it's just something you have to say.

"You can be counted on or not. There is no middle ground to that," she said. "Now finish up that tea."

Obediently, I drained my cup. I needed to swallow something to get rid of the knot in my throat. I didn't want Miss Nadia mad, not because I feared her famous temper, but because if the Hand had brought me the job it would be foolhardy to lose it. Well, maybe it's a good thing Aunt Phyllis snatched me, I thought. Staying in town, I can get here in five minutes. I never have to be late another time.

I put the cup on its saucer and stood up. She smiled. "Ready, then?" she said.

"Ready," I replied.

13
MISS NADIA PLAYS HOOKY

"The thing is this," Miss Nadia explained. "I have my methods. If someone looks over my shoulder I will become impatient, and I don't want to be rude to Mrs. Dell. You see?"

I didn't, quite, but she didn't owe me explanations. I was being paid to lie. We were going to photograph Isaac Duvall the bellboy, and Mrs. Dell didn't need to know about it. If she called, I was to say that Miss Nadia was out, but really we were covering the windows with a black velvet drape. Miss Nadia clambered from chair to table, balancing herself against the rainy windowpane. Deft as a sailor, she twisted the velvet around the curtain rod and jammed a hatpin to fasten it.

Someone was knocking. "I need three minutes before I'm ready," she said, stepping down. "You were so good with little Clara. Do the same with Mr. Duvall. Talk to him about the wonders of his heart." She shut herself into the darkroom.

Wonders of his heart! Why would he want to talk to me about them? Clara was easy. All little children like rocks.

"Miss Nadia will be out in a minute," I said, letting him in. "This is where she wants you to sit. Or you don't have to if you'd rather stretch your legs while you're waiting. I always look at the lake if I don't have anything else to do. I mean, you never know what it'll be up to on any given day. People say it looks as big as the ocean, but an ocean's a thousand times bigger. Have you ever seen one? An ocean?"

"No, Miss Blake. I never have." He stood stiff as a soldier. He was not relaxed. Neither of us had teacups to arrange or luggage to lift.

"Where do you live? When you're not here, I mean. You're not from Pigeon Harbor, are you?" It sounded wrong, like I was snooping.

"That's right, Miss. I'm from Alabama. Tuscaloosa."

Geography was my best subject, but I didn't know anything about Tuscaloosa, and nothing about Alabama except it was just about as far down south as you could get.

I kept on. "Does it ever snow? Here it snows for about seven months straight and the snowdrifts are taller than a man. I get to school by snowshoe."

"We get some snow," he said. He wasn't getting relaxed in the slightest. I couldn't ask anything I wanted to know. Had his parents been slaves when they were children? Was his family richer than ours? We didn't have money for sugar most of the time, and colleges aren't free, and you can't work every minute when you have to study, and that's why my father only went for one year, because my grandfather died and there was nobody else to run the farm.

How did my mother always get people talking, even Mrs. Peterssen sometimes? She'd ask about their ailing mother or how often do you have to sharpen those butcher knives of yours. She'd butter them up: that green brings out your eyes, that marrow bone made such good soup, what a handsome little boy you have.

"How did you decide to be a doctor?" I said to Isaac Duvall. "You must be really brave."

He smiled, finally. "It's what I always wanted to be. My father—"

Miss Nadia's door opened. She was carrying one of her wooden crates. "I've got it," she said when I started over to help her. "Thank you for your patience, Mr. Duvall. Keep on with your conversation. Don't let me interrupt you." She ducked beneath the camera cloth.

"You were saying about your father," I said to Isaac Duvall.

"Yes, Miss. He's a doctor, so he used to take me around with him ever since I was little, and I got used to being around sickness. It doesn't bother me. So it isn't really brave."

I knew little of doctors. My mother treated our sniffs and fevers with tea and cloths of just the right temperature, warm or cool, whichever was needed. The only time we had the doctor was when Aunt Phyllis brought him to see my mother. "You look peaked, Georgia," Aunt Phyllis had said. "Humor me. I just want you looked at."

My aunt didn't know that my mother slept late into the morning and didn't ever sing, but she could see the crumbs on the table and the wash not done. The doctor gave my mother a powder that she threw away and said was poison and cried for days because Aunt Phyllis had paid the doctor to come. But soon after, my father was home and gray days turned green, and in no time at all she was mending his work clothes and giving us all haircuts and making angel cakes.

"Left hand down, please, Mr. Duvall," Miss Nadia was saying. "More down. Stop. Don't move. Perfect."

Most anybody would have said Isaac Duvall was black. But up against that velvet, the matter wasn't so straightforward. His face was brown, mostly, with possible tones of blue, perhaps a cast of maroon. I thought of how a lake can be so dark from far away, but if you row to the middle and look down, the water's barely any color, or how your foot can be sun-dark on the beach, then white as a mushroom underwater.

I scrambled to fetch things for Miss Nadia: the brush to dust the camera, a hatbox to serve as a footstool, the plates that took the pictures. She took picture after picture, a tilt to the head, eyes downcast, an adjustment of the curtain. The foghorn wailed.

When he was being a bellboy, Isaac Duvall could deaden up his face so that nothing caused his eyes to smile or flash or sadly sag. If you didn't know him you'd think he didn't think about anything. When he talked to Miss Nadia, his eyes helped tell how he loved reading Cicero in Latin, how proud he was to have a mother whose singing made a queen cry.

"I should be getting back," he said after a time. "The boss won't like me being gone so long, Miss Zalzman."

She unhitched the latches of a metal box and removed a slim canister. "Your boss is who?" she said.

"Mr. Nickels, ma'am. The bell captain."

"If I could just do one with the flash," she said. "It won't take two minutes. Why don't I give your Mr. Nickels a call and explain that I have kept you? Then he won't think you're shirking. Shall I?"

"Well, he doesn't like us being singled out by a guest. He says it leads to misunderstandings. And he isn't too favorably inclined toward me in the first place."

"But you're so pleasant and intelligent and a hard worker." She put a scale on the table and steadied its shuddering imbalance with a finger. "Not to mention careful with my equipment. How can he not think well of you?"

"In his opinion, I'm full of myself. My kind shouldn't be doctors. And also he already fired my cousin."

"Your cousin! Why?"

"A ring went missing, and he'd been in the room. So that was it. And I went to Mr. Nickels and told him Joseph wouldn't steal. Even when he was little, he wouldn't take an apple off someone else's tree, even if all the rest of us were doing it. No matter if he was hungry. He's always been like that. If anyone took a ring, it wasn't Joseph."

"And what did Mr. Nickels say when you stood up for your cousin's character?"

" 'One more word, boy, you're on the next train out of here.' So I clammed right up and begged his pardon. And Joseph won't have money for school next year unless he finds something back home, and he'll be lucky if he does. And I don't want to lose this job or I'll be in the same boat. So I do everything just the way Mr. Nickels likes it done."

"Eyes right here, Mr. Duvall." She flicked her hand. Light burst the room bright. I jumped. The room smelled of burned hair. "Wonderful," she declared. "Mr. Duvall, please get up and move around. Violet, let's get the windows open."

Miss Nadia was cloaked in white smoke. The rest of the room swirled with soot flakes. There was a rapping at the door.

"Nadia!" said a voice. The rapping was louder.

"It's Mrs. Dell," Miss Nadia said to me. "Go ahead and let her in."

A tall, long-faced fair-haired lady stood in the hall, dripping with lace from the elbows down. She was a blue heron, moving slowly but with steady purpose through the door and past me into the cloudy room.

"Nadia!" the lady exclaimed. "What are you up to? Setting the hotel on fire?" Plucking up the camera cloth, she ducked under it. Ash was still aloft. A piece of it landed on a frill cascading from a narrow shoulder.

"Alice!" Miss Nadia said. "*Alice!* Come out of there at once. I don't allow anyone to touch my cameras."

The lacy lady was Mrs. Guy Dell, then. I recognized her spit gob of a pearl ring. She was the lady in white who bought the stack of boxes from Lucy Thornwood and her grandmother when we were talking about where my mother had gone off to.

"Oh, Nadia, don't be fussy." Mrs. Dell emerged from beneath the cloth. "I've been around a camera or two, you know. But I don't understand. What's the picture?"

"Mr. Duvall has been kind enough to help me with some lighting tests," Miss Nadia said, straightening the folds of the camera cloth. Isaac Duvall was at the open window, waving smoke out, his back to the proceedings.

"Nadia," Mrs. Dell said. "We must strategize about tomorrow."

"What strategizing?" Miss Nadia said.

Most of the smoke had been coaxed out by Isaac Duvall. He shut the window. The rain had stopped, and the sky was patchy over the lake. "That will be all," Mrs. Dell told him with a wave of her hand.

Miss Nadia opened her mouth and closed it again. She looked mad, but she thanked Isaac Duvall. He let himself out. The door closed behind him.

"I told you," Mrs. Dell said. "Guy's arriving."

"No," Miss Nadia said. "You didn't mention it."

"I absolutely did, I'm sure," Mrs. Dell said. "He wants to see you as soon as he gets in tomorrow morning. The baby on the beach and whatever else you have. I must say, I didn't expect you to spend your time on bellboys. I don't feel that Guy would want you wasting film on subjects more appropriate to street photography than promotion of the hotel."

"I hope that my pictures transcend subject," Miss Nadia said coldly.

"Oh, Nadia," said Mrs. Dell, taking up Miss Nadia's elbows in her white-gloved hands. "Don't be offended. You artists are so awfully sensitive. Let's see what you've got. I'll choose the crème de la crème for Guy to look at. I know exactly his taste."

Mostly a heron, once the fish is caught, will toss it up and snap it down, but once at the swamp I saw a heron spear a fish with spines all down its back. She knew not to swallow it, but took it to shore and stabbed it over and over. When it stopped flopping, she tore it apart to eat it.

Miss Nadia made herself smile. "I wasn't expecting to show things already," she said. "Not all the pictures are developed yet. I'll be in the darkroom all night."

"One of these days you'll have to let me watch you. I'm sure it's fascinating," said Mrs. Dell. Miss Nadia opened the door for her to make her lacy exit.

The darkroom was thrilling. Everything had to be just so, with gloves and measuring and not spilling a drop, and setting the timer, and pictures blooming in the trays, and the light always stayed the same so there wasn't any way to tell how late it was.

When we ran out of places to hang wet prints, Miss Nadia had me order tea, and after we had it she said I could go. Outside, it was barely raining. My father's going to miss me, I thought as I walked along Front Street. Or he'll need the help, anyway. He'll come to get me. Maybe he'll be there when I get there. He'll tell Aunt Phyllis I have to be at home, and she won't pitch a fit, because she doesn't really want me with her. I'll give Bonny a good rubdown as soon as we get home, because she doesn't like rain. He'll have made corn chowder with bacon, milky and flecked with pepper.

But by suppertime he hadn't come, and good thing I'd had some cake with Miss Nadia, as Aunt Phyllis had out-done herself on fish balls in a crunchy puddle she called piquante. My uncle was working late, because he had to track down a mad dog that had run away from whoever owned it. Being sheriff, he had to do those kinds of things, and my aunt didn't stop saying how brave he was, and how he was too good for the county we lived in, and how nobody appreciated all he did. I'd have wagered that he worked late to avoid the suppers his wife came up with.

By bedtime my father was still not in evidence. He's glad I'm gone, I thought. Good riddance to us all.

My bed was on a scratchy narrow couch in the room Aunt Phyllis called the sewing room, though she never sewed. I despaired of ever having a decent meal again. On a summer night like this, my mother would have made a feast of freshness—buttered green beans, tomatoes warm from the sun, melon chilled in the stream.

There was a tune I used to hum when Fry couldn't sleep. Maybe he's having trouble sleeping too, I thought. He's missing me even more than I'm missing him, because he's little. When my mother couldn't stop being sad, sometimes she was asleep at his bedtime. I would get him washed and tucked in and read to. It was me he called for in the night.

In the morning, I was curled beneath the covers like a fox cub. The foghorn sounded its pining groan. I could smell the gluey porridge that Aunt Phyllis always made when there was rain or any kind of chill. I told her I couldn't eat it, because I had to be at Miss Nadia's early to help her get ready for Mr. Dell. Of course, Aunt Phyllis only cared about Mr. Dell being happy and satisfied in the world, not whether I starved to death, so she didn't argue.

I was interested to meet the man my father called a famous swindler. Swindler or not, I hoped he'd like the pictures.

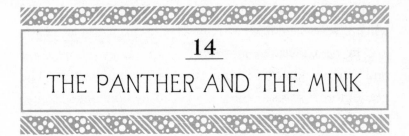

14
THE PANTHER AND THE MINK

But Miss Nadia had forgotten about breakfast. The whole room was so festooned with pictures, you had to duck under and skirt around them. She had run lines from wherever twine could be fastened—chair to dresser, curtain rod to transom—and clipped the pictures on with tiny metal clothespins.

I unclipped pictures from the twine one at a time the way Miss Nadia showed me, so as not to smudge them with the oil of my fingerprints. Some were of empty rooms in the hotel: the ballroom, bowling alley, casino. I remembered those being taken. Others she'd done without me, like one of the sun edging through clouds over the lake, torching the cresting waves.

"These are not for Mr. Dell." Miss Nadia put a stack on a chair. The top one was of Isaac Duvall. It didn't look like him in the least, though the nose was his nose and the chin, his chin. The real Isaac Duvall wasn't handsome, but his picture was of a nobleman from an ancient, wise nation.

The next picture on the line was of Lucy Thornwood and her grandmother with the hotel behind them. The grandmother was scowling. Lucy Thornwood looked something like my mother, with the same dark eyes and hair, though my mother never wore it in two braids.

Miss Nadia took the picture from me and frowned at it. "If I am Mr. Dell, this is the picture I want." She held it out. "Not with these ladies, but happy children on the sand, or a young lady with an umbrella. But see how the hotel isn't so clear? Too far from the lens. If I focus on the people, the hotel's soft. If I focus on the hotel, the people aren't sharp. We'll hope he likes a different idea." I hid the Lucy Thornwood pictures in the darkroom along with the others that Mr. Dell wasn't supposed to see.

You could tell from Mr. Dell's knock that he was a man without a tick of extra time on his hands. Miss Nadia smoothed her hair. She looked more like a mink than ever, sleek and bright-eyed. Mr. Dell was all cat, from his wide light eyes to his hands as big as loaves. If he'd had a tail, it would have been twitching.

"Nadia!" Mrs. Dell exclaimed. "These pictures are sublime. Didn't I tell you that child was out of this world?" She meant Clara, who indeed was the spit of a cherub on a gravestone.

Mr. Dell came at me with his hand out. "Who's this pretty thing?" he said. I'd never had occasion to shake a man's hand before, but I did what was expected. I hadn't been called pretty, much, but sometimes people said I looked like my mother, who absolutely was.

"Mr. Dell, I'd like you to meet Miss Violet Blake," Miss Nadia said. "Without her, this series of little Clara on the beach would not be so successful. Miss Blake was able to keep the subject on land, when all the child wanted was to play she was a fish."

"Isn't she a vision?" said Mrs. Dell, a picture of Clara balanced on her palm.

He wasn't careful snatching up the picture. "If I saw this in a magazine, I'd think it was to sell soap," he said. "Use our soap every day, your husband won't stray, your hair won't go gray. But where's the hotel? If the hotel was in the picture, I'd like it fine."

"She's got the dunes in the background," said Mrs. Dell. "You definitely know you're somewhere remote."

"That's what those are? Dunes?" he said. "You've got to realize, Alice, most people are louts like me. They don't see all the little nuances. You notice this beautiful brand-new hotel's not fully occupied in the middle of the season? I need a picture that'll make people hightail it up here and sit on the biggest porch in the whole damn country! Let's see the damn porch! You take a hell of a picture. Now take one with my hotel in it!"

"Let's look at one more thing," said Miss Nadia. "Violet, bring us the ones we were talking about before, with the hotel background."

I hurried to the darkroom and shuffled through the stack. There they were, Lucy Thornwood and her grandmother. Islands up north, I thought. What islands?

I handed the pictures to Miss Nadia. She put them on the table. "What were these hidden away for?" Mr. Dell said. "This is what I'm talking about!"

"Guy, you're absolutely infuriating," said his wife. "The hotel's massive in the background, and it's not in focus."

"So focus it!" he said.

"If I'm not mistaken," Mrs. Dell said, "it's too far from the foreground subject."

"Then get closer! Put the young Indian in front, not the old squaw. Give it to me Wednesday noon at the latest."

Miss Nadia looked up from the picture. "I'm glad there is a plan to pursue," she said to Mr. Dell. "As for Wednesday, I can't promise."

"Why not?" he said. His eyes turned on me. He yawned, his fingers spread across his wide mouth. One of his back teeth was gold.

"Things have to be arranged," Miss Nadia said. "I don't know if Mrs. Thornwood will be willing to pose, or what her schedule is. Even if I—"

"Dig up another squaw," he said. "Your Miss Violet has an exotic complexion. Put her in some fringe and use her."

Mrs. Dell turned her round bird eye on me then, and smiled at me, scrutinizing. "What do you think, Nadia? She looks more or less authentic. *Are* you part Indian, dear? Or have you just had sun?"

My impulse was to lie, as I didn't think she ought to

know a thing about me, but I didn't like to mislead Miss Nadia. "My grandmother was Odawa, but I never met her," I said. I had no inclination to have my picture made. Staying still always made me want to kick something. I much preferred to hand Miss Nadia the plates while someone else got a stiff neck.

"I think we all like Lucy Thornwood," Miss Nadia said. "The same lady as before. Perhaps she'll be here again tomorrow with her beautiful boxes."

"They're like gypsies," pronounced Mrs. Dell. "They don't live anywhere. We don't want to waste time waiting for her if she's off to the next town. Let's try your little assistant. She'll do nicely. Don't you think so, Guy?"

"I just said so," he growled.

"Lucy Thornwood lives on the river road," I offered, to get myself off the hook. "In a house," I added.

"There you have it," said Mr. Dell. "See you Wednesday."

"Not Wednesday," Miss Nadia said firmly. "A good print takes time. My work does not go out unless I'm happy with it."

"Quality's a good thing," he said. "So's time. Let's not spend all summer on this. I'm sure you have other fish to fry, and I do too. Alice, I want you to help this thing along. Nadia, make use of my wife. Alice should be at your side whenever you take a picture. She knows what I'm after."

"I believe I'm clear on what you want," she said in a clipped kind of way. "Not on the sentimental side, but showing off the natural beauty. The hotel featured."

"Don't you worry, Nadia," Mrs. Dell said. "We'll do something marvelous together. You let me know when you get the pretty squaw. Guy, you're late already."

Miss Nadia turned away from Mrs. Dell in order not to snarl. This didn't escape Mrs. Dell. Heron as she was, she didn't like the backs of peoples' heads in her face. The heron spends her days standing above the water, contemplating reflections. She considers herself superior to other creatures in sense and comeliness, and doesn't take to being slighted. A mink like Miss Nadia would have a time evading her: the wide wings above, scouting the shadows, the dive and the scissored beak.

"Nadia, you're going to make me a masterpiece," said Mr. Dell. "And that will make me a happy man." His bow was graceful. The tip of his tail, had it been there, would have ever so slowly waved.

Then he and his wife were gone, and Miss Nadia was in a state. "Pfah!" She tossed the stack of pictures on the table. "Why did I show him this?" She picked up the picture of Lucy Thornwood and her grandmother. "It's not possible, what he wants, and for not being able to bring him what can't be done, I'll be blackballed. It's no use explaining to such a man. He doesn't want to know the difficulties. Just solve it!" She flicked the foggy hotel with a stained fingernail.

"It's too bad you can't just cut them out, like paper dolls," I said before I thought I'd better not.

"How do you mean?" she said.

"I—I know you can't," I stammered.

"Tell me anyway," she said.

I hesitated. In school sometimes the teacher tries to trip you up by asking you to try to unravel your wrong answer.

"You had a thought," she said. "Explain."

"Just—when I was little, I used to cut people out from magazines, and then I could put them on top of pictures so it would seem like the cutout people went to different places. It was just to pretend. It's not the same thing, what you have to do."

She narrowed her eyes at me. "Yes," she said. "Photography is like pretending. You try to make something look the way you want it to look, even if it doesn't look like that in life. And maybe this is something I can figure out. Thank you, Miss Blake."

Maybe it's the Hand's doing, I thought. Maybe it knows I like Miss Nadia, and so it gave her something that she wanted.

"So," Miss Nadia said, "let's track down Lucy Thornwood."

15

PAYDAY

Miss Nadia and I got into a buggy. I was instructed to show the driver the way. I wasn't at all certain I knew it, as I'd been to the place a year ago or two, and only the once.

We clacked through Pigeon Harbor. The sun was ablaze in the bleached sky. There was Ingie Peterssen staring at the boats. Her mother came out of the store, snatched the broom from Ingie's slack grasp, and shoved her at the door. We passed the undertaker's and the shop that made my aunt's overwrought hats. A dirty boy came out of the Greek's with a white paper parcel. Ingie often had sour balls and conversation hearts from the Greek's and would share, but it was a high price for having to listen to her dull talk. Mercy the preacher girl wasn't anywhere close to dull.

I found the house without a snag, even though it was off the river road on a narrow lane, with willows draping over. Once I saw the place, I remembered everything about the time I'd been there—jars of maple syrup in a dark glossy row, flat chewy bread to dip in stew broth, black walnuts and a stone to bash them with, dry wrinkled red plums. It had been a cold dark day. My mother and Lucy Thornwood's grandmother had gone off together and left Fry and me with Lucy Thornwood. She had fed us. The stew had been dark and sweet.

I was empty inside. I almost wished I'd taken up Aunt Phyllis on the gluey oatmeal.

Miss Nadia told the driver to please wait. The door to the cabin was open. Lucy Thornwood's grandmother was inside, stirring something on the stove. She looked over at us. "Yes," was all she said. She reached into the pot with two spoons and brought up a spiky bunch of porcupine quills, red and dripping red, as if she'd been cooking them in blood.

"Hello, Mrs. Agosa," Miss Nadia said. "It's Nadia Zalzman. You were kind enough yesterday to let me take your photograph. You and Mrs. Thornwood. By the hotel."

Mrs. Agosa banged the spoon on the side of the pot. I could tell Miss Nadia wished she had her camera, but she'd left it in the buggy.

"Good color," Miss Nadia said. "That's for your boxes?"

"We have to make more. One lady, she took almost all we had." Mrs. Agosa took a quill off the spoon, put the rest back, held the red quill up to the light from the doorway that we stood in. The dye smelled like one of my father's tree concoctions.

"I see you have work to do," Miss Nadia said. "We won't keep you. I'm interested in taking your granddaughter's picture in my studio. I would pay for her time, of course."

But Mrs. Agosa was looking at me. "You've got a memory," she said. "It's a long time ago you were here before."

"Nothing gets past Violet," Miss Nadia said. "She is a sharp young lady."

"Watch out for ghosts out by you," Mrs. Agosa said to me. "I hear they're digging up Indian graves over by the lake there."

It took all my strength to keep my face a stone. She was looking straight at me. My blood pounded.

"Indian graves?" Miss Nadia said.

"That's what I heard." Mrs. Agosa shrugged and stirred. "You live up there by the new summer people, don't you?" she said to me. "They're the ones doing this digging up. Mad ghosts can throw out curses, some people believe. You see any ghosts, just tell them it's not you doing the digging. They'll leave you alone then."

She couldn't know about the feather lady. She was just the kind of mean crone who likes to scare children. "My father's making them stop digging," I said. I wanted to believe it.

"Who buys your pictures?" Mrs. Agosa said to Miss Nadia, ignoring me.

"Different people. People pay me for a portrait sometimes. Right now the man who owns the hotel wants a picture for an advertisement."

"A pretty Indian girl makes them want to spend money," Mrs. Agosa said. "I used to be as pretty as anybody, but you missed your chance on that one." She smiled. Her teeth were white and strong, not the teeth of someone old.

"You're still very beautiful," Miss Nadia said.

"What's the pay?" Mrs. Agosa said, waving us inside.

"That's a powerful color," Miss Nadia said.

Mrs. Agosa took up a handful of something out of a basket. "This will come out purple." It looked like bits of rotten stump. "And this—" She shook the other basket. "Almost like gold. You'll never see boxes like these."

When I was there before, dried-out stalks and leaves hung from walls and were bundled in the overhead beams. It must have been fall then. Now the kitchen was crowded with baskets of fresh grass and coils of white bark. Mrs. Agosa reached into the pot of quills and shook a handful as if she was about to throw a game of jackstraws.

"Would you let me make a picture of you with your quills?" Miss Nadia said. "Your kitchen is beautiful, so many patterns. It won't take any time. Just go ahead with your work and I won't get in your way. No, you stay here, Violet. I know where everything is and it's not much to carry."

Was I supposed to put Mrs. Agosa at her ease, like with Isaac Duvall? I only had a minute, if even that. Miss Nadia wasn't one for dawdling. Mrs. Agosa pulled out another fistful of quills. The scarlet spikes looked like they'd poison you if you even touched them.

I couldn't ask about the feather lady. She'd wonder why I cared.

"Your granddaughter said you might know where my mother went," I said all in a rush. I didn't care for Miss Nadia to know my business.

"Lucy said that?"

"She said there's islands up north. Maybe you'd re-member which one my mother went to. And my little brother."

"Your father doesn't know?"

"The paper it was written down on got eaten by mice and we can't read it."

Her eyes were on me like they were looking for lies. When Aunt Phyllis looked at me like that, my hopeful innocent quarter-smile threw her off the scent. Mrs. Agosa's eyes went further into me.

"She doesn't write you?" she said.

"Not lately," I said.

"Oh," she said.

Miss Nadia was back. "Mrs. Agosa, don't pay any atten-tion to us," she said. "We're not even here. You're alone in your kitchen."

I knew what to do and gave Miss Nadia what she needed, but I wanted to stab Mrs. Agosa with one of her poison quills. She was the kind of person who liked to know every-thing about everybody, and it amused her to scare children with ghost stories, and she wasn't even a good liar.

Lucy Thornwood came in just as Miss Nadia and I were finishing packing up, and smiled at me in a kindly fashion, and she and Miss Nadia agreed on Monday. "I look forward to it," Miss Nadia said. Mrs. Agosa was turned away from us, busying her hands.

The buggy started off. Miss Nadia went into her bag and took out the black leather notebook she wrote things down in. "We might as well settle up," she said. "It's payday." She wrote, then showed me the notebook. "Is that how you remember it?"

"Well, Thursday I left before six," I said. "Ten of, I think. And Friday I was late."

"I don't like to penny-pinch," she said. "I want you happy so you don't go looking for something better." She looked at her watch. "One-thirty. By the time we get to town let's say it's two." She wrote in the book. "That's seven and a half hours. Right?"

"Isn't there more to do today?" I said.

"Not for you. I need you strong and bright-eyed for Monday. Tomorrow's Sunday anyway—the day of rest, yes?"

Rest! Aunt Phyllis would dose me with castor oil and give me a swampy supper of jelly made of baby cows' feet, and the next day I'd be dragged to church and made to sit in a stuffy pew for an entire morning and pretend to know the hymns, because if I didn't, Aunt Phyllis would spend the afternoon at the piano to clank them into my head, and by the time Monday came, I'd have nothing in me but Bible verses. I could have said I was staying at my real house, but there might have been awkwardness, and my father might have been rude to Miss Nadia. I considered hurling myself out of the buggy.

"Girls your age," Miss Nadia said, "sometimes they don't know when they're tired. I've maybe been wearing you out. And next week will be more grueling than this one. Much more." She took two dollar bills out of her handbag and held them out.

"I owe you fifty cents," I said.

"No," she said. "We're even. You are a conscientious worker. You pay attention. You think about what you're doing. And anyhow, if you have a whole dollar, it's easier to keep. Maybe you'll save for something."

I'd never considered that money could be had in such quantity that it could be hoarded. I would save it up and take a train to wherever Fry was. Or maybe I wouldn't have to. Maybe the copper hand would bring him home. I folded up the money and slid it in my shoe. My aunt didn't have to know I had it.

The driver pulled up by the herringbone brick house with the jail in back. Miss Nadia didn't offer to walk me to the door. Even she didn't want to contend with Aunt Phyllis.

I rapped lightly. Nobody answered, so I let myself in. "He said he'd pay for everything. Whatever it takes!" I recognized Uncle Fowler's throaty laugh. My aunt was laughing too. They were in the kitchen.

"I knew it!" my aunt exclaimed. "I never doubted for a—" She gasped and giggled. In the kitchen I found my uncle lifting my aunt off her feet with his arms around her waist and kissing her on the mouth. She saw me and squirmed away from him. She didn't believe children should know that such things went on.

"My favorite niece!" Uncle Fowler said. He always said that. He had no others.

"What are you doing creeping around, Violet?" Aunt Phyllis said. She was rumpled from being twirled. "Why aren't you with Miss Zalzman? Don't tell me you've gotten yourself fired the first week."

"No, ma'am. She let me leave early. I was thinking I'd run home and help out with the chores, but I didn't want to go without permission."

"You may," Aunt Phyllis said, smoothing her skirt. "Uncle Fowler and I have been invited to dine with the Dells tonight, and we wouldn't want to leave you here by yourself. Your uncle's going to be a senator!"

"Hold on, now, Phyllis. I have to win first." Uncle Fowler smoothed his moustache. He was vain, my uncle, with his waxed moustache and brilliantined hair.

"Well, you will." She beamed. "No question, with Guy Dell behind you."

Dining at the Dells! Aunt Phyllis's deepest dream had come true. Everybody's getting what they want today, I thought. Miss Nadia got Lucy Thornwood, Mrs. Agosa got her purple and yellow quills, Uncle Fowler gets to be a senator, I got extra money. The copper hand likes making everything better. That's its job.

"We'll come and fetch you in the morning in time for church," my aunt said. "Go up and get what you need for tonight. I'll bring your church clothes tomorrow."

I was out of the kitchen like a shot, so I could be long gone before she reconsidered, and I'd only just started up the stairs when someone was at the door, knocking. My aunt bustled into the parlor to answer, and it was my father.

"You commandeered my daughter," he said to my aunt. "She belongs at home."

"We were just discussing having her stay at your place tonight," Aunt Phyllis said.

"Like a furlough?" he said. "No. We're not talking about one night."

"It's just so much easier for her, Henry, being here. She should stay until her job is over, at least. It saves her all that walking. When is Miss Zalzman leaving, Violet?" I was leaning over the banister, listening.

"The end of August," I said. Miss Nadia had told me the twentieth of July, less than a week away, but surely she'd stay until Mr. Dell had a picture that he liked. For all I knew, that would take a year. "Maybe even into September," I added. "This is the most beautiful place she's ever been. She tells everyone that. She wants to come next summer too." The lie wasn't a good one, too easily found out.

It worked, though. Weeks and weeks, my aunt was thinking. The food, the washing, the comings and goings, all the snags and complications. "If you insist, Henry," she said. "But we'll take her to church. You can't just keep letting her grow up without any religious instruction whatsoever."

"I have my beliefs," my father said.

My aunt snorted. "Socialism! Anarchism! Lawless, murderous . . ."

While they were hashing it over, I got myself to that sewing room and jammed my things into the bag my aunt had brought them in.

Bonny clopped along at a good pace, like she always did if she knew she was headed for home. The biggest stars were out, early as it was, and I could exactly smell Blue Lake before I could even see it from the crest of the hill. Our little lake smelled nothing like the big one, with its depths and billows and fish as big as children.

He was in a mope, didn't ask about my day, didn't sing a song he'd make up as he went along and pretend to have trouble with the rhymes so I'd have to fling something in and make us both laugh. I'd been so young then.

"Everybody in town is talking about that skeleton," I said. "It's famous already. And I met the swindler. Guy Dell. He shook my hand."

"The railroad pirate! Boss of your boss, isn't he? And now he's got your uncle in his big old bag."

"What's a railroad pirate?"

"The game is, they gobble up the competition until there isn't any. Then they've got it sewed up from both ends. Everybody's got to buy from them and everybody's got to work for them. They can charge any price they want and also starve the workers."

"What's a senator do?"

"You get to make laws. Whatever makes the capitalists happy, that's what Fowler's for. Phyllis can have a big house in Lansing and hobnob around with the other politicians' wives. *She'll* be in heaven. And Fowler, he'll just grease the wheels for Dell and his type to run roughshod over the little folk."

"Well, you won't let him, will you? Did you find the papers for the land?"

"Oh, there's *papers. They've* got papers. The preacher man put them under my nose. All sewed up from their end. That whole strip by the lake."

"But what about our stream?" I said. "Your father wouldn't sell that land behind your back!"

"I told you! Nobody can prove anything! Old deeds. Pay a lawyer. Get rooked from every angle!"

I felt poisoned inside. Where would magic even start? We were passing the graveyard, always dark under the swooping trees. Bonny turned us in at our road and stopped by the barn.

"Violet," he said before I could turn away and get down. He reached into his pocket and pulled out a crumple of paper and pulled at its corners to straighten it. It was a torn envelope. I could see the writing on it, the certain way she always wrote in her delicate hand. *Henry and Violet Blake.*

"I picked up the mail," he said. So that's what he was doing in town.

It was from her.

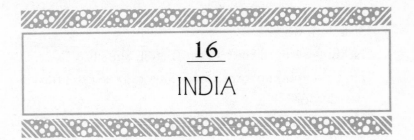

16
INDIA

"Let me read it," I said. My voice was hollow and hoarse in the way of first waking.

"It's not all for you." He fanned out the pages, three ledger papers torn from a book, and drew one page out. The wind flapped it as he handed it to me. He stuffed the other pages and the envelope back in his pocket.

The writing was shaky, like she'd been jaggled on a train.

My darling daughter, I hope you are getting along all right. You would like it here. It's wild and beautiful with lots of birds. I will have so much to tell you when I see you again. I don't know how long it will be, but it's going to be awhile. I hope you are reading some good books and keeping your mind strong. I am so proud to be your Loving Mother.

"Why doesn't she know when they're coming back?" I said.

"She was sick," he said. "She can't travel yet."

"Sick with what?"

"Nothing serious. She's getting better. She's fine."

"How do you know she's fine? She says she can't travel! Is Fry sick too?"

"He's happy. Her sister's wild about him."

Was she giving away my brother to *another* kidnapping aunt?

"Well, when are they coming back? When?"

"I'm no mind reader." He shrugged, as if it didn't matter.

"But where *are* they?"

"Up north somewhere. Like I said."

"But where? What's the place called?"

"It's not called anything. It's the middle of the woods."

"What woods? What does the postmark say? Isn't there a postmark on the envelope? Can I—may I—see it?" I was wheedling. Sometimes wheedling worked on him.

"Later," he said. "Won't be light much longer." He stalked off to coddle his trees.

Cold flashed through me. I set my teeth together hard so I wouldn't shriek or bite. I was like the wounded fox I'd run across once in the woods, mad at trees and sky. I ran upstairs and lifted the mattress. The Hand tumbled free onto the slats. I snatched it up. It didn't look magical in the slightest.

I wanted to wish. My mother wasn't dead, so wishing her back wouldn't bring us a ghost to gloom around the kitchen. But how to say it? Bring Mama and Fry home and make her completely well? Make everybody get along?

Make Aunt Phyllis move to Lansing? No, make Aunt Phyllis part of the everybody getting along and while you're at it make the cherry trees prosper?

I pressed my lips together. I couldn't just go around wishing. My mother didn't want to be with me, so why should I want her? I felt the chill of rage again. If I'd been holding anything but the Hand, I would have hurled it through the window.

Just Fry then. But how could he return without her? I traced the spirals in the copper with a finger. The copper was dull and cool. The Hand was out of magic maybe, or maybe there hadn't ever been any. My head hurt and my throat hurt. I hid the Hand away.

It was past suppertime. The kitchen was empty and the stove cold. The only bread was a moldy heel. So now he was starving me. The trees were his only children. I went out with the egg basket. He'd probably eaten all the hens by now.

Through the partly opened door to the shed I saw his back. He was slumped on the crate we used for milking, since the stool had lost a leg sometime that spring and he hadn't got around to mending it. His head was against the cow's flank. I thought at first that sleep had overtaken him, but I saw his shoulders heaving and heard the strangled gasp. The edge of his boot crumpled the torn paper beneath it.

I couldn't move. I knew if he saw me, he'd be ashamed. He needs her, I thought, even if I don't.

I went back inside with the empty egg basket and eased the screen door so it wouldn't bang. My heart wouldn't stop beating too fast. Even after I'd washed all the dishes, it was still throbbing in my throat.

His face was red when he came in, as if he'd run a long hot way. We had a silent supper of tomatoes he'd picked, and a jar of soup from last year's garden. He said nothing about the letter. I was glad.

Upstairs again, I couldn't stay asleep. The creaking house and wind in the trees and the croaking of frogs and bird-calls kept waking me. Surely if I looked out my window, the feather lady would be standing below, cursing all of us for generations to come. I had to get back in the magic's good graces, if I'd ever been in them.

I lit the lamp. My mother's sewing box was still on the dresser from when I cut up her old shirtwaist. From my grandmother's linen napkin I made a soft pouch for the Hand and sewed on a loop of thin white ribbon so I could wear it like a quiver. I even embroidered a wavy border in blue chain stitch, the only stitch I could reasonably execute. For once I was careful with my stitches, and I didn't have to rip out any mistakes, because I didn't make them.

I wouldn't have to leave the Hand abandoned and alone. It would be nicely concealed. We'd get to know each other and serve each other well. In the early mists of morning I'd take it to the rat root place, where I'd wished before. My dress wish had come true when I wished there. If the Hand had anything left in it, it would be most alive by water and trees. It would bring my mother and brother back and they would be well and happy. It could do that. It would want to.

* * *

I'd intended to be back from the rat root place before my father got up, but I didn't wake until well into the morning. Something was baking downstairs that wasn't bread. I put on a clean shift and the Hand in its pouch over it, then my ratty work dress.

There was a large round blueberry cake for breakfast, exactly a quarter gone. I hadn't had half a bite when my father came in with a bushel of green beans to be put up in crocks, and of course that meant that I had to do all the snapping.

The stove clattered as he heaved our biggest pot on it for the beans to cook in. He looked gray around the edges, as if he hadn't slept. My lungs clutched, remembering his head on Moony's flank. It was even worse than Mama crying. Hers made me mad, at least. His made me scared that nothing could ever be right.

"There's a girl on the road," he said. "Must be preacher spawn. You'd think they'd make her read scripture all the livelong day on the Sabbath."

He could see the lake road from the window by the stove. I couldn't tell him not to snarl at her or make her feel made fun of. He always hated everybody even when he didn't even know their names yet.

But he went out the back door before she arrived. "Give me a shout when you're done," he said. "And don't let the water boil over."

I heard her footsteps coming up the stairs. Her face was at the screen door, smiling. "Can you come out?" she said.

"I have chores," I said.

"Well, I could help if you show me what to do. Then we'd be done faster. I've never worked on a farm before. Will your father mind? Maybe you should ask."

It was hard to say with him. Sometimes he was reasonable. "He won't mind," I said, opening the screen door to let her in.

She leaned toward me to whisper. "I've got something to show you when we're done. I think you'll like it. Don't ask me what it is. You'll never guess. I made it." She was smiling again. It was good to see a smile that someone really meant.

"You could get stuck here forever," I said. "This job's just the first one of the day."

"I'm good at jobs. Well, certain ones. Oh, beans." She seemed somewhat disappointed, but sat down and took up a handful.

"I love your house," she said, looking at the window by the stove and not at the dirty floor and unwashed cake bowl. "You can see the lake and sky every minute. How sublime can you get? When we build our cottage I hope we can see the lake from it, but I think it's going to be way back in the forest on the other side of the road. But maybe that will be good because there might be more wildlife. So far I've seen just little things, like chipmunks. What's the most exciting animal you've ever seen in real life? You know, not stuffed or in the zoo."

"Wolverine," I said without hesitation. I'd never been to a zoo. "It's kind of rare to see them. They don't like people."

"Why would they?" she said. "People are always plotting

against animals. My father says there aren't any bears or panthers or wolves around here anymore, because they all got killed off."

"Sometimes a bear will come around," I said. "I've seen them lots of times—well, twice." There was no need to lie, though I often did so without reason.

"Lucky! I'd give anything to see a panther. I think they're probably so graceful and majestic. My brother Willis is scared to death of them. He pretends he isn't, but he is. The only wild animals in a city are rats. They're *not* exciting. Where would you go if you could go anywhere?" She took up another fistful of beans.

To find Fry, I thought. Wherever that is. "Just about anywhere," I said. "San Francisco or Paris or Egypt. Or the South Pole, but not on an expedition or anything. I'd just like to see it, but not stay too long."

"Me too! It's on my list. It must be so amazingly quiet. Maybe the ice floes creak around and the polar bears roar once in a while. But India's my number one. They've got the Taj Mahal, and elephants and Bengal tigers and fakirs. If I was a missionary I could go there, but I don't want to be a missionary. But I want to see the world more than anything. But not cities so much. I'm tired to death of cities. Except traveling's expensive. I might have to marry an heir or something, maybe a nice elderly crippled one who'd be so grateful that I married him he'd let me gad about. Or become a famous actress. Either way, my mother will be appalled. She says riches corrupt. Do you agree?"

"I don't really know anybody rich," I said. "Maybe the

lady I work for is, and she's nice. At least to me she is. I don't know if she's exactly rich, though. If you're really rich, you don't have a job, right? She has a job."

"Also you can be nice and corrupt both at once," Mercy said. "Extra nice to cover up, so nobody suspects. I'm not saying the lady you work for is. You'd know if she was, because you notice things. I do too. Not everybody does. Have you noticed that?"

We laughed, both of us at the same time. She was three times faster than I was at snapping off the stems, but tended to drop them on the floor. It didn't matter.

"You know what?" she said. "Being here is the most exciting thing that's ever happened to me so far. It might be as exciting as India, for all I know. I never got to sleep in the woods or go places by myself before. And meeting you, obviously. What's your most exciting thing that ever happened?"

Finding the Hand, of course. Even if it wasn't magic, it was ancient and mysterious. But I couldn't tell her.

"My job's kind of exciting," I said. "I get to work in the darkroom and see pictures appear out of nothing, and when I help Miss Nadia take them, everything has to be done fast and exactly perfectly. And she's from Russia."

"Russia! That's not on my list. The people I've seen pictures of look completely gloomy, probably because it's never warm. India's constantly warm. Oh! My mother said to invite you to have supper with us. Do you want to?"

"If my father lets me," I said. Our meals together were mostly dismal. I didn't mind missing one.

We talked about whether we'd ever get to climb the

Himalayas or the pyramids and finished the beans before the water on the stove was even close to boiling. She asked if she could come with me to tell my father, so I let her. He didn't say anything insulting to Mercy and gave permission about supper.

"Go play," he said, waving us off.

Play! I didn't know he'd ever heard of it.

"I'll show you what I made now," Mercy said when we were out of earshot.

She had us go along the road toward the preacher camp, then led me by the arm into the woods. She stopped to look and listen. Voices from the preacher tents were thin. The wind was making the lake roar and trees bend.

"We're almost there," she said in a low voice. "You have to absolutely promise you won't tell anyone or let anyone see it, even at the end of the summer when I leave. Or ever. But you can use it anytime, whether I'm here or not. And then every year it can be for just the two of us. Hand on your heart."

I did what she said. "I'm an expert at keeping secrets," I told her.

I was. I kept my mother's sadness to myself and made Fry forget that she was crying upstairs and never told my father or anybody.

"From now until the end of time," Mercy said.

"From now until the end of time," I said too.

Her hand was held out for me to shake. We clasped hands. Her grip was solid. It was exciting to have a secret with somebody. She smiled and let go.

We continued up a slope, where the roots of a grand maple clung to the hillside. "This is it," she said, touching the trunk. "Watch."

She stepped over to a tumble of boughs and lifted one away and laid it to the side. The other boughs made a large nest with a hollow in the center. From there she drew out a ladder of two stout branches with narrower lengths of wood lashed on for rungs.

"You made that?" I said.

"I couldn't use any nails," she said. "Hammering's too noisy. The last people I want to find out about this are my vile and hideous brothers." She lifted the ladder and fitted the top rails into notches she'd cut in the bark of the maple. "Yank it around and make sure it's in there solid," she told me.

The ladder was sturdy against the tree. She clambered up to the lowest branch and waited for me to join her. It was an easy climb with the ladder and would have been impossible without it.

"This part's tricky," she said, and with a stick that was up there for that very purpose, she snagged a loop of rope that was attached to the ladder, prodded the ladder away, and hauled it up, securing it to a branch with a strap that was almost exactly bark-colored.

We continued up. She'd made footholds exactly where they were needed. She wasn't the least afraid and barely held on.

"Here's where we can leave messages," she said, indicating a cracker tin camouflaged by a hank of wood that ingeniously swung aside if you knew to do so.

I ascended slowly, not looking down. Then we were both on a platform of fallen wood that anyone could have mistaken for part of the very tree. We were up as high as the branches would allow. She'd made it so we both could lean against the trunk with our legs outstretched. You could stay up there forever, invisible, inspecting the vastness of the world. Blue Lake glinted between the trees.

"There's heaps more to do, obviously," she said. "Pillows would be ideal, and storage. We could keep food up here or anything."

"Fry would love this," I said. "I mean, of course he won't know about it."

"Who's Fry?" she said.

What was wrong with me all of a sudden? I never let things slip out. But with Mercy it didn't matter. She wouldn't scoff or treat me like I was soft in the head.

"My little brother," I said. "He's gone."

"Oh." Mercy looked abashed. "I'm sorry. You're mother's dead *and* your brother? That must be awful."

Through the leaves below I could see the ferns and ripples in the stream by the rat root place, right where my mother used to go to listen to the wind in the leaves and the water in the rocks.

"My mother—" I began. "She isn't dead, really. She took my brother to visit people and I don't even know where, and they've been gone a long time. So I thought something was wrong. And—maybe there is. And it's—" I had to stop. My throat burned.

"It seems really confusing," Mercy said. "And scary."

It was. I caught my breath.

"We got a letter," I said. "But I wasn't allowed to read all of it, or even see the postmark. Nobody ever tells me anything."

"They never do," Mercy said. "It's despicable how grown-ups treat us like we have no sense. Everything's always so hush-hush. It's made me into a perfect sneak. I have to be, or I'd never find out that we're moving to a new state until we're on our way there. So do you know when they're coming back?"

Maybe never, I thought. Or maybe soon, if the Hand can do it, if I wish right. . . .

"I'm sorry," Mercy said. "You don't have to talk about it. My mother's always admonishing me not to ask questions. I'm rabidly inquisitive."

She wasn't being nosy. She just wanted to know me. I wanted her to. The ache ebbed.

"It's all right," I said. Below, Blue Lake danced in the wind. Clouds shadowed the water. A warbler made its lilting call. "It's as good as India up here," I said. We were invisible creatures of the air, not clumsy, noisy, two-legged brutes.

"It's really kind of magical," she said, smiling just a little.

"Not kind of," I said. I wasn't lying. It really was.

17

THE SWINDLER

"So when you say magic," I said. "Do you think there's really such a thing?"

"Of course," she said. "Don't you?"

"Mostly," I said. "I mean, I guess it depends on what you mean by magic."

"You can't laugh," she said. She had taken off her shoes. Her feet were very white.

"I won't laugh," I said.

"I've thought about this quite a bit," she said. "Where I live, it's city all around. Noisy and smoky and hardly anything green, except in a park. And we don't even get to go there very often. But when we do go there, I always get this feeling that magic is nearby, in the trees or the air or something. And up here in the woods it feels like that too, but even more. And I think it's real—whatever it is. Because in ancient times, magic was just normal and common—sorcerers and soothsayers and magic carpets and whatnot all over the place. And then it went out of fashion, or went into hiding, or who knows. But that doesn't mean magic is dead, and just because hardly anybody ever sees a fairy doesn't mean there aren't any. And I don't care if it's babyish to think so."

"It isn't," I said. "Lots of people have seen them."

"Have *you*?"

"No. But it even says so in books. Or at least one that I know of. *The Yellow Fairy Book*. I've got it at home. It's one of my favorite books. Have you ever read it?"

"Probably not. I hardly ever read. I'm not saying books are bad, but I'd rather do things. Reading makes me twitchy. I didn't mean to get off the subject. You were saying about your mother's letter. Can't you snag the rest of it from your father's grasp and find out where she is?"

"He's probably burned it in the stove by now. I think that's what he does with them, or he's got a really good hiding place. I've looked for every letter that he doesn't let me read."

"Maybe she told a friend where she was going."

"She doesn't have any."

"Really? How come?"

"People in town don't like her and she doesn't like them either. Because my father used to be really handsome when he was younger, and just about every girl in the state wanted to marry him, and then he picked somebody who isn't from around here. And Indian to boot, even though she's only half. And they say nasty stupid things that she can hear. And so can I sometimes."

"How dare they! Like what?"

"Oh, you know. Names. Half-breed. Heathen. That kind of thing. She made him go broke, she brought the family bad luck. My mother says people around here are small-minded and my father says it's not just around here, people are like that everywhere. And *she* says she's been places where they aren't. It's one of the things they argue about."

"Maybe she had to escape from here because she hates it so much. Maybe she's finding another place for you to live. Maybe it's somewhere exciting that you're going to really like."

"Then why didn't she take me, and not just my brother?"

She narrowed her eyes. "Is Fry—that's his name, Fry? Is he her favorite?"

I considered. "I don't know if she has a favorite. I guess she'd pretend she didn't if she did, so maybe she does."

"You'd be able to tell. They can't hide it. My father likes Willis best and then Emmet and then me, and for my mother it's Emmet, Willis, me. But it's not terrible, because they don't care if I learn Latin, which I'd be awful at, and the boys have to get perfect grades, and they don't mind so much with me. If Fry's not her favorite, she'll be back or she'll send for you. But I could help you look for the letter or anything else that would help."

I was used to keeping matters to myself. But there are certain things you shouldn't attempt alone. If you go out in a boat and a wind comes up, you might need someone on the tiller and someone on the sail. Mercy was good at figuring things out and seeing what was true and what were just maybes.

I reached for the copper hand in its pouch against my side. Warmth came into me.

"All right," I said. "I do need help with something. It can never be spoken of to a living soul. Promise. So help you to the sky above."

"I promise. So help me to the sky above."

"I found something. And I think it really is magic, and it might grant wishes. I think it gave me one already. But I don't know what it can do. I have to be careful with it. Magic can turn on a person."

"Of course," she said.

"I might have made everything up, though, and made myself believe it."

"So you might not really have wished for something that actually came true?"

"No. I did. But it was the kind of thing that could have happened without wishing for it. It was a dumb wish."

"Well, listen to this," she said. There were two things I wanted terribly badly this summer. And I wished for them. I did. Not prayed for, because you're supposed to pray for others, not yourself. It was absolutely wishing. I wanted something exciting to happen. That was one. And two, I wanted a friend. And both came true. So maybe the magic's contagious."

"Maybe. I don't know how it's supposed to work. That's what I have to find out. But when I first found the thing, it *felt* like it was magic, just to touch it. And now it doesn't. So I think I have to take it to where I found it, because that's where it was acting magical in the first place. Maybe you could go with me."

"Well, of course! When?"

"Now," I said. "If nobody's there."

I couldn't exactly tell, even from our lofty perch. I could see where the stream emptied into the lake, but not the mossy clearing or the hole of bones. I couldn't tell for sure if anyone was down there, digging further. If someone was, we would be two summer friends out on a stroll, just happening by.

We were deathly quiet, descending the ladder, hiding it away in its nest, moving through the woods with stealth. Almost to the stream, we stopped to listen. Nothing rustled. We came through a copse of young trees to the ferns and the rat root, taller than last time I'd seen it. There was the hole, covered in its green canvas. No excavators were in evidence.

She wouldn't say I was touched in the head, no matter what the Hand did or didn't do. She believed in fairies, after all. I reached for the cord of the Hand's pouch and drew the pouch up around my arm and toward the collar of my dress. I drew out the Hand. The thumb caught on the cloth. I freed it gently, weighing the Hand with my fingers so the wind wouldn't take it.

"Copper," she said. "Like the beads."

"But does it seem magical?" I said.

She leaned over it. "Well, the designs could be a spell or an incantation or something." With beaver fastidiousness, she traced a snaky line with her smallest finger. The Hand lay in my outstretched hand, not fluttering, not bringing winter.

"Try this," I told her. I pressed the Hand between my palms and raised my hands to the sky just as the feather lady had done, if I'd really seen her. The Hand shuddered between my palms and warmth filled me. I wasn't imagining. I brought my hands down and opened them.

"You now," I told Mercy. "Don't wish. Not even in your mind."

I offered her the Hand. Sun caught the copper edge. She slid it from my hand to hers and closed the copper between her palms and raised her arms as I had shown her. Her eyes were closed. She took a sharp breath and her eyes came open. Copper fingers splayed like rays of the sun. She brought her arms down. The Hand was still between her palms.

Her eyes met mine. "It feels alive," she said.

Something rushed us from behind, a tumble of limbs. I fell, my face hit moss. It filled my mouth.

"You can't!" Mercy shrieked. "It's not yours!"

"It isn't *yours*," said Willis. One hand held the copper hand above his head. With the other hand he twisted Mercy's arm behind her back.

I stared at my enemy like a wolf on the stalk. "It's mine," I said.

"It's not," he retorted. "It's an artifact. It's for people to study."

"Let go of her," I said. Instead, he yanked her arm. She winced. He was a head taller than either of us.

"Look," said hideous Willis, waving the Hand aloft. "I'm doing you a favor. If anybody found out you had this thing, you'd be in trouble with the law, since you stole it. Girls never think rationally about anything. You just want it because you think it's pretty."

"That isn't why!" I ran at him. He held it away and kept me off with one arm, one foot. I grabbed his arm with both hands and dug my nails into his flesh. He threw me. He was strong.

"Ooh! It's *magic*! It's *alive*!" he jeered.

"That's right! And it'll *curse you*, you pig!"

"Ooh, I'm *frightened*!"

"It's Violet's! Give it back!" Mercy kicked him hard. He stumbled but didn't go down. I knotted up my fist and bashed it between his eyes. Blood splashed from his nose. He staggered back, dropping the Hand. Mercy scurried for it. Willis was faster. He dove, and the Hand was under him.

"It'll break!" I cried. Mercy was already pulling at his shoulder. "Don't break it, don't break it," I said, pushing at him. His face was in the moss, bleeding on it. He wasn't light. He twisted around and elbowed me in the neck. Mercy tried to shove him and he shoved her hard. She fell.

He was laughing. I hurled myself at him, pounding at his arm. He clutched the Hand to his chest, his trophy.

"You hurt it!" Mercy cried.

The copper thumb jutted. It was bent. So was the finger next to it. Trying to get the Hand away would only hurt it more.

"It's broken," I said. "You've got the curse on you now. I hope it tortures you before you die."

"Oh, yes! The famous curse nobody's ever heard of! Because there's no such thing!"

He ran down the beach with it. I hoped I'd knocked a tooth out. I hoped the Hand would destroy him. I wished it. I wished it like anything.

Mercy was breathing hard beside me. "I'm telling Father," she declared.

"Don't," I said. "It won't do any good."

"But it's yours," she said. "He stole it! My father will be furious. All we have to do is say you found it digging in your garden. Nobody can prove you didn't."

"No. Don't say anything. It'll be worse if the grown-ups are fighting over it. Let's go see what he says and where he puts it. We'll get it back."

We quickly brushed the dirt and moss off ourselves and ran for the road. We slowed as we approached the preacher camp. Mercy took my hand and squeezed it. The preacher camp was a cluster of half a dozen tents, a long table with splintery benches on either side, and a smoky cook fire being prodded by Mrs. Rankin. Mercy's father sat on a camp stool, a stack of books at his feet. He was inspecting the Hand. Willis hovered, keeping Emmet and two other little boys from getting too close by elbowing them.

"This is quite a find," Reverend Rankin said. "Excellent workmanship. Well-preserved."

Mercy and I edged our way in. "What *is* that?" said Mercy. Anyone would have believed she'd never seen it in her life. Willis threw us a cool stare.

"Grave goods," said Willis.

"Your brother has found something that may be quite rare," said Reverend Rankin. He turned the Hand over carefully, peering at it. The bent thumb and fingers had been straightened back to how they were supposed to be, but there was a faint crease at the base of the thumb. I wanted to crack Willis's head open with a rock.

"What's it for?" said Emmet.

"Hush," said hideous Willis. "It's that repoussé technique, Father. I was just reading about it. They used to pound the copper into sheets and cut out shapes, like warriors and serpents."

"The human hand," his father said. "Supplication. Where was it exactly?"

"Near the southeast corner of the excavation. Under a thin layer of dirt."

"What's it for?" Emmet said again.

"It's not *for* anything," Willis said. "Decoration. To show how important the person was."

"Most likely it stands for something," their father said. "Privilege. Knowledge—a diploma of sorts, perhaps. Or an amulet to ward off evil spirits. People will debate the significance for years to come, no doubt."

"To the table, please!" Mrs. Rankin called.

"Well done, Willis," the reverend said, giving the Hand to the swindling boy. "Go put it in the box with the other things."

"Both hands, Mercy!" Mrs. Rankin gave Mercy a bowl of potatoes. "This can go on the table, please. Violet, how nice that you could join us. Sit right here." Willis scurried into one of the tents with the Hand pinched between two fingers like a dirty rag.

Before the food was served, everyone had to hold hands

with the people next to them and close their eyes while somebody blessed the food. The meat was tender, the potatoes charred but uncooked. Everybody wanted to know all about the Hand. Willis got to spew his lies. Mercy nudged my foot with hers every time he told one.

"Will you have it looked at by an expert to determine its value and significance?" said one of the ladies.

"We'll see," said Reverend Rankin, and he launched into a lengthy account of the book he had just started reading. I figured he didn't care to discuss the future of the Hand in my presence. He didn't want any trouble from my father, who was too busy with his green beans to bother with anything important.

The Hand was so close, captured by the foe. The tent where Willis had stowed the Hand was behind me, and I couldn't even look at it. I was expert at pretending not to be mad. It took forever for everyone to finish eating, and the grown-up conversation was too loud, and then there was cake. The cake was from the bakery in town and almost made up for the potatoes.

There was work waiting for me at home. Mercy was given leave to walk me to the road, barely any distance.

"It won't be hard to get the Hand," she said when it was safe to speak. "It's just in a box. All we have to do is take it. It has to be at night, obviously, and we can't be suspected. We could fake a bear attack—get some kind of furry blanket, or—"

It wasn't funny, but it was. We let ourselves laugh a little. "It has to be foolproof," I said. "If we get caught, it's no good for the Hand. We have to rescue it for its own good."

"Of course," she said. "We'll think our heads off. But we have to do it fast, before they figure out what expert they're going to show the Hand to. When are you done with work tomorrow?"

"It's different every day, and sometimes my aunt makes me stay with her."

"Leave notes in the tree then," she said. "Remember where I showed you?"

"Don't say anything revealing. Your brother's a really good spy."

"We're better," she said.

I told my father exactly nothing, except about the charred and rocky potatoes. It got him to crack a smile. There weren't as many chores as I had feared. I told him I was tired and went up to bed well before dark.

I already had a scheme, or part of one. I'd read a story once about jewel thieves making fakes and switching them with real diamonds. Somebody back in ancient times had made that copper hand. Why couldn't someone from a time of telephones and factories make one exactly like it?

Copper—surely I could get some. Didn't we have a broken copper kettle with the other junk in the shed? And Mercy was good at making things. Together we could do the miraculous. I would get the Hand back. I had to.

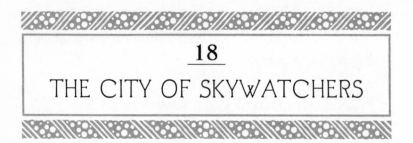

18

THE CITY OF SKYWATCHERS

It took four days for everyone to tell how things had been. The first to speak were those who had made the longest journeys, those from the warmer south, those from the dry west. Then the people from the eastern shore, then the mountain people. Then Greenstone and others from the north, and finally the people of the plains and rivers.

They gathered at the place that once had been the city of skywatchers. Councils in every region sent the most highly respected healers and sages, dreamers and seers, root workers and tent shakers, the men and women who did their best to keep things in order. As many of them as there were, the great circle could have held ten times their number. Grass grew tall where once hundreds had danced the earth bare.

The worst news was from the eastern shore. The burning rash was a wildfire. Bands and clans and families—thousands gone. The dead became wolf food. Nobody was left to bury anyone. Some people got sick and didn't die, some people stayed well, but they were the rare few.

Everyone who gathered at the city of skywatchers had a chance to speak. Some were in favor of revenge. The invaders had forced themselves on countless women. They had kidnapped warriors to take across the sea as curiosities. Whirlpools could dash their ships on the rocks. Crops could be poisoned. Tornadoes could lift every one of their settlements away.

Some said it was the only way, others said it would be dangerous and wrong. They weren't able to agree. Some would do one thing, some another.

Greenstone was someone who could help messages be heard and understood. Greenstone had copper knowledge, ways of listening, ways of bringing things together. She was the one chosen to lead them all in song.

There was nothing else to do but sing. So they sang.

The next day was Monday. I woke early. My idea was possibly ridiculous, possibly a stroke of genius. If only I could talk it over with Mercy, I'd know one way or the other. Meanwhile, I had to get my hands on some copper.

The broken kettle was in the shed, beneath an old shelf that gave me a splinter. Only the bottom part of the kettle was copper, and it had a hole in it. Still, copper abounded. I would get some. Copper mines were to the north, not so very far. Copper was around.

I was early for Miss Nadia, but not by much. It was the day of Lucy Thornwood's sitting. Her grandmother Mrs. Agosa arrived with her.

"Mrs. Agosa," Miss Nadia said. "How good to see you. How did your purple come out?"

"Not so bad," Mrs. Agosa said.

"That must mean it's perfect. Do you have some boxes with you we can use in the picture?"

The bark boxes were packed inside a big woven basket. Lucy Thornwood put them out on the table and Miss Nadia looked them over. Mrs. Agosa sat drinking her coffee like it was medicine. I gave her more. She didn't look at me, but out the window at the lake.

"We haven't had the time to make more fancy ones," Lucy Thornwood said. "These are kind of plain."

"They're wonderful," Miss Nadia said. "No two alike. The purple—it's so deep it makes me want to cry. Keeping the design plain is right for that kind of color. All your colors are from plants?"

"My grandmother likes it done that way," Lucy Thornwood said. "Some people use dye from the store. It's easier, but it doesn't look the same."

"I don't always like things too easy, myself," Miss Nadia said. "For example, this picture we are taking. You're supposed to be outside the hotel. But, with any luck, we can make a better picture by having you pose inside, right here. Then I can put people and hotel and sky together afterward, and they don't all have to be taken at the same time."

She had Lucy Thornwood sit on her mat and pretend to be working on a bark box that actually was finished, while keeping as still as she could and not moving her fingers or eyes.

"So," Miss Nadia said, "you are in the outdoors. You can hear the waves from the lake. You can feel the wind on your face. And people are all around, coming, going, talking. That's good, looking down like that, but up one half inch with the chin. Yes. And Miss Blake, if you will take the braid on the right shoulder and let it fall to the front. No. Back where it was."

Someone was at the door. "That will be Mrs. Dell," Miss Nadia said. "You'll let her in, Miss Blake. Mrs. Thornwood, are you uncomfortable at all?"

"I think my hand's asleep," Lucy Thornwood said.

"Oh, dear. Please shake it. Make a fist."

"Nadia!" Mrs. Dell exclaimed, looking at the black-draped room. "It looks like you're about to have a funeral. I sincerely hope that my husband hasn't caused you to take leave of your senses. He's been known to have that effect."

"Do you know Mrs. Agosa and Mrs. Thornwood?" Miss Nadia said.

"I'm a great admirer of their exquisite baskets," said Mrs. Dell. She pursed her lips at the one Lucy Thornwood had put down. "They have much nicer ones than that," she said. "I bought some the other day that we can use. There's one with a crested bird that would be perfect."

Mrs. Agosa was looking at Mrs. Dell intently. I tried to figure what animal Mrs. Agosa was—bear, maybe. But smarter than bear. Maybe wolf.

"I don't think you'll see the box so much," Miss Nadia said. "The box isn't the point of the picture. But if you want it, let's get it. Miss Blake can go."

"No. You're right. It's too vivid. I'm sure this one is fine." Mrs. Dell regarded Lucy Thornwood with her heron eyes. "I still don't understand how this is going to work," she said.

"Darkroom magic." Miss Nadia peered over the camera

at Lucy Thornwood. "Now, everybody please will be quiet a minute."

Just then the telephone rang. I hurried to it and answered in a soft voice, so as not to rattle Miss Nadia. She hadn't said who she would talk to or not, because she didn't like for Mrs. Dell to know that there was such a thing as a talk-to list.

"Miss Violet," a man purred. "Is the lovely Alice Dell up there with you, by chance?"

"Yes, sir," I said to the railroad pirate. "Mrs. Dell, it's your husband."

Mrs. Agosa watched Mrs. Dell cross the room at her heron-like stalk. Wolf for sure, I thought. Not bear in the slightest.

"How's your hand?" Miss Nadia said to Lucy Thornwood.

"Awake." Lucy Thornwood took up the box again and resumed the pose.

"Perfect," Miss Nadia said. "Miss Blake, if you would—"

"I've been summoned," Mrs. Dell said, hanging up the phone. "Wasn't I just saying that Guy can drive a person mad? He's got *another* project he wants me to take care of. He wouldn't say what it was. He can be so mysterious and clandestine. Well, I'll be off, then. Try to manage without me."

I let her out. When I turned back to the room, Mrs. Agosa was looking out the window again at the lake. I felt hate swell up in me for Mrs. Agosa for not saying what she knew and just letting a girl be motherless.

"Mrs. Thornwood," Miss Nadia said. "You will have to stay quite still. We're having a long exposure, so any move you make will be a blur. Are you ready?"

Lucy Thornwood said she was. Miss Nadia set the camera. "Nobody move or walk around, please, until I say so. Now. Mrs. Agosa. Did you grow up around here?"

"Around here," Mrs. Agosa said. "Other places too."

"You've seen some changes, I imagine. This place hasn't been a town so long, has it?"

"Depends what you call long," Mrs. Agosa said.

"The buildings don't seem so old," Miss Nadia said. "I'd guess most of them were put up after your War Between the States."

"Could be," Mrs. Agosa said. "I didn't keep track."

"I was born in a city hundreds of years old," Miss Nadia said. "So forty years, a hundred, to me is young for a town."

"You're a long way from home," Mrs. Agosa said. "Russia, it's the other side of the world, isn't it?"

"For me it's no longer home." Miss Nadia looked at her watch. "My people are persecuted there. It's better in America for us, though many things aren't fair in this country either, with one way for some and another way for others. Maybe you've seen that yourself."

"You're around as long as me, you see a thing or two," Mrs. Agosa said.

"What can we do about this world?" Miss Nadia said. "Twisted, ignorant people. They don't like Indians. They don't like Jews, Chinese, Italians, anybody. Do you believe this is human nature?"

"Maybe," Mrs. Agosa said. "For some humans it is."

"I want to think it's what people are taught, not how

they're made. But we can't know. So this town here. You remember when there was nothing here, maybe?"

"It wasn't nothing." Mrs. Agosa's wolf eyes were hard dark rocks again.

"I'm sorry," Miss Nadia said. "I didn't say it how I meant it. There was no street. No mill. No stores. You remember how it was then?"

"Sure," Mrs. Agosa said. "Where this hotel is, it used to be a sand dune. When I was young, we used to come to that beach there for the sturgeon." She waved her arm at the window. "There's hardly any sturgeons now. We used to climb on the dune to see when the canoes were coming back. You could see everything from up there."

"Sturgeon! I know sturgeon. Where I'm from, it was always for the royals. They're gone from here now, the sturgeon?"

"There's still some. The old smart ones go deep, where the nets can't go. The pigeons, they weren't so lucky. The pigeons used to like the dune, and all the trees around that got cut down for lumber. The pigeons made the sky dark, there were so many. White people named the town for the pigeons. Then they hunted them all."

"What happened to the dune?" Miss Nadia said.

I remembered the dune myself. One day I was in town with my mother and Fry and it was gone. My father had railed for weeks about it.

"They took it away in wagons so it would be flat for the hotel," Mrs. Agosa said. "I watched them. Days and days it took. I asked one of the men: where are they taking the sand? They sold it for making glass. Somebody made a lot of money off that dune."

"That must have been hard to watch."

Mrs. Agosa shrugged. "You don't watch, you don't know what they're up to."

"That's very true," Miss Nadia said. "I didn't mean to bring up memories of sorrow. I ask too many questions sometimes."

"That's all right," Mrs. Agosa said. "Even hard things have to be remembered. You want to know what it was like here before white people made a town. This was our summer place. Winters, we went south more, where it's not so cold with the wind from the lake. It was more quiet back then. No horses. No mills."

Miss Nadia turned the camera on its legs away from the black drapery where Lucy Thornwood had been sitting on her mat and pointed it at Mrs. Agosa's chair.

"Mrs. Thornwood, that's all we need. Please stretch yourself. Thank you for your patience. You're an excellent model. Sit yourself where it's comfortable. Violet will give you coffee."

I poured a cup for Lucy Thornwood and gave it to her. I could see she felt sorry for me. I hated when people did that, but she didn't mean any harm by it.

"Mrs. Agosa," Miss Nadia was saying. "How about we take your picture now? You don't have to move. Exactly where you're sitting is perfect."

"I'm no advertisement." Mrs. Agosa shook her head. "I'd scare them all off."

"Not at all," Miss Nadia said. "I'd like to have your picture. Please. No posing or fiddling, nothing fancy."

"We have to go," Mrs. Agosa said.

"The train's not in for a while yet," Lucy Thornwood said. "Have your picture taken, Grandma. It won't take any time."

"It always takes longer than you think," Miss Nadia said. "You're right, Mrs. Agosa. Soon the people will be coming to wait for the train. You don't want to miss them. We'll all go down together. Can you believe this sky?"

And she plucked the camera off the tripod, put the camera on the table without even cleaning the lens, gave Lucy Thornwood an envelope for her time and trouble, and then all of us were in the hallway.

"Run, Violet! Tell him to wait!" Miss Nadia grabbed the case I was carrying so I could move faster. She meant the elevator man, who had stopped on our floor. We all piled in. I had to stand next to Mrs. Agosa. Our arms touched. The cloth of her dress was soft from many washings. I edged away.

The doors opened in the lobby and smack in the middle of it where before there had been a cluster of chairs was a long narrow box of glass. Mrs. Dell was half inside it, as if it was eating her alive. She pulled herself out and saw us.

"Nadia!" she cried. "Just who I was pining for. You've got to lend me your eye."

Lying in the glass box was a skeleton. I went completely cold. I knew who it was, her bones mounted on a board with wire.

"Isn't it something?" Mrs. Dell said. "A boy found it in

the woods not far from here. He did a marvelous job putting all the bones in the right places. What do you think of the presentation—the forest motif? Tell the truth, Nadia. You might as well. You're terribly transparent. I'll know if you're humoring me."

Mrs. Dell had put pine needles and branches in there with the bones, trying to make it seem like forest floor. The copper beads and knife were arranged on hunks of moss. On a piece of stump by the skull lay the copper hand.

"I'd like to have a careful look," Miss Nadia said. "But I've got to take advantage of the light. In less than an hour it's gone."

"*This* is the find," Mrs. Dell said, tapping on the glass to indicate the Hand. "Isn't it nicely crafted?"

"Lovely," Miss Nadia said, but she was looking out the window at the day.

"I don't know about these pinecones," Mrs. Dell said.

"They're fine," Miss Nadia said. "But I can't linger. The light is perfect."

I blazed with rage. The bones weren't flowers to be pressed in a scrapbook or seashells to be lined up on a shelf. And the Hand! It wasn't for decoration.

Mrs. Dell gave my arm a ladylike prod. "I wouldn't lean on the glass," she told me.

I wanted to smash through it and grab the Hand. It was so close. Miss Nadia started off. I knew I should follow, but I couldn't move.

Mrs. Agosa frowned, her jaw tight. "These bones will

bring bad luck," she said. "They should go back in the ground where they were."

"I don't believe in such things." Mrs. Dell's arms were inside the glass box, adjusting and arranging. "People make their own luck."

"Grandma," Lucy Thornwood said, taking her grandmother by the arm. "The train will be here soon."

Mrs. Agosa looked up from the glass. I could see beneath her wrinkled skin and pouched eyes what maybe she had looked like when she was my age, when she was on the big dune looking to see if her father's canoe was on its way to shore.

Her eyes met mine. They looked more weary than mean. She turned away. Lucy Thornwood was already at the door. A bellboy held it open for them.

I placed a hand on the glass. *I'll get you out of here,* I said to the Hand in my mind, and ran to catch up with Miss Nadia.

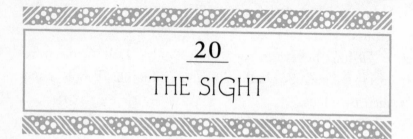

20
THE SIGHT

All that afternoon, Miss Nadia took more pictures than you'd ever think someone could take in half a day. Crowds of people sat beneath umbrellas and splashed around in the water. The big lake was smooth, with low streaks of cloud over it. Miss Nadia strode across the sand with the heavy wooden tripod hoisted on a shoulder, then stopped and thrust it into the sand when she wanted to take a picture. Some were of clouds, but mostly they were of the hotel from as far away as you could get without being in the water. When she was finished, hardly anyone was on the beach anymore. The sun was low.

"Now for the darkroom," Miss Nadia said. "If you would just help me put everything away before you leave. Then tomorrow we start early and already we're organized. Can you be here by six?"

"Of course, Miss Nadia," I said.

We got in the elevator. The elevator man knew better than to ask Miss Nadia if she needed help. She never needed any.

The doors opened on the second floor and there stood Mrs. Agosa. "I've got something to tell you," she said to Miss Nadia. "In private."

I knew it was about the Hand somehow. My heart was in my ears, my throat.

"Please sit where you like, Mrs. Agosa," Miss Nadia said when we were in the studio. "I need Miss Blake for a minute to help put things away, and then we can send her home and have a talk."

"She can listen," Mrs. Agosa said. "I won't keep you long. Tell you what. You can have Lucy's picture any time. Or mine, if you want. No charge. But first make a picture of those bones."

"The skeleton, you mean?" Miss Nadia was frowning.

Mrs. Agosa gave a nod. I clenched my hands so they wouldn't shake.

"But why?" Miss Nadia said.

"I'll tell you the truth," Mrs. Agosa said. "I don't care so much about a picture. I just want to see. My eyes aren't so good these days, and the glass gets reflections on it so you don't know what you're looking at. I think the wife of your boss will open up the glass for you, but not for me."

"What's so interesting about the bones?" Miss Nadia said. She had the camera out of its crate, dusting it off with its soft little brush.

"That skeleton is someone important," Mrs. Agosa said. "Someone with power. That copper hand isn't for just anybody. *It* has power. People fool around with these things, you don't know what could happen."

"Like what?" I said before I could stop myself.

"Who knows? Anything. Disease could come. The world could stop."

"How?" I said. I couldn't help it. "How can something that's just a piece of metal do things like that?"

"I don't know what it can do," she said. "But I know one thing. The bones should get buried in a proper kind of way before bad things start to happen."

"I'm not understanding completely," Miss Nadia said. "You want a picture why?"

"A reason I can have it in my hand. I might find out something. Give me yours," she said to Miss Nadia. "Your hand."

Miss Nadia came over to Mrs. Agosa's chair and held out her hand, stained brown at the tips. It was a tired-looking hand, but delicate and strong.

Mrs. Agosa took the hand in hers and looked out the window at maroon sky over the big lake. "Losses," she said. "Family lost. Sudden deaths. You've known hunger. You try to forget by working. But for you, work is more than just money. Love—you're new at love. You're careful with it." She turned away from the lake and looked at Miss Nadia.

"You have the sight," Miss Nadia said.

"Not sight. Sometimes I can feel things. I can feel something about those bones, and especially about the hand of copper. But through the glass, it's faint. If I can touch that hand, something might come to me."

"All right," Miss Nadia said. "Let's see what can be done." She went to the telephone.

I felt Mrs. Agosa's eyes on me, but I couldn't look at her. I fiddled with the camera case instead, lifting up the lid and pretending to make an adjustment.

"Alice," Miss Nadia said into the telephone. "I had a thought. This remarkable find of the skeleton, and how you made it so intriguing to look at. The display. This must be documented. I want to re-create this, the artistry of Mrs. Dell, and the ancient mysterious traditions. Right now, if you have nothing that will interfere. I'll be down immediately."

She rang off and then rang the bell captain to say that Mrs. Dell required two bellboys to move something heavy in the lobby. Then she gave a quick mink smile to Mrs. Agosa, and she picked up her burdens and I picked up mine and the three of us went down the hall.

"I'll walk. I don't trust those elevators," Mrs. Agosa said, and turned from us.

Miss Nadia and I loaded ourselves in the elevator and came out into the lobby, where two bellboys who weren't Isaac Duvall were stiffly waiting for Miss Nadia to tell them what to do. Mrs. Dell already had the case open and was inside it, arranging pine boughs and jostling the Hand around. Next to her foot on the floor was a tiny padlock that fastened into a hasp on the sliding door of the case. It looked like it would break if you hit it hard with a rock.

Miss Nadia had the bellboys move the case closer to the window. The Hand shuddered when the case was lifted.

"Isn't that copper piece exquisite?" Mrs. Dell said. "Definitely rare. Guy will find an expert to tell us how old it is and so forth. Maybe we'll put on a lecture series. There's so much interest in this kind of thing now. You must know someone, Nadia. You travel in such erudite circles."

Miss Nadia had the camera in place. "That's perfect," she said. "Be still, Alice. Hold your breath."

The camera clicked. If she'd really wanted a photograph of Mrs. Dell, she'd have taken many more. Miss Nadia reached into the box of glass, plucked up the Hand with her thumb and one stained finger, and held it out to Mrs. Agosa. "Would you mind?" she said in the distracted way she had when she was thinking of the picture she wanted.

"Be careful, now," Mrs. Dell said. "That's a valuable artifact."

"She knows," Miss Nadia said.

Mrs. Agosa went to sit down on a chair, the copper hand wrapped in her shawl. Miss Nadia followed with the camera. Mrs. Agosa sat. The Hand was on her lap. She touched it lightly and closed her eyes. To some she might have looked like an old lady dozing, but she looked like the feather lady to me, casting a curse on those who dared disturb bones.

"Not one of those stuffy museum people," Mrs. Dell went on. "Someone who won't put the audience to sleep. For heaven's sake, Nadia, how long is this going to take? I have to dress for dinner."

"That was the last one," Miss Nadia said. "Go ahead and put everything back in the case. Thank you, Mrs. Agosa."

Mrs. Agosa gave me the Hand. She wanted to see me with it. It's nothing special, I told myself. It's a book, a piece of bread. I kept myself steady. It was mine again, but it wasn't. I had to bring it to Mrs. Dell, who snatched it from me and tossed it among the pine boughs.

"Oh, Nadia!" she cried. "Before I forget. I spoke to the man from the little paper here in town and told him you would take a picture of the boy who found all this. He needs it by Friday. The boy is with that settlement over by the little lake just north of here. Any of the drivers can take you there. You'll go and get the boy's picture, won't you?"

"Certainly," Miss Nadia said.

My stomach went sour. Hideous Willis in the paper? I couldn't bear it. His squirrel mother would snip it out and save it in the family Bible, and show it proudly off to anyone who came to visit, and his grandchildren would exclaim, and it was all a lie.

Mrs. Dell shut the glass door and hinged the hasp and stuck the little padlock through and drifted on her lacy way.

"Do you have time for coffee upstairs?" Miss Nadia said to Mrs. Agosa.

"I'll start up," Mrs. Agosa said. "Elevators make my head go around."

So when Mrs. Agosa arrived, I was on the telephone doing the ordering and had to listen extra hard to what Mrs. Agosa and Miss Nadia were saying to each other and say what I was saying in between.

"What did you find out?" Miss Nadia said.

"The copper is for deep purposes," Mrs. Agosa said. "It isn't to be seen by people unless they're trained to know. Even in a picture. And especially it shouldn't be touched."

I almost dropped the receiver. She was trying to scare me. I could feel her stare.

"Why not touched?" Miss Nadia said.

I had to talk to the man in the kitchen. My voice was too low and he couldn't understand me. Finally he did. I hung up.

"—dangerous if you don't understand it," Mrs. Agosa was saying. "If you haven't been taught. When people play with something like that, its power gets confused."

"I'm quite interested in the metaphysical," Miss Nadia said. "At first glance it seems to be an ornament. But no holes are in it for fastening onto whatever's to be decorated. Why then was it made? Your theory seems possible. Deep purposes. Yes."

Mrs. Agosa cast me a glance. She wanted the Hand for herself, of course. She knew of its powers. She had her own heart's desire and didn't want me getting mine.

"It's a caller, this Hand," Mrs. Agosa said. "Friendly with water beings."

"What are water beings?" Miss Nadia said.

"I was taught to believe there are many different ones," Mrs. Agosa said. "You might say it's superstition."

"I wouldn't," said Miss Nadia.

"Would you?" Mrs. Agosa turned her wolf eyes on me.

"No, ma'am," I said. I was a deer, stunned by my killer's gaze.

"Where this copper hand was found is a sacred place from far back," Mrs. Agosa said. "Maybe it was something to do with what happened there, when Blue Lake spilled out."

"I don't know that story," Miss Nadia said.

"It's not a story. It happened. Not so long ago, thirty years maybe. They were logging over by Blue Lake. The big pine trees. They were long and heavy, these trunks, and they had to drag them through the woods to get them to the mill. So then they thought if they just cut between Blue Lake and the river that goes into the harbor, the logs could go from Blue Lake down the new river to the old river to the harbor. That's how they figured it. The mill would saw up the logs and then the wood would be right where the ships are and they could just load it all up. They got a surveyor and they took their measurements and they staked it all out and they cleared a strip of land and they started digging. And the surveyors and the county men, they didn't want to hear about Blue Lake being holy or how the water that's so clear in that lake wouldn't be clear anymore from the sawdust and dumping the logs. They had their plans drawn up on a big rolled-up piece of paper and they were going to get the pine trees over to the mill faster with this new river of theirs."

This didn't seem to have anything to do with the Hand. She was just blathering. I wondered if my father had a tool that would break that little padlock quietly. If I could only slip my arm into the case . . .

"They dug for a long time," Mrs. Agosa said. "Many men, horses, loads of dirt. The day came where they were going to carve away the last part between Blue Lake and the river they were making. People came from all over to watch. They thought the water would come gently out of Blue Lake and fill up this channel they'd been digging and then they could float those logs down. A man was making a speech. He barely got started, and the waters of Blue Lake came rushing, rushing out, flooding out. Water came fast. It was loud. People ran from there. It seemed like it would end up with a big hole where the lake was. But after a while the water stopped pouring out. The lake's still there, but not as deep as it used to be. The water, it's still clear, though."

"That must have scared everybody," Miss Nadia said.

"Good," Mrs. Agosa said. "People maybe learned something."

"Did they find out why it didn't work?"

"Depends who you talk to. Some people said their figuring was wrong. The lake was too high up, so it just spilled out. Some people say there's somebody in the lake, somebody who didn't like this digging, and it put a stop to it. So, anyway. That's all I know. The copper maybe called out to the underwater beings, got them riled. I'm just saying it should be all put back—her bones and everything that belongs to her, so power doesn't get disrupted."

"Why do you say she?" Miss Nadia said.

Mrs. Agosa pushed herself up from her chair. "It's what I think," she said.

"Don't leave yet. There's coffee coming," Miss Nadia said.

"Not for me. I'll go have my granddaughter's cooking. You have a talk with the boss lady. People already say there's a curse on this hotel. Her husband doesn't need another one, I bet. No good for business."

All I wanted was for her to go. Miss Nadia was walking her to the door, offering to get a buggy to take her home.

Mrs. Agosa was refusing. Maybe Miss Nadia had a tool to knock off the lock with. I didn't like the thought of stealing from her, but it would really be borrowing, and I was doing it for the good of us all, not just from selfishness.

"Violet," Miss Nadia said. "That will be all for today. You and Mrs. Agosa could walk down together. Mrs. Agosa prefers the stairs."

"But, Miss Nadia! Don't you need—?"

"Not a thing. It will all wait. Six tomorrow, yes?"

Mrs. Agosa and I were alone in the hall. She grabbed my arm and twined our elbows. We made our way along as a shuffling four-footed creature. Her hands were strong, clutching at my arm. It wouldn't have been easy to pry her off.

"I thought so," she said. "You're like your mother. You see what others don't. You hear things."

She wouldn't find anything out. I could lie even to someone with the sight, whatever that was, because I was an expert. "I'm just like anybody," I said.

"You're just like anybody, and the copper hand's a piece of metal. No. Everything is more than what it is. A shirt worn by a sick person makes someone else get sick or even die, but it's just a piece of cloth. Don't you think that copper hand is more than what it seems to be?"

"It doesn't look like anything special," I said. We were at the staircase. She let go of me with one hand and reached for the banister with it. We started down.

"All right," she said. "I thought you were someone I could talk to about these kinds of things. I guess you're not, though. All right."

"What do you mean talk to? About what?"

She shrugged. "Nothing. You don't know anything, so what's there to talk about?"

"I could listen," I said.

We were at the landing that overlooked the lobby. I could see white bones, spiky pine needles, evening clouds reflected in the glass. We kept going. She was surefooted and swift and in no need of a supporting elbow.

"Some people," she said, "they go into a house. If somebody died in that house they know something happened there. Your mother's that way. You say you're not. I must be wrong about you. I thought for sure you got a feeling off that copper hand. I thought maybe you wanted to have it for yourself."

"That wouldn't be right," I said. But I wasn't fooling her.

"That doesn't always stop people," she said. "This kind of thing, if it's treated wrong, it can't do anything for anybody."

"I don't know what it can do," I said. "All I know about it is what you said."

We were almost to the bottom of the stairs. The summer people were hungry from their long day sprawled in the sun. A line of them waited to be let into the dining room.

"I'm getting old," Mrs. Agosa said. Her voice was low and I had to bend toward her to hear. "More and more these days I get suspicions that are wrong. I had a feeling you'd been around that copper hand. I thought you wanted to have it just like I want to have it. Not just for me, but for everybody."

"It's with a dead person," I whispered. "I don't think I want anything like that."

"Some things should belong to everyone. Georgia knows that."

I lifted my chin and straightened myself. Georgia Blake's not here to say so, I thought. I make my own rules now.

"I'll tell you this, though." We were on the last stair. She let go of my arm. "If the copper hand goes missing, I'll know who took it."

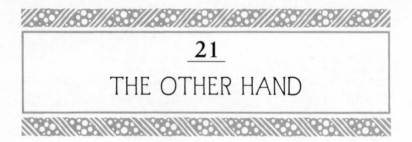

21

THE OTHER HAND

I wasn't going to let Mrs. Agosa make me scared. She wouldn't even know the Hand was gone. She'd be fooled like everyone else. And even if she did find out, what could she do to me? I would rescue the Hand. I would listen to it. It would reward me.

I went out in the dead of night with a lantern and searched the shed for a padlock to practice on. I found two. You could bang and pry around on one of those things for a year and never get it to open without a key.

The next day I was twelve minutes early by the lobby clock. The lobby was empty but for a man at the desk, who recognized me and said good morning. I was annoyed that he knew me. I would have to blend with the summer people if I was ever going to get into the glass case. I gazed down at it from the staircase landing. The feather lady's skull seemed to be glaring my way. I took the rest of the stairs two at a time.

I helped Miss Nadia in the darkroom all morning. Conversation wasn't possible, unless you call asking for the tongs conversation. Thinking about padlocks wasn't all that possible either, or the tongs would get misplaced.

"So this famous Blue Lake," Miss Nadia said as we sat down for lunch, which was something called schnitzel. "You've lived by it all your life?"

"Yes," I said.

"You must know this boy who found the Indian grave."

"Not really," I said. "I know his sister a little."

"Well, we're doing a picture of him. A silly thing. Half an hour to get there, ten minutes for the picture, and then back again. The newspaper man could take the same picture I could take. But Mrs. Dell, she pays the bills, she makes the plans. Maybe afterward, you'll show me where you live. I'd like to meet the father of such a bright girl."

"He wants to meet you too. Except he's up at the river today, fishing. He won't be back until after dark."

"Another day, then." She didn't look fooled. I swallowed hard, too loud. Nobody believed me anymore, even when I told them something not hard to believe.

Miss Nadia hired a buggy. The big lake was dashing and leaping, and the clouds were massive and bright, and the sky had part of the moon in it, even though it was daytime. The buggy jounced along. We got to the preacher camp. Reverend Rankin came to greet us.

"Miss Zalzman! It's an honor. Alice Dell said we should expect you one of these days." He rumpled the top of my head. "And how are you, little miss? *Willis!*" he bellowed, and waved at a group of men and boys who were hammering at a stack of lumber. Willis was wielding a saw. I hoped it would slip and take both his legs off.

"I'd like to have your son pose where the skeleton was found," Miss Nadia was saying.

"It's awfully dark there, Miss Nadia," I blurted. "It's in the woods."

"Let's have a look," she said. When we got there, sun was coming through the trees in patches. There was even a wide bright stripe right across the canvas covering the hole.

"Not bad light," Miss Nadia pronounced, "but it will leave us, if we're not quick. Everybody pay attention, please."

It was almost like church, with everything hushed and nobody talking but Miss Nadia. Even Reverend Rankin didn't speak. Miss Nadia had Willis and Emmet pull the canvas away. The hole gaped, deeper than it had been. I put the tripod where Miss Nadia pointed with her toe. She brought the camera over and I got a plate ready. Miss Nadia told Willis to sit on the ground right by the hole.

I caught Mercy's eye. She stuck her tongue out, but barely, to indicate the hideousness we were forced to behold.

I had my job to do. If the light stopped being perfect, I didn't want to be the reason. I was dying to talk to her. Maybe she had a scheme better than mine.

"Willis," Miss Nadia said. She took a cigar box from her bag. "So. You were digging. You find something. You take it from the ground and look at it more closely. You never saw anything like it before, yes? That is our picture today." She opened the cigar box. Inside was the copper hand.

I almost fell into the hole. How did Miss Nadia have the Hand, and how had I not known it was at my feet in the cigar box in her bag in the buggy we'd ridden in from town? I felt Mercy behind me. She nudged my foot with hers. Miss Nadia took the Hand from the box and gave it to Willis.

"Everybody very quiet," she said sternly. "We're exposing for one minute. There can be no talking, nobody moving. Willis, you especially."

All of our eyes were fixed on Willis, the copper hand on his hand, his elbow on his knee, his knee crushing a fern. He couldn't manage to look awed or amazed, but only smirked. "Mouth closed, please," Miss Nadia ordered Willis. Again we all were statues.

Then Miss Nadia came out from beneath the camera cloth, the Hand went back into the cigar box, the cigar box went back into her bag, and all thoughts I may have had of snatching the Hand from box or bag were unthinkable. I couldn't do such a thing to Miss Nadia, could I? All I could do right then was to hope that none of the magic had rubbed off on hideous Willis, because he was the last person who deserved to get what he wanted in life.

But it seemed for a while that the magic was meant to be for me, if anyone, because Miss Nadia politely refused the offer of cake and conversation, and said she really had to get into the darkroom, and that I might as well have the rest of the day off. Mrs. Rankin said that Mercy was free until five o'clock, and Miss Nadia said she didn't need help getting the one camera back to the buggy, and that we girls should have a lovely afternoon. And at first it seemed that we would, because Willis was waylaid by the reverend to chop wood. But then it seemed we couldn't, because just as the two of us were about to disappear into the trees, Mrs. Rankin told us to take Emmet to the beach.

"But we don't want to go to the beach," Mercy said. "We want to look for raspberries. Violet knows where there might be some." Mercy wasn't good at lying, I noted. Raspberries wouldn't be ripe for weeks.

"You can do that later," Mrs. Rankin said. "Emmet needs to practice. Father won't let him go out in any boat until he can stay afloat for ten minutes."

But it was all right. Mercy and Emmet and I went down to the shore of Blue Lake, and Emmet went splashing into the water while Mercy and I sprawled ourselves on the warm sand, far away from any bushes or beach grass where anyone might hide and listen.

"Can you believe it?" she said. "Didn't you want to just grab the copper hand and run for your life? It was so nearby, I wanted to scream. Too bad we can't disguise ourselves as highway bandits and hold up Miss Nadia on the road back to town."

I laughed. It was terrible—wide-eyed Miss Nadia with her hands up, Mercy and me in big disguising hats and goggles. I hadn't laughed in years, it felt like.

"At least Willis doesn't have it anymore," I said.

"We took it to the Voyageur Hotel yesterday to show Mr. Dell," she said. "Because it used to be his land where it was buried, before he sold it to us. My father thought maybe his crew found other things when they put the road in. Of course Willis is desperate to know how old it is and all that. I insisted on going along so I could keep an eye on it. We had to lend it to that awful Mrs. Dell, plus the bones. She said it should benefit the public—whatever *that* means. She couldn't stop drooling over Willis. I almost asked her if she wanted to adopt him. He'd have every advantage."

"It's in a display," I said. "In a glass case in the lobby. Mrs. Dell has the key."

"That's perfect, then. All you have to do is borrow the key and put it back once you've got the Hand. We could go to the hotel in the dead of night and give the desk clerk a sleeping potion. Nobody would ever suspect us."

"Willis would," I said. And Mrs. Agosa, I thought.

"Well, let them search all they want," Mercy said. "You'll hide it somewhere, and after a while everybody will forget about it."

I'd been sifting through the sand, making a pile of tiny white shells. I smoothed the sand and began pressing the shells into a circle. I didn't want Mercy to want the Hand too much, only enough to help me figure out how to get it.

"What if we had a replica?" I said. "Replace the real one with the fake one. We'd have to get some copper and cut it and make it look old and everything."

"Easy," she said. "Making a hand like that would be nothing. Sheet copper. You mend pans with it. Gypsies! Do you have gypsies around here?"

"I think so," I said. "On the other side of the harbor."

"How do you get there? Is there a boat? I've got thirty-five cents left over from my birthday money. We should get as much as we've got money for, in case I make a mistake."

"I have my pay from last week," I said. "I'll get more on Saturday."

"We can't wait that long. What if they send it to a museum or to some collector? We have to move like wildfire. And I'll need photographs of the real Hand, so I can copy it exactly. We could use the ones Miss Nadia just took!"

"Except they're going to the newspaper," I said. "And I don't know if the Hand shows that much. Willis was holding it."

"Right. And smearing it with his hairy paws," she said. "Well, we could take our own photographs. Miss Stebbins has a Brownie camera. I could sneak it."

I remembered my father saying that preachers' boys were always bad. It seemed to be true for preachers' girls as well. She was a born criminal.

Then I remembered. "Miss Nadia took pictures of the Hand yesterday," I said. "They're not developed yet, but they might work. I'll have to see how they come out."

I hadn't lied to Miss Nadia so far. Not really. Just little lies. I'd tried not to. But maybe I wouldn't have to lie. I'd just be borrowing, not stealing. She'd never know.

"Let's go tomorrow," Mercy said. "I'll offer to do my mother's errands in town. She'll think I'm being helpful. I'll ask the gypsies what tools to use. We'll pretend we're making doll dishes or some charming little thing. Once we've got the copper and the tools, you'll borrow the photograph of the Hand from Miss Nadia. I'll just need it for a couple of hours. And we'll hide everything up in the tree, of course."

Emmet came out of the water and started racing up the beach. "Meet at five in the morning on the road behind my house," I whispered in a rush. "If you can get away."

"She'll let me," she said. "She'll be ecstatic."

Emmet threw himself on the sand. Without Willis around he seemed a nice enough boy, freckle-faced, nose peeling from sunburn, eager as a dog to chase something.

At home, I cleaned and scrubbed and weeded so that the Hand would know I wasn't an idler who expected magic to do everything. I told my father I had to be to work extra early. He barely heard me. For once, I didn't worry about him, as I had my own thoughts. There were many ways that it could all go wrong, but if I prevailed, the Hand would put everything to rights and I wouldn't lose hold of it again. It would be mine for always.

At ten to five in the morning, I ran up the hill behind my house. The sun was a scarlet sliver on the far side of Blue Lake. Swallows swooped and dipped into the hovering mist. Mercy appeared, cresting the rise in the road.

"So what will you do with the Hand when you get it back?" she said. "Hide it, of course. But what about the magic? How do we find out what kind of magic it's got and make it work exactly perfectly?"

Maybe I shouldn't have talked about it with anyone. But she wanted to help, and she was full of ideas. I didn't have to tell her about Mrs. Agosa's dire pronouncements.

"Magic's like anything," I said. "It has to get to know you. Like a wild animal that won't let you see it unless you sit still for a long time."

"That's what I think too. And it'll appreciate being rescued. We need Houdini, The Handcuff King. He can open any lock. They say he bribes people, though. Maybe we could bribe someone. Mr. Dell, perhaps. 'Mr. Dell, we can offer you *thirty-five cents* to open up your fancy glass case and never tell a soul!' How's that for a good idea?"

We laughed and plotted. Before any time at all had gone by, we were at the harbor. Fishermen were winding their ropes and spitting in the water. I recognized Lucy Thornwood's husband, with his fishy whiskers and furrowed brow. I asked him if he was going across, and he said he had a man to see on the other side, so he could take us. He helped us into his boat and didn't ask a single question about anything, and the wind smelled of far-off places.

The gypsy man gave us three big sheets of copper for the money we had, and showed Mercy how to cut the metal with a clipper.

"You can get one at the hardware store," the man said. He wrapped the copper in brown paper and gave it to Mercy.

We didn't have to wait long for Mr. Thornwood to return from his errand, and the return crossing was as swift and smooth as the other. We said our brief good-byes and

Mercy went off to do her mother's errands with the brown paper parcel held tightly beneath an arm.

I passed the glass case in the lobby and gave the Hand a nod. I didn't want it to forget me or think I'd forgotten it. Breakfast was a platter of cinnamon rolls. I was itchy to look for the picture of Mrs. Dell with the Hand. It was taken on a pretense, so that Mrs. Agosa could have a moment with the Hand. Miss Nadia wouldn't care if it was missing, if she ever even noticed.

Sadly, though, it was a day with the kind of light Miss Nadia liked, and we had to go outside and take endless dreary photographs featuring the handsomeness and vastness of the hotel. After that, I was given the Willis photographs to take to the newspaper office. I couldn't see them, as Miss Nadia had printed them and wrapped them up without my assistance. The parcel was firmly taped, and I didn't care to try to open it. For the rest of the day, Miss Nadia and I went around the hotel taking photographs of carved doors and wafting curtains, and there was no opportunity to look for the pictures of the Hand.

But the next day there was. Shortly after my arrival, Miss Nadia went into the next room to make a call. Keeping an ear out for her return, I shuffled through a stack of photographs on the table. Tennis court, bowling alley, stables. Sunset over the big lake. Clouds.

There was a smart knock on the door. I dropped the stack. Pictures scattered. "Breakfast," said a voice from the hall.

"I'll be right there," I called. The slippery pictures slid around. I had to get them gathered. Miss Nadia hadn't told me to do anything with them. One time when I straightened out a haphazard pile, she told me not to. Most likely she'd notice that they weren't how she'd left them.

The door to the room came open. Isaac Duvall came in with the breakfast tray. He held the door with his foot as he withdrew a key from the lock.

He had a passkey! Of course he did! How else would a bellboy get to the bags and boxes he was expected to load up and move around? My mother had used a passkey when she was a maid at the hotel, I suddenly remembered, and had thought it quite a smart invention.

Everything imaginable all at once seemed likely then. I could figure out a way to get Isaac Duvall's key, just for the brief moment it would take to get to wherever Mrs. Dell's key to the padlock happened to be, and he'd never know what I'd done, and nobody would, and the Hand would be mine again forever. I gave Isaac Duvall my sweetest smile as he departed.

I had the photographs put back just as Miss Nadia came out of her room with another stack of prints, and she showed me how she wanted them organized in shallow boxes. She leafed through the stack I'd dropped, frowning at a picture that was upside down as she righted it. Then she left for an appointment and said she'd be back in half an hour.

In twenty minutes I'd looked at every photograph in the entire two rooms. Some were stored, some were on tables, some were drying in the darkroom. There were none of the Hand. There was nothing for it but to inquire, but Miss Nadia returned from her appointment in no frame of mind for chatting, so I waited until she was cheerier. "Did you ever show Mrs. Dell those pictures of her with the display?" I asked.

"There was only one, thank goodness," Miss Nadia said. "I had to destroy. She would cry if she saw it. Not flattering in the least. Bad light for her, and an unfortunate reflection from that glass case."

"What about the ones of Mrs. Agosa you took that same day?" I said.

"Not developed yet," she said. "They're not for Mr. Dell, so they must wait."

And maybe it was because I had planted the idea in her mind, but the very next day they were hanging up to dry, three photographs of Mrs. Agosa's hands holding the copper one. And later that afternoon I had the opportunity. I took them all, because if Miss Nadia found just one of them she would be apt to wonder where the rest of them had gotten to. She was only in the washroom and I had to move fast. I slid the photographs into the back of my dress and hoped they wouldn't rustle. They barely did.

That night I found the ladder to the tree house and put the photographs in the hidden tin. I had to roll them up so they would fit. And the next day Miss Nadia sent me into the darkroom, because everything was in disarray and we hadn't had a chance to tidy up, and among the plates that were lying around waiting to be put away were the ones of Mrs. Agosa and the Hand that the pictures I'd taken were made from, and I got so rattled that I knocked over a bottle of developer. There wasn't much left in it, but what there was splashed over the floor and onto my white stockings, staining them the same brown that Miss Nadia had on her fingers. I took the stockings off and used them to clean my shoes and mop up the floor, and when I was done I had brown fingers myself. The stain didn't come off with soap. And it gave me an idea, and I thought I'd be right about it, and later I found out that I was.

I hoped Mercy would be done with her handiwork by the next day, but she wasn't, and the day after that was Sunday, and in the morning Mercy had to sing hymns and so on, and Miss Nadia had me come in for the afternoon because we still had so much to do to get ready for Mr. Dell to see new photographs on Monday. I couldn't get to the tree house until after my father was asleep, and he was up forever. Finally I got there.

She'd left me the photographs of Mrs. Agosa and the Hand, rolled up to fit in the tin, and a flat parcel. My lantern was barely sufficient, but I slowly unwrapped the paper to look. It wasn't quite exactly it. First, it was shiny new copper. The real one looked old, because it was. But also the thumb stuck too far out. One finger was too broad. Fear clamped me. I'd made up a baby fairy game and spent my money on a foolhardy folly. If I went on with it, I'd be caught, imprisoned, would never see Fry again. The best thing to do would be to throw this other hand in the lake, weighted with stones.

But I did no such thing. I wrapped it back up, took it home, and looked it over again. Even imperfect, it was close, and once it wasn't shiny and new it might be even closer, and who would think that anyone would substitute a replica for the real one, and who had studied the shape of the real Hand as carefully as I had?

I tried to sleep. A hundred times that night I took the false hand out, looked it over, tried to recall just exactly how the real Hand appeared and felt, traced the shape of how I thought the thumb should be, doubted my memory of it. I practiced sliding the false hand into the pouch with the blue stitching. I practiced leaning down as if to scratch my knee, as if to pull my stockings up, as if to straighten my skirt. I watched myself in the mirror in the shadowy lamplight, and did it until it was fast and smooth each time.

The Hand wants me to get it back, I told myself. It will make it come about. I won't let it get away again. But first I couldn't forget to make the false hand look old before I made the switch. I couldn't forget. I wouldn't.

I blew out the lamp. The rain lulled me into the little sleep that was left to me in the disappearing night.

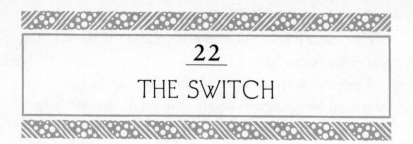

All foreboding dissolved with the light of day. Even though I knew the copper hand I had wasn't the real one, having it with me made it seem that things were right with the world.

I slid on my shift with the fake in its pocket, and then the dress from Mr. Fairchild's store. I'd thought the whole thing through. The switch itself would be easy, once I got my hands on Mrs. Dell's keys. She was forever being careless with her things, leaving her handbag on the floor by the glass case or on the chair in Miss Nadia's room.

All along the road I soared with certainty, plummeted into despair, clambered out, was swept along by the competing winds of hope and hopelessness. I had to get the key, then get the Hand, and first I had to get rid of the coppery sheen of the fake one. I'd seen how Miss Nadia's developer stained fingers brown and figured it might work on copper too, and I'd tried it on a penny and made the penny turn dull and brown. But what if it didn't work? What if Miss Nadia caught me?

But by the time the spires of town were in sight, I was confident. Magic would prevail. And it seemed to. Little miracles kept sprouting up, and each time one did, it seemed more likely that my mission was sanctioned. Not a soul was in the lobby but for the desk clerk, who didn't even look up as I passed. The sun came through the big windows and striped the case. The back of the case was made up of two sliding panels, which were prevented from opening by a small hasp secured by the tiny padlock. I cradled the padlock in my hand and felt its cool weight. The place where the key went in was like a crooked grinning baby mouth gapped with missing teeth.

The ding of the elevator made me look up. The doors creaked open and out came Mrs. Dell. I snatched my hand off the lock. Had her heron eyes seen?

"Oh, Violet," she said. "Good. Don't go running off. Miss Zalzman can wait for two minutes." She glided up to the case. "I need a pair of eyes. Hold this for me. Don't wrinkle it." She handed me a square cut from a newspaper. It was the picture Miss Nadia had taken of hideous Willis. He held the copper hand like a dead pelt.

She took the picture from me and taped it to the glass. And there he was, the usurper and pretender. The copper hand would be sullied and insulted to be within his realm. It was my duty to remove it. Mrs. Dell peered at the ring of keys in her hand and picked out the small one that opened up the case. It would be harder to hide a whole wad of keys instead of just the one, but I could do it. The case slid open. She arranged beach stones around the skeleton.

"We need some texture," she said. "I think the rocks help, don't you?" She stepped back from the case, looking from this angle and that, and all the time the case was wide open, with the copper hand mere inches away with no glass or lock between us. It seemed that the Hand had brought her there so I could be closer to it. The Hand surely knew that what I was going to do was for its good, and not just for my own designs. Then she was finished, and she waved me away just as the elevator opened up its doors to let me in.

Miss Nadia's room was a spiderweb. String looped from every knob and drawer pull, with pictures clipped on every inch of drooping line. She looked wild, as if she'd been sleeping in the woods, but she hadn't slept at all. Strands of hair had come loose. New brown stains blotched her fingers and the neckline of her wrinkled rumpled dress. Her eyes were darker than ever, with shadows underneath, but they glistened. I took pictures down when they were all the way dry and put them in piles, which Miss Nadia shuffled through and left in disarray for me to neaten up again.

Mr. Dell was late, but that gave Miss Nadia a chance to take down her hair and brush it out and put it up again. And while she was doing that, I was charged with cleaning up the darkroom. And what was in the darkroom but a made-up tray of developer, which was the very substance that turned new copper ancient-looking brown. I extracted the false copper hand from its pocket, dipped it in, swirled it with the tongs, fished it out, dried it with a rag.

The new hand looked old as the hills. I felt like singing.

When I came out, Miss Nadia had changed into a dove-colored dress I hadn't seen before, and was more elegant and refined than someone who'd been working all night long had a right to be. The Dells had arrived. Mrs. Dell's outfit made her resemble a banana. Her handbag bulgingly slumped on a chair, tantalizingly half open.

Mr. Dell said nothing as he looked at the pictures. This time he was careful with them, and didn't fling them about or flick a finger at a bothersome one. When he had looked at all that Miss Nadia had left out for him to see, he took one of the pictures and handed it to his wife.

"That's it. Just what I was looking for." He rapped the table with his broad fingertips. "I knew you'd pull it off, Nadia," he said. "All this it-can't-be-done business. I didn't buy it. If this picture doesn't bring people streaming into this place, nothing will."

"I still don't understand the technique, Nadia," Mrs. Dell said.

"Just a parlor trick," Miss Nadia said. "You take the people separately from the background, like paper dolls. Then you can manipulate in the darkroom."

"Marvelous," Mrs. Dell said.

"This isn't a final print," Miss Nadia said. "There are some imperfections. I'll need some time to fuss around in the darkroom more. But I can do that back in Chicago."

"Not so fast," said Mr. Dell. "You're not in a hurry to leave us, are you? I think we should put together an exhibition. Don't you, Alice? The woods. The farms. Let's see what else you've taken. Don't waste my time pretending you don't know what I mean. The harbor and so forth. All the local color you're so interested in. Bring it all out."

He must have had spies everywhere, reporting on Miss Nadia's localities. Her objections made him impatient. "Do I have to search this whole twenty-dollar suite myself? I want to see what you've been up to when you were supposed to be working for me. And no editorializing. You either, Alice. Come on! I've got too much to do today. Chop chop!"

And so she had to. Miss Nadia brought him the pictures of Isaac Duvall, of the fishermen and their wet nets, a gypsy child with her three skirts, Ingie Peterssen barely sweeping, a lean sallow shirtless boy on the beach.

"Ha!" he blasted. "Now this is something like it! This man—he's the spit of my great-uncle the blacksmith. People who work with their sweat!" He glared at Miss Nadia. "Why didn't you tell me that this is what you're good at? These have something to them. Keep on with it. Alice, you know what I like. You two stick together and we'll have something in no time. Something brilliant!"

And having instructed his wife to take Miss Nadia out to the golf course and have her take a look at his caddie, who had the map of Ireland on his face—because Miss Nadia would be staying an extra couple of weeks, wouldn't she, on his dime, same pay as before and all the extras?—he winked at me and strode out, swiftly, graceful as a panther gliding through a grove.

"Well now, Nadia!" Mrs. Dell exclaimed. "What did I tell you was going to happen? I knew you were just the right one for this job. I can't *wait* to see your work at the Art Institute. A one-woman show!"

"I have you to thank," Miss Nadia murmured, but she wasn't as happy as she might have been about the pronouncement. She didn't like being saddled with Mrs. Dell, and now she'd have to be. As for me, my mind was on Mrs. Dell's handbag. I willed her to leave it behind, and after some rummaging around and the extraction of a handkerchief, which she tucked into her yellow sleeve, she did.

I spent the next hour or so contriving how I could get away, but Miss Nadia made a drawn-out to-do of everything from packing up the cameras to getting ourselves in the elevator to getting to the golf course to posing the caddie, all in the hope that Mrs. Dell would become bored, or would remember an appointment that she had to run off to. But she didn't, because the copper hand was stronger than mere mortals' will, and all of us were paper dolls to be moved about and placed in rooms and on grassy hills at the copper hand's pleasure.

At last Miss Nadia had the caddie right where she wanted him, beneath a tree so that the leaf shadows patterned his craggy cheeks. Mrs. Dell all at once looked stricken.

"My mind's left me!" she exclaimed. "Did I or did I not tell Guy about dinner tonight? I think I mentioned it to him this morning, but perhaps I didn't. Violet, you can take a message, can't you? You have some paper, don't you, Nadia? Rip out a page from your notebook."

"And while you're at it," Miss Nadia said, "get another set of plates." She tossed me the key to her room.

I subdued myself from running all the way back to the

hotel. I let myself in, took a deep breath to slow the drum of my heart, and went straight for Mrs. Dell's bag. I remembered the case of plates for Miss Nadia and went back out into the hall, Mrs. Dell's keys in the secret pocket with the false hand. I took the stairs down. I kept myself calm by thinking of how the copper hand was bringing everything about. The copper hand wouldn't let me get caught. I would use Mrs. Dell's key to the case, make the switch, run upstairs and put the keys straight back in her handbag. Nobody would ever know.

The lobby was almost empty. Almost everyone was out in the sunny day, but for two ladies walking slowly across the lobby, deep in conversation. I sidled up to the glass case and got the keys out of the secret pocket. I felt for the tiny one that belonged to the padlock and maneuvered it in. The padlock opened.

Keeping my eyes on the two ladies, I tried prying the padlock out of the hasp, but it was a tight fit and I had to pull at it. Just when I was sure it would never come free, it suddenly jarred out of the metal brace and clattered to the floor, and the keys too. The sound seemed enormous.

The desk clerk looked around, then sneezed three times. I felt for the keys with my foot and covered them from view. The face of hideous Willis scowled at me from the newspaper clipping taped to the glass. The front door opened and a man came in, flanked by two boys. The three of them went to the desk. The clerk nodded and jutted his chin at the man. I slid the case open just enough to reach in. My hand covered the copper one. I brought it out.

I had it. Oh, I had it.

One of the boys at the desk looked right at me. I had the real copper hand in one hand and the false one in the other. I put the real one in the secret pocket just as the two boys came running across the lobby straight for the case. I got the fake one in the case and closed it back up before they got to me. But I couldn't lock it, because the lock and its key were beneath my foot, and then the boys were leaning on the glass, banging on it, exclaiming over the skeleton.

The elevator dinged. The Hand was safe in its pocket, but I couldn't take my foot off the evidence of my cleverness. The boys' faces were right on the glass, steaming it up. I couldn't pick up the keys with them right there. Or could I? They didn't know the keys weren't mine. But the elevator! I heard the doors open behind me. I turned to look. Out came Mr. Dell.

There was nothing to be done about the keys. I kicked them just underneath the case. I'd have to retrieve them later. Mr. Dell frowned at me as I came toward him. I fumbled in my pocket for the paper Mrs. Dell had given me. The copper hand, the real one, knocked against my ribs with every step.

"A message from your wife, sir," I said. He took it, didn't read it, and strode across the lobby to the front door. One of the bellboys opened the door and Mr. Dell went through it out into the bright blue day.

The copper hand and I, we did the same.

I had it. It was mine again and for always, and nobody would ever have to know. I would get my brother back, and Mama too. My father would have more money, not as much as a capitalist, but enough for comforts. I had done it, I had it, it was mine. I felt its little weight in its pocket against my back. I would hold it in my hands the way Mrs. Agosa had done. I would listen to it. It would know I had its best interests at heart.

"Violet!" Miss Nadia said. "Please ask at the desk for messages."

She was finished with the outdoors for the morning. The sun was too high for good light. Isaac Duvall had somehow appeared and was carrying Miss Nadia's camera case. He pressed the elevator button.

There were two messages for Miss Nadia, each in a cunning little envelope. It was magical how handy it was to have them. I took the little envelopes over to the glass case and let them slip from my hand, pretending a mistake. I crouched down to see beneath the case. No keys were under there.

I stood up fast. I'd have seen them if they'd been there. I leaned on the case. The face of Willis stared from the newspaper clipping taped onto the glass.

I was marked. I'd returned to the scene of the crime, as the empty-headed do. Soon I'd be in handcuffs, and Uncle Fowler would get to use his jail for once. Aunt Phyllis was always crowing about it, how the people of the county were so lucky and grateful to finally have it and how nobody had been able to figure out where to get the money to build it until her husband came along. But my uncle had never arrested anyone, and the jail up to now had never been used, and now I'd be the one to initiate it.

I crossed the lobby to the stairs. From the balcony I could see the glass case as a crow would see it, flying over. The skeleton's skull eyes seemed to be aimed my way. I ran the rest of the way up.

Miss Nadia and Isaac Duvall were moving furniture around. Mrs. Dell's handbag rested on the same chair where I'd rifled it and taken out the keys that now were missing. But maybe someone had found them underneath the case and returned them to her, and she'd already forgotten about the little inconvenience and mystery, and was thinking about what to wear or what to spend her money on.

The telephone rang. "Hello, Violet," said Mrs. Dell.

"I think Miss Nadia—" I faltered.

"It's you I want to talk to," she said.

"Oh," I gulped. I felt like a frog lurking in the silent

swamp, soon to be speared by the heron huntress. But I was the expert liar. Lying hardly ever failed me. I formulated my story in a flash. I'd found the lost keys, then had lost them myself. I should have confessed at the time it happened. Please, Mrs. Dell, forgive the addled orphan girl. I bit my tongue to work up tears.

"It's all settled," she said. "I spoke with your aunt."

My aunt! Already I was doomed. There was a tap on the door. Was it my uncle, coming to put me in chains? Miss Nadia went to answer.

"I'm having a little beach soiree," Mrs. Dell went on. "Your aunt has given you permission to attend. There's a girl visiting from Chicago who you can keep an eye on. Seven o'clock. We'll all meet up in the lobby. And tell Nadia she doesn't have to join us if she has too much to do—I'll absolutely understand. I'm so glad you can be there. And come hungry. The kitchen's outdoing itself beyond the wildest expectation."

She rang off. My father was right. Rich people got whatever they wanted, because everyone belonged to them some way or another.

The furniture was where Miss Nadia wanted it. "One more thing, Mr. Duvall," she said. "I have your portrait. If it's not so easy for you to keep it now, I can send it in the mail. Maybe to your mother, or the most convenient."

It was a good picture, like all of hers were. He regarded it. "You're a magician, Miss Zalzman," he said. "If you wouldn't mind, my mother will want to have it. It's better if Mr. Nickels doesn't know."

"I understand. It's a shame about your Mr. Nickels, what he doesn't see." She circled above the picture with a finger. "A serious young man who is kind. There is pride, but not arrogance. That's what I see. Before I forget. Would it be too much out of your way to take something to Mrs. Dell's room?"

"Not at all," he said.

"That bag." She pointed. "On that chair. Probably she's wondering what she did with it. Thank you, Mr. Duvall." He picked up the bag and hooked it by its handle on the cart.

"I don't like this Mr. Nickels's way of thinking," Miss Nadia went on. "People are not parts to a machine, a pair of arms, nothing under the ribs. Not just anyone can be a doctor. Everybody has their gifts to be celebrated, not to be ashamed of."

She held out money for him, but he waved it away. "That's all right," he said. "You're too generous."

"Take it," she said. "For books. You can't ever have too many, yes?" It went into his pocket. He thanked her and the door closed behind him.

Miss Nadia and I spent the afternoon taking pictures at the harbor of men rolling barrels up gangplanks and lowering crates on pulleys and shouting good-naturedly at each other and squinting from the sun. There was plenty to think about other than Mrs. Dell and her keys, and I tried to be distracted, but I couldn't be and wasn't. When the fishing boats began to come in, Miss Nadia realized the time was almost six o'clock, and she remembered that I was meeting up with Mrs. Dell and the others at seven.

"But the fishermen," I said.

"Another day. I'll forego them and the lighthouse for a bath and a book. For me, a lighthouse isn't so exciting. But you'll have a good time."

I doubted that I would. And when we went into the hotel lobby, I suspected I wouldn't ever have a good time for the rest of my born days. My uncle the sheriff was with Mrs. Dell at the glass case, talking together in low voices.

"What's Alice doing with such a handsome man that she isn't married to?" Miss Nadia said.

"That's my uncle," I said. Everyone always said what a picture he and Aunt Phyllis made. I supposed he was handsome, with his dark thick waxed moustache and his long fox nose and narrow fox eyes. His hair was even rusty like a fox pelt. If I have to be arrested, I begged the Hand, don't let it happen in front of Miss Nadia.

He always had a smile for everybody. "You must be Miss Zalzman," he said, his eyes glinting. "I'm Fowler Wilmot. I hope this little scamp hasn't been giving you any trouble."

"On the contrary," Miss Nadia said. "She's a lifesaver."

"You won't believe what's happened," Mrs. Dell breathed. "Someone almost made off with the artifacts. In broad daylight!"

"Right here?" Miss Nadia said. "How?"

"Reckless is the word," Mrs. Dell said. "It's a wonder we're not all murdered in our beds. Someone was terribly desperate to—"

"If I may," Uncle Fowler said. "We don't want to draw attention to the situation, make folks nervous. Not that there's anything to be nervous about. The would-be thief's an amateur. Careless. We'll catch him in a flash."

"This is the last thing the hotel needs," Mrs. Dell said. "I'm sick about it."

"Put it out of your head," Uncle Fowler told her. "The new lock's in place." He pulled on the hasp. "New key. If anybody made a copy of the old one, it won't do them any good. Mrs. Dell, if we could speak somewhere quiet? I'll need some details. Excuse us, Miss Zalzman. A pleasure. You'll keep our girl in line, I hope."

"Keep your doors locked," Mrs. Dell whispered. "I mean it, Nadia." She whisked away at Uncle Fowler's side.

The false copper hand was dull and clumsy beneath the glass. You could tell it wasn't magical and never would be.

Upstairs, there was a message tucked beneath Miss Nadia's door. It was for me. The note inside the little envelope said Aunt Phyllis had called. *Important,* the note said. My heart sank. Did she know what I had done? But before I had a chance to pick up the telephone and find out my fate, there was a knock at the door. Miss Nadia put a finger to her lips and slipped into the next room.

I opened the door. There stood Aunt Phyllis, carrying something draped over her arm and out of breath. "You were supposed to call," she began. "Didn't you get my message?"

"Just this second," I said. "We just got in."

She glared at me, not liking my tone. "Is Miss Zalzman here?" she said, swishing her way inside. A hat all loops and ribbons perched on her curls.

"In the darkroom," I whispered. "She can't be disturbed."

"All afternoon I had to run around trying to find you something to wear tonight." She was shaking out a pink dress with an absurd ruffle. "I have no idea if it will fit you, and now there's no time to do anything about it. Put it on. Quickly, now. We're meeting the Dells in half an hour." She picked at a thread hanging from a buttonhole.

"I can just wear what I have on," I said. Aunt Phyllis would surely find the Hand in its pouch with all her tugging and gussying.

"Don't be a dunce. Just take your dress off! Hold still!"

I backed away. She would have slapped me if Miss Nadia hadn't been in earshot. She pinched me instead on the neck, hard, and scratched me with her scrabbly blue jay claws. I heard the door to the darkroom open. Miss Nadia emerged.

"Miss Zalzman!" Aunt Phyllis's voice was all sugar. "How have you been? Alice Dell doesn't stop talking about how well the pictures are coming out."

"It's beautiful, this place, Mrs. Wilmot. The pictures can't help it to be nice."

Nobody ever thought my aunt was mean, because of her dimples and curls, and the way she could look perfectly delicious when she wasn't being anything like it, but nothing got past Miss Nadia.

"You've brought Miss Blake a change of costume," she said. "Please feel free to go into the next room, Violet, and put it on."

"I saw you downstairs as I came in," Aunt Phyllis said as I slipped into the washroom with the vile pink dress and closed the door. "You were waiting for the elevator. I waved, but you didn't see me. Then who should I run into but my own husband! He had some business with the clerk at the front desk. That husband of mine does nothing but work his fingers to the bone for the people of this town. Wherever there's a need, that's where he is. He's exactly what they had in mind when they thought up the term public servant."

I looked around for a hiding place for the Hand. A mirror hung on the wall from a wire. Nobody would ever look behind it, would they? I had to climb onto the sink in order to lift the mirror off its nail. It was heavier than I expected, and I almost fell off my perch. I climbed down quietly and propped the mirror against the wall. Then I took the Hand from its pouch.

Please, I begged it. *If there's anyone you don't want to know about you, it's Aunt Phyllis. Just stay quiet. Don't do anything.*

Attaching the Hand to the back of the mirror would be tricky. If I bent the thumb a little, I could hook the Hand into a crack in the wood. There was no other way to secure it, but the Hand wouldn't like being bent, I knew.

"Violet? Are you almost ready?" Miss Nadia was tiring of Aunt Phyllis.

"Yes, Miss Nadia," I said. My skin pricked. The Hand wouldn't stay put. Then I remembered my sash. I untied it, wrapped it around the Hand, wound the sash onto the mirror's wire. I put the mirror back up and slipped into the ruffled dress and buttoned up and went out.

"This girl is like a little snail." Aunt Phyllis sniffed. "Everything she does takes forever."

"In my line of work, it is good to be deliberate," Miss Nadia said. "Violet is careful. She doesn't make mistakes."

I'm not a careless thief, I thought.

"Good night, Miss Zalzman. We'll leave you to your solitude," my aunt said, whisking me out the door.

"You've made us late," she hissed, yanking me down the hallway and past the elevator. "We'll be waiting all night for that thing." I hoped she'd trip on her skirt and cannonball downstairs.

Outside, at the end of the walk, three buggies waited in a row. Mrs. Dell flitted about the gathered guests and greeted my aunt by kissing her cheek and whispering something in her ear, to which my aunt nodded. I found myself in a buggy with Aunt Phyllis and Mrs. Dell and nobody else but the driver up front.

"Now, Phyllis," Mrs. Dell said, once the buggies had started out along the road in a line. "You too, Violet. I'm going to take you into my confidence. We've barely escaped falling victim to a felon."

"I had a feeling," Aunt Phyllis said. "I ran into Fowler just a little bit ago at the hotel. All he would say was that he had some business to conduct, but I wondered if it wasn't something sinister. Has anyone been hurt?"

"Only my nerves have been affected," Mrs. Dell said, a hand at her throat. "Nobody's been injured. But there's been a theft. A serious one."

"My! We've never had that kind of thing here, Alice. At

the logging camps you find all manner of hooliganism, but in our little town—"

"I know. And that's exactly why I told Guy from the start not to bring in a hundred colored boys to wait tables and carry luggage. This area's crawling with farm boys, boys from good families who would work hard and be grateful for the opportunity. He claimed it would be hard to train them. The colored are used to service work, and you can get them for a price. Guy had his reasons, but I'll have to bite my little tongue in order not to say I told you so. But fortunately, I know who did it."

"Who?" I blurted.

"I don't believe anyone was addressing you," said my aunt, throwing me a glare.

My chest stabbed. What would happen to the one who was accused?

"I know exactly which boy it was," said Mrs. Dell. "Isaac something. He went through my bag and got the key to the display case. He tried to open it, but something must have scared him off."

The buggy went over a rut and we all were jostled.

"What display case?" Aunt Phyllis said, straightening her hat.

"In the lobby. A nice Chicago boy found an Indian skeleton by that charming lake just over the hill a mile or two. Do you know that area?"

"Oh, yes," Aunt Phyllis said. "The house I grew up in is practically on the beach."

"I didn't realize you hadn't seen the display," Mrs. Dell

said. "It's tucked away in a corner of the lobby because I thought it best to put it out of the way of children bashing into it and so forth, but little did I realize I was making it easier for the unscrupulous. The boy must have gotten startled or lost his nerve, and he dropped the keys and left them for all to see. Someone found them, of course, and turned them in to the desk. I suppose he thought nobody would put two and two together. Heaven knows what would have happened if he'd gotten in. He was planning a voodoo ritual with the bones, no doubt."

"No!" my aunt exclaimed, making a show of shuddering. She always pretended to be scandalized or revolted because she thought a lady would be, but she could gut a chicken faster than my father.

"Not only that," Mrs. Dell said. "He took quite a bit of cash. I was careless to have so much in my bag—I'd meant to put it somewhere safer and it slipped my mind."

My chest felt full of stones. Isaac Duvall! He was the last person who would steal.

"What will happen to him?" I said.

"Your uncle's making the arrest," Mrs. Dell said. "We can all sleep tonight, knowing he's been apprehended. A thief is often unbalanced, you know, or on the hop."

"He wouldn't do anything like that," I said. "Ask Miss Nadia. She knows him."

"When your opinion is required," Aunt Phyllis said tartly, "it will be requested." She gave me another you're-in-trouble glare and pressed the heel of her shoe against my leg and scraped it up and down.

"Unfortunately, the whole family is a little crooked," Mrs. Dell said. "This boy's cousin stole a ring from me. The important thing is to keep this under our hats. I'm relying on you both not to breathe a word of this to a single soul. If word gets out that criminals work at the hotel, there's no retracting it. You see?" She patted Aunt Phyllis on the arm.

"Of course," said Aunt Phyllis.

"Violet," said Mrs. Dell. "I want your solemn word that this matter stays between us."

A vow to her meant nothing to me. She was the kind of person my father always railed about, who thought they knew all about someone when they didn't know a thing, and who never admitted they made a mistake. Aunt Phyllis was that kind too. I hated them both, and Aunt Phyllis could switch my legs until her arm fell off for all I cared.

"Violet!" Aunt Phyllis said. "Mrs. Dell is speaking to you."

"I promise," I had to say, and bit my tongue and kept it between my teeth so that I wouldn't say anything further. I promise I'll get the copper hand to make the rest of your days miserable. I promise all your money will disappear. I promise you and Aunt Phyllis will have to be washerwomen and live on moldy crusts.

Rich people go to a lot of trouble for some supper. Horses slogged our buggies along the sandy road to the lighthouse beach, where cooks in white aprons flourished forks as long as lances over a row of camp stoves. Waiters passed platters abounding with trout and buttery cob corn and deep red sliced tomatoes and it would have been delicious if I'd deserved to be fed, if my insides hadn't been a tangle.

In my mind I kept envisioning the canny capture. Uncle Fowler would get the boss Mr. Nickels to bring the unsuspecting suspect into a room. The small journey up the street to the jailhouse would be conducted in the dead of night. Abject secrecy. No frightening the guests, no rumors, no possibility of escape.

The little girl I was charged with watching was afraid of waves and sand, and didn't want to play tag or skip stones or anything that Fry would have jumped in glee to do, so I was obliged to priss around with the dolls she'd brought with her and make silly voices for them and hop them to their stupid parties. They were beautiful dolls, with pale china faces and stiff little hands. The mother had shiny china hair, the children had flaxen locks that could be combed, their clothes were trimmed in fine tiny lace and wee blue satin bows. My mother had made my dolls of muslin and yarn. The stains on their faces wouldn't wash off and their hair couldn't curl.

I kept an eye out for my uncle, who my aunt said would join us if his duties came to an end at a reasonable time. If only I could get him alone, he might listen and believe. He wasn't mean like Aunt Phyllis.

But he didn't come. The waiters brought slabs of cherry pie. Mr. Dell made jokes that everybody laughed at. The sun hovered over the big lake, blasting orange and purple streaks across the sky. Everyone exclaimed at the splendor. From our house you couldn't see the setting sun for the hills. You could only see the sky get ruddy and deepen.

I made myself not look at the magnificence of sky and

lake. Isaac Duvall would never see the light of day again, wouldn't become a doctor, would be a disgrace to his family. What if he had tried to run and gotten shot? His blood would be on my hands. I felt spinny and sick.

My aunt had arranged to keep me for the night. We were crammed in the buggy with the little girl and her mother and father. The girl was afraid of the dark. Her father circled her in his arm. She burrowed in. My aunt's sharp elbow was in my side. All evening she'd given me black looks for my insolence to Mrs. Dell. My aunt would never disbelieve anything Mrs. Dell would ever say. If Mrs. Dell said the sun was a triangle, my aunt would declare her a genius.

Aunt Phyllis and I disembarked from the buggy. The house was dark and quiet.

"Oh, heavens," my aunt said, snatching up a note from Uncle Fowler. "Go on up, Violet. Your uncle's guarding the prisoner. I'll go see if he wants a sandwich."

"I'll help you," I said. I could maybe steal the key and free Isaac Duvall, or at least make sure he got a sandwich too.

"It's after ten," my aunt said. "Bed. Now." She shooed me off.

Upstairs, I opened windows to see what I could hear. There was only the wind and the clopping of a horse way up the street. The jail was behind the house and my room was in front. If I'd had the Hand, I would have held it to the sky and wished, but it was behind the mirror, down the street at the hotel.

If you can hear me, I pleaded with the Hand. *Let him go free. Clear his name.*

The Hand will comply, I thought. If not tonight, first thing tomorrow when I rescue it from behind the mirror. If it's my last wish, then that's the way it is. Mrs. Dell will realize her mistake. Everyone will forget it ever happened. Magic can do that.

That's what I still believed.

24

BRAMBLES AND SHADOWS

All I thought about and dreamed about all night was Isaac Duvall, cold and starving in his barren cell because of what I'd done. Rain had started in the night. The morning was a gray one. The lake was and the sky was and my mood was. I succumbed to my aunt's oatmeal, because if Isaac Duvall had to suffer, I should do the same. Outside, the wind was a wall I had to push against, and I had to leap over the little rivers that the street had become, and my shoes got wet, and I didn't care.

Miss Nadia had a camera pointed out the open window, with a cover draped over the lens to keep the rain off.

"Hand me a plate, will you?" she called out cheerfully. Rain had come through the window and her wet footprints were all about. She ducked under the cloth and took a picture of the white-capped lake hovered over by clouds.

She doesn't know, I thought. If she did, she wouldn't stand by. Even if she bites my head off, I can't stand by either.

"Please, Miss Nadia," I said. "Isaac Duvall's in jail."

"Jail! What do you mean jail?"

"Mrs. Dell said he took her keys and money, and so he got arrested. But she doesn't have any proof. Isaac wouldn't take anything. Can't you do something, Miss Nadia? You're the only one she'll listen to."

"I doubt that very much," she said, but she was already at the telephone with the receiver to her ear. First she called Mrs. Dell, who wasn't in, so Miss Nadia left a message. Then she called Mr. Nickels, the boss of the bellboys.

"According to Mr. Nickels," she said, hanging up, "Mr. Duvall's gone home to Alabama. A personal matter, he said."

"That's not true!" I said. "They don't just let people out! He didn't do anything! You could call my uncle and find out what's going on. Will you, Miss Nadia? Please!"

She frowned. "Yesterday we were at the golf course with Mrs. Dell, yes? Do you remember if she had her keys with her?"

Of course she didn't have them, I thought. They were in the handbag, which I took them out of.

"She had them in the morning," I said. "When I was coming through the lobby, she was putting rocks in the display. Maybe she left the keys there by mistake."

Miss Nadia looked at me for a long time before she said anything. "Let's say Mrs. Dell lost her keys," she said. "It would be embarrassing to admit. If I can just get Mr. Duvall out, that would be something to begin. Now, where is this jail?"

"Right on Front Street, across from the bandstand."

"All right then," she said, taking up her hat. "I'll be back as soon as I can. Better you stay here. It might be awkward for you with your uncle. I might have to make a scene."

Truth to tell, I was certainly relieved. I didn't want to face anyone.

"Think hard where those keys of Mrs. Dell's might have gotten to," she said. "She left them somewhere. They dropped from her bag maybe. Try to remember or find something out."

I've tried not to lie to Miss Nadia, I thought, not really. But I have to start, or I'll be the one sent to the reformatory.

"I saw some boys by the glass case," I said. "Later in the day. One of them was kind of pulling at the door where the lock goes. They saw me looking at them and they ran. They had something that rattled and sort of clanked, like keys. I didn't really see. But it could have been. Maybe they found them there and they were trying to open the case, but then I came along. Boys are crazy for keys. My little brother was. Is."

"Why didn't you say so before? This isn't a game, you know, Violet." By the way she thrust her hatpin, I could tell Miss Nadia was mad.

"Just now it came to me. And I'm not completely sure. It could have been keys, or maybe it wasn't. I wasn't thinking about keys at the time, so I didn't try to really find out."

It all seemed perfectly real, as a good lie will. I could see the boys, spitting images of Willis and Emmet, and how they ran through the throngs of people and out the front door along the boardwalk and across the sand. It was just like remembering.

"These boys," Miss Nadia said. "You remember what they looked like?"

"Brown hair," I said. "One of them had a white sailor suit."

Every boy on the beach wore a white sailor suit.

"It could be something," she said. "I will see what can be done about Mr. Duvall. You will look around for the boys who maybe had those keys. Tell the mother I must arrange a sitting—or mothers. Say I have admired their charming handsome sons. And get the names, room numbers, where they're from, and write it all down. All right? You are a spy now, or a scout. If Mrs. Dell calls, don't say anything about it. Just tell her I went to run an errand."

She went into the room where she slept and came out wearing a nifty slicker that was half a cape. There was a knock at the door. She nodded for me to get it.

"Nadia!" Mrs. Dell sailed into the room. "Guy has a mission for us. There's a place up the coast where the Indians do dances. Guy wants—"

"Excuse me, Alice," Miss Nadia said. "I understand that Isaac Duvall's in jail."

Mrs. Dell frowned. "If you mean that thief of a—"

"Thief! What did he steal?"

"My dear! He tried to take the antiquities. He stole my keys—took them right out of my handbag, bold as brass. And a good amount of cash."

"Did someone see this?"

"Nobody had to. Don't you remember? You gave him my handbag to bring me. Clearly he took the keys out, went downstairs, and opened up the case. The boy's not terribly clever."

"But how do you know the keys were in the bag when you left it upstairs?"

"Well, of course they were. Where else would they be? I'm no detective, Nadia, but the matter is absolutely straightforward."

Miss Nadia gathered herself. "But, Alice. I've known you to forget where you put things sometimes. Your keys. A hat. Your sketchbook. Isn't it possible that you—"

Mrs. Dell waved at Miss Nadia as if she were a spiderweb. "I can't imagine why you're concerning yourself with this. We have to go immediately. They start their dancing at noon."

"I'm afraid no," said Miss Nadia. "This young man has been jailed with no evidence. You and I must go and get him out."

"Nadia! That's ludicrous."

But Miss Nadia was buttoning up her slicker. "By myself then," she said.

"I'm shocked," Mrs. Dell gasped. "This inordinate concern is really—"

Miss Nadia swept out the door. Mrs. Dell shook her head. Seeing me standing against the wall where I'd tried to make myself inconspicuous, she gave off a weak laugh.

"This weather makes people moody, doesn't it? It's the barometric pressure. Call me, please, when Miss Zalzman has returned." She let herself out. The door closed behind her.

Nothing was right. Mrs. Agosa had said that anything could happen, and the magic was making everything haywire.

Well, I couldn't let it. Magic was to be managed. I would have to be firm with it, and tell it just what I expected, or it would run me.

Magic was full of brambles and shadows. It could help you keep to the path or it could make you lost. It could let you find berries or it could let you starve. It could eat you or seize your mind or break your bones or shelter you. The worst thing was to be afraid of it. Once you let fear take hold, fear would be the conqueror. If you're lost, my mother used to tell me, talk to the trees. Tell the woods to pity you. Give something. Listen. Help may come your way then.

I went into the washroom, closed the door, and lifted the mirror away from the wall. My breath steamed the glass. The Hand was still safely tied to the back of the mirror with my sash. I untied it and reached into its pouch. I put the Hand between my palms. Nothing surged to chill or warm me. It was just metal on skin.

I could have just gone ahead and wished anyway. But what if Miss Nadia got everything fixed and I wouldn't have to waste a wish on something that could happen without magical interference? If anyone could persuade anyone, it was Miss Nadia.

A whole day was unfurling, and it was still early. Besides, I'd more or less wished from the lumpy couch in my aunt's sewing room. Maybe the magic was already at work. It might be offended if I doubted it.

"I'll take you back to my house later," I said. "You like it there, by the woods and Blue Lake, don't you?"

The rat root place. The magic was strongest there. I remembered moss on my bare feet, the fragrant icy stream, the gulping frogs.

I maneuvered the mirror straight again on the wall. Miss Nadia hadn't left me a key, so I couldn't really leave the room without being locked out, and they wouldn't give me a key at the desk without Miss Nadia's say-so. Besides, there were no sailor suit boys to look for, and I didn't want to have to face the glass case full of bones. Instead, I looked out the window at the gray day. Nobody was on the beach. Clouds suffocated the sun. Rain pocked the sand.

Miss Nadia came back wet and somber. "I saw Mr. Duvall," she said.

"Did they give him anything to eat?" I'd been worried about what my aunt might provide—gut stew, snail pie.

"The food is fine," Miss Nadia said. No fish balls for the prisoners then, only for blood relatives. "Of course he knows nothing about these keys or money. I tried to pay bail, but it's more than I have, and anyway, where would he go? He won't have his job, and he wouldn't be able to leave the state until the trial."

"He could stay with us," I said. "My father wouldn't mind." He was always going on about the working man getting a bad shake and how the bosses kept everybody clawing at each other for crumbs. He'd be on Isaac Duvall's side no matter what some rich lady said he'd done.

"Your uncle the sheriff might not like that," she said. "Anyway, Mr. Duvall must stay in jail until the judge comes. There's just one judge for the county, and he's thirty miles north today and has business up there tomorrow also. Your uncle said he told the judge on the telephone he should hurry. If people find out, there is scandal for the hotel. So maybe the judge is here tomorrow, and if he's a fair man, he drops the case. But it's no good for Mr. Duvall either way. He's been disgraced. The shadow is on him. And it's my fault." She looked worn and angry, her eyes dark and the skin beneath them dark.

"Miss Nadia! It's not *your* fault." Why was she taking blame, when I was the one who should have?

"But it is," she said. "His boss thought Mr. Duvall pushed himself on me for a helper. Then when the mystery of the keys occurs, Mr. Duvall comes to his mind as someone sneaky. Often I'm too much an interference."

"You're not," I said. "You just help people."

She smiled a little. "That's nice for you to say. Any luck with the sailor suit boys?"

"I looked all over," I said. "I didn't see the ones I saw before."

"Maybe later you will," she said. "If you were in jail, what food would you want?"

"Pie," I said.

"Of course pie." She wrote it on a paper. "Mr. Duvall

should be cheered up. Pie is good for that. And cookies. Sandwiches—he can eat at any time of day. One ham. One turkey. One cheese. One tomato and lettuce. A Thermos of hot tea and a Thermos of lemonade, yes? Maybe some apples."

She handed me the paper. "Call downstairs and have them pack these things, and anything else you think. And of course I don't need to say this, but nobody must know about Mr. Duvall's situation. It's no good for the hotel, for Mr. Dell and the workers here, if there is accusation of stealing. So to anyone who wants to know, we are preparing for a long day of work, not bringing food to somebody."

"Of course, Miss Nadia," I said. I was making everyone into liars.

I was then dispatched to the reading room for books to divert Isaac Duvall's attention from his plight. The reading room was empty but for an elderly bearded gentleman engrossed in a crumpled newspaper, who made no objection to my staggering out with as many books as I could carry.

Miss Nadia approved of my selection. "So many!" she exclaimed. "But all to the good. We don't know his tastes in reading, and there may be many hours to fill. Do you have a wrap with you? I think this rain will be all day."

"I don't think I should go," I said. "My aunt won't like it. Mrs. Dell is her friend." What could I possibly say to Isaac Duvall?

"Your uncle gave permission. It will be instructive for you, he believes. So you'll always walk the straight and narrow, yes? This will keep you warm." She handed me a thick dark green shawl.

I put the shawl over my shoulders but didn't wrap it around myself. I was the one who should have been in the dankness with the cold iron bars and shadowy echoes. I should witness the desolation. My bones should chill there. The rain could freeze me all it wanted.

Miss Nadia hoisted the box of books and I took the carpet bag that we'd put the food in. We went by the stairs instead of waiting for the elevator. The bag wouldn't have been heavy but for the two big Thermoses, each as long as an arm. From the landing I could see the glass case, surrounded by a batch of summer people with nothing to do on a rainy day but rest up for the next tennis match. Out the big windows, past the wide veranda, rain pelted the beach.

Miss Nadia had ordered a buggy to take us the short distance up the street. Bellboys who weren't Isaac Duvall shielded us with umbrellas as we got in. The big lake was almost black under the heavy clouds. Miss Nadia saw that I had left the shawl loose and wrapped it snugly around me. It took less time to get there than it did to load the buggy and get in. Rain sheeted down, cold and sharp.

Uncle Fowler had instructed Miss Nadia to come to the front door of the house as if she was paying a call. Mercifully, Aunt Phyllis wasn't home. The hired girl, Ingie's cousin whose name I always forgot, showed us through the side door to the jailhouse in back.

Uncle Fowler let us in. The front part was the office, which was practically a cell with its high barred windows and metal doors. My uncle took the box of books from Miss

Nadia and put it on a table and indicated to me where to put the carpet bag.

"We're required to inspect everything that's brought in," he said. "Have your visit while I'm doing that, if you like."

"Certainly," Miss Nadia said. "Thank you."

He unlocked the sliding metal door that let us into the corridor where the two cells were. Each had a cot and metal pail. Isaac Duvall's also had a chair with a folded newspaper on it. The other cell was uninhabited, except probably by vermin and slugs. Isaac Duvall's blue jacket and trousers were rumpled. He looked tired.

"Thank you for coming over here in the rain," he said.

"It's nothing," Miss Nadia said. "Just a little summer downpour. I spoke to a friend in Chicago, one of these people who knows everybody. He is finding out the best lawyer nearby, someone with the highest reputation. I will make arrangements—with your permission, of course."

"I appreciate it," Isaac Duvall said. "But lawyers are expensive."

"That won't be your concern. I understand pride, but you must put it away. This could go badly for you. You *did* have the handbag. So I insist. Please."

"That's right," Isaac Duvall said. "I had the bag. The best lawyer in the world can't prove I didn't do it."

"That's no way to think about it," Miss Nadia said. "In this country, they must prove guilt beyond the shadow of a doubt. And maybe there is evidence of the real culprit."

Maybe there was. My fingerprints. A witness. More

misfortune was coming everyone's way because of what I'd done. Miss Nadia would lose her job with Mr. Dell for standing up for Isaac Duvall, and she'd end up in the poorhouse. I was glad I had pulled her shawl open to get the rain on me when we went from the house to the jail. I was soaked and frozen. Maybe I'd get pneumonia and serve me right.

"Violet! Your lips are blue," Miss Nadia said. "I should have given you something warmer. How can it be this cold? Yesterday it's too hot and today it's almost winter."

"I-I'm fine," I stammered. Shudders came from my depths. The one narrow window showed a strip of gray sky and the green waving edge of what must have been a tree. To be enclosed in a box, no distant hills, no nests of birds, no sound of waves—it wasn't bearable. I wanted to run back out into the rain. Isaac Duvall looked mad and sad. Cold bars were between us.

My uncle slid open the metal door and brought in the box of books and the carpet bag. He put the things down next to Miss Nadia. She handed the packets of food to Isaac Duvall through the bars and told him what was in each packet. We had wrapped the sandwiches and cookies in napkins from the hotel. The pie was a whole apple one. My uncle wouldn't let Isaac Duvall have the knife and fork we'd brought to cut and eat with.

"Regulations," he said. "We'll get him a spoon." He didn't leave to fetch it, but stood watching us. My heart was a hummingbird. I was hot suddenly, the kind of hot that you get before you're sick to your stomach. My throat was too dry to swallow.

"Violet chose some books for you," Miss Nadia told Isaac Duvall, and so I had to hand the books to him through the bars, and each one was a mistake. *Great Expectations* had a convict in it! *Moby Dick* would make him crave the freedom of the sea. Jo March and her sisters would make him miss his own family. Sherlock Holmes would give him bad dreams.

Reaching through the bars was unbearable. Even that much of myself inside the cell that should have been mine made my liver tremble. Isaac Duvall stacked the books on the floor by his feet, then rose and stood stiffly as if awaiting orders at the front door of the hotel.

Miss Nadia put a hand on my shoulder. "This girl needs to get warm," she said. "We'll come back another time. Please let us know whatever you need. And don't worry. This is just an unfortunate misunderstanding that will be straightened up. All right?"

"Thank you." His voice was low and hoarse. "Both of you."

I felt that I would choke. I made myself not run. I couldn't have, as Uncle Fowler had to unlock us out. The doors clanged shut. I was out in the wind and rain and Isaac Duvall was not. I sloshed through the mud to follow Miss Nadia to the buggy and got in.

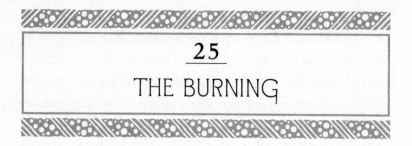

All afternoon Miss Nadia called people on the telephone and left messages and waited for them to call back and not all of them did. I organized photographs and dusted the equipment. Miss Nadia wrote down everything she found out, but she didn't find out anything that would help Isaac Duvall. She remembered that Isaac Duvall had taken the handbag to Mrs. Dell's room at around four-fifteen. The man who found the keys beneath the case had turned them in to the front desk at five-thirty. So Isaac Duvall could have had plenty of time to try to steal the artifacts if that's what he'd done.

The lawyer that Miss Nadia's friend said was the best in the state wouldn't take the case. Nobody would. Miss Nadia must have called twenty lawyers. Everybody was too busy or too far away or just said no without a reason. Then it was after office hours and nobody was answering the telephone. Miss Nadia was hoarse. Her tea had gone cold with a scum of milk on top, but she drained the cup.

"That's all we can do today," she said. "Tomorrow not too early, let's say nine. Let's get you a cab. This rain is crazy."

"Oh, no, Miss Nadia. I'm staying at my aunt's," I lied. I wasn't planning to go straight home. I was taking the Hand to the rat root place, where maybe it would be magic enough to wish on.

"But it's so wet! The street's all mud." She was dialing the phone.

"No, please. It's one minute away. My aunt will say I'm taking advantage. I'm used to rain."

She put the telephone down. "Well, take the green shawl. Are your clothes dry?"

She had given me a dressing gown to wear while my clothes hung from the curtain rod. My dress was still damp on its hanger. "Bone dry," I told her.

In the washroom, I recovered the Hand from behind the mirror. I slipped it into its pocket beneath the clammy dress and put the ribbon around my shoulder and put the mirror back on the wall as quietly as I could. The washroom window rattled as the wind hit it.

Miss Nadia stood at the window watching lightning slash the tumbling sky. "Look at that magnificence," she said. "Be careful out there."

I said I would. It was just some rain. City people don't have to feed the chickens no matter what it's doing out.

The elevator dinged just as I was leaving Miss Nadia's room. Two young city ladies came out, arm in arm, and swept down the hall with their heads together. I got in.

"Going down," the elevator man said. The metal doors

clanged shut. The elevator jolted downward. The light flickered and went out. The elevator stopped hard. It was dark, dark as a cave.

"Power's down," the elevator man said. "We'll just sit tight a minute." There was a breaking noise. We shook in our cage.

"We have to get out," I said.

"Wouldn't recommend it. We won't drop to the bottom or nothing like that. Nothing to be scared of. Best to wait."

I couldn't. All day I'd had to think of being in a cell instead of Isaac Duvall, and the elevator was a cell, wasn't it, made of metal but suspended in the air like a fly in a web? If the elevator fell and I was crushed to death, Isaac Duvall would never get out. It was up to me and up to the Hand. I had to really wish where the Hand would really listen.

"Open the door," I said. "I have to get out. There's an emergency."

"Let's see where we are then," he said. Metal screeched as he pulled the doors open. He struck a match. Through the partly opened doors there was a dark expanse and then a platform high above my head.

"Too high up," the elevator man said. "Even a little stick of a girl like you couldn't squeeze in there. And no telling what'll happen if the power comes back on. You'd get squashed like a bug."

"Please! I have to get home. My mother—my—" I said it to pretend to be crying. I almost was.

He made a cradle of his hands for me to step in, and hoisted me. "Go fast. If the power goes up, you'll get sliced in half. Hurry, now."

I raised my arms and felt up into the dark cold chasm, groping for something to touch. It was all one huge shaft, an endless well.

"Higher!" I urged him. He grunted, lifted me an inch. My fingers felt a surface. I gripped it. My arms wouldn't pull me up, and my feet hunted in black space. Anything could have come at me—snakes, bats, razor teeth, hairy spiders, human bones with scraps of flesh clinging to the gristle.

I somehow clutched the floor above and wrestled my way upward. I stood up. All was blackness. I heard the voices of people making their way in the dark. There was a splintering crash—a falling chandelier, a broken window. I'd witnessed many storms, but at home there was no electricity to go out, and lamps and candles and matches were always close at hand, and on a stormy night there were fires in the stove and in the fireplace too. Thunder rumbled and burst. Lightning flashed. I could see now where the stairs were. Then it was darker than ever. Hands in front of me like a drifting swimmer, I made my way along, found the banister, and started down. The lobby was lit with kerosene lamps, casting pools of pulsing light. The glass case glinted and shone in the flickering, as if the bones inside were aflame.

Outside, the rain needled my face. A sizzling bolt speared the sand. Everything flashed blue. The big lake was a frantic panting beast. In the sudden crackling light, I might have seen a pair of giant wings stirring the dark clouds. I might have seen a shadowy massive tail rise from the depths and whack back under with a colossal splash.

Every building in town was dark but for the flickering of

candles or lanterns in a window here or there. The electric streetlights that Aunt Phyllis was so proud of were out. Rain slammed down. The wind made my thin dress into a sail and hurled me in directions not of my choosing.

It was slow going. The road was a river, and the wind pushed at me so that I was hurried along too fast, then changed direction to become an opponent. I thought I must be almost there, and yet I didn't get anywhere, and then I thought I certainly had lost my way and was bound to wander in an endless downpour until I collapsed in the mire and sank beneath the flood.

I would have missed the path to the stream entirely had it not been for the preachers. The rain had let up some, and I could see the hulks of trees. Before me, moving across the road in a line, were lights—fireflies, I thought at first, though they didn't flit, and then I thought they must be ghostly presences, especially because the lights seemed to be singing. It was a hymn of some kind, and the lights were lanterns carried by people crossing the road.

"I don't hear you, boys!" a man shouted. I recognized the booming voice of Mercy's father. It was a bleak and lonely feeling to know that Mercy was passing by so close to me and I couldn't even wave. The lights disappeared into what I then discerned was their big church tent, which began to glow from the lanterns hung within as the singing swelled. I wondered what had possessed them to hold a service at that hour, but couldn't say I wasn't grateful. I had my bearings then. I'd almost bypassed the path.

Branches clawed me from their trees. I tripped over fallen

ones. Wind wailed. The trees creaked and cracked. I felt along the ground for the place where I'd found the Hand. If it had power, it would be strong there.

The canvas over the hole had blown into a soggy knot, one corner held by the heaviest stone. The hole was a swamp of leaves and mud. I wrestled the Hand out of its soaked bag. I could feel the etchings in the copper. I remembered the lady with the white feather cape and tattoos on her chin, how she held the Hand to the sky between her palms. I did the same.

"I wish for Isaac Duvall to be unaccused," I said. "Like it never happened. His name has to be cleared. And soon. Please."

There was no icy jolt, but magic seemed to flow from my hands to the metal and from the metal to the sky and from the sky to everywhere. I was a sapling, gaining strength from the water that threatened to uproot me. I was a spiral etched in copper. I was an eddy in a stream making my way to a river to a lake to the sea. If it was my last wish, then that's how it had to be.

My arms were stiff when I finally brought them down. I tucked the Hand beneath Miss Nadia's shawl. Even in the dark, my feet knew the path through the woods to the house.

My father was with his trees, of course, draping sheets and quilts around branches to protect them from the battering wind. I saw him in a flash of lightning as I passed. It seemed a useless effort. The wind whipped and yanked and stole my grandmother's linen tablecloth and threw others in the mud. He didn't see me.

Upstairs, I wrung out my garments into the basin, then

put the basin beneath the leak in the corner. I had to move my bed away from a new leak. Finally I was under the covers, the Hand beneath the mattress. Even with the thunder bellowing and the wind tearing around, I fell right asleep.

The rain stopped during the night. When I got up, my father was out. I found him with his trees, of course, unwrapping them from the sheets and tablecloths that he'd cocooned them in to keep them from the storm. Some of the trees were tilted and he was heaving dirt around their stunted trunks to help them straighten up.

"She works you too hard," he said. "You weren't back until late."

"I don't mind," I said. He didn't either, not really. He just thought he should. It didn't matter to me either way. The magic would unaccuse Isaac Duvall with more wishes to come, surely. It would fix the trees if I asked it to.

The road was a slippery sloshing bog. The wind had strewn branches everywhere. Others were dangling from their trees like dislocated arms. In town, Front Street was a river. Men in hip boots were bailing with buckets.

I passed through the double doors of the hotel. The lobby was thronged with people arranging to leave and talking about how it could take the rest of the summer for the electricity to be fixed. Wires were down all over the county. Branches had to be cleared off the tracks, so the train was late. It maybe wouldn't come at all. More rain was expected. The lobby was dim with only the gray outdoors for light.

Miss Nadia was sitting at the table closest to the window, looking at a photograph. She flung it down. It slid across the table, knocking other photographs to the floor. I bent to pick them up.

"Just leave them," Miss Nadia said. "Don't bother yourself. We're dead in the water today. No darkroom. No telephone. I waited twenty-five minutes downstairs to order breakfast to be brought up. And where is it? And no light! I can't see what I'm looking at. Pfah!" She banged the table.

"We could visit Isaac Duvall," I suggested. "Maybe the judge came."

"No! I went already. I couldn't sleep for all this. The judge—who knows if his business is finished up north or he can even get here! Nobody knows if the train is coming or when. Nobody knows anything. And no phone for calling any lawyers. And I went over the head of Alice Dell to her husband. He knows she forgets, she loses things. But to him Isaac Duvall is just a bellboy. If his wife doesn't like him, too bad then."

I'd asked for the Hand to work quickly. It didn't seem to be listening to me.

"I'm sorry, Miss Nadia," I said.

"For what? I'm sorry for my mood. I don't like sitting on my hands. I wish there was something we could do, but I think we just have to wait."

Someone was knocking.

"Finally!" Miss Nadia said. "It's just toast and sausage. I knew eggs would get here cold, they're so busy downstairs. The kitchen must be wild today. Nothing working—and dark. Let's hope the tea is hot, at least."

But it wasn't the tea. It was Mrs. Agosa. She strode past me as I held the door for her to come in. She was out of breath a little. Miss Nadia was gathering papers from the table to make room for the tray. She saw Mrs. Agosa and straightened up. Mrs. Agosa put her hands on Miss Nadia's shoulders and looked into her face.

"Try to believe what I'm telling you," she said. "The bones downstairs. The copper things. They're sacred, like I told you before. They have to be treated right or powers could get shook up."

"What do you mean?" Miss Nadia said. "What happened? Please sit, Mrs. Agosa."

Mrs. Agosa didn't sit. "The bones, they should be put back in the ground in a proper way. Your Alice Dell's in charge of them. Tell her. She won't listen to me."

"But, Mrs. Agosa. Is it hurting the bones just for people to see them?"

"Do you want the bones of your great-grandmother looked at for a curiosity? Your mother? Sister? Talk to the Dell woman. Explain to her it's wrong."

Miss Nadia raised her eyebrows. "She's not easy to convince."

"You have to try," Mrs. Agosa said. "That's a holy woman, those bones."

"All right. Help me understand. In churches there are sacred things displayed. Bones from saints, sometimes. People are interested to know about times gone by and other ways of life."

"Too bad for them," Mrs. Agosa said. "I'm saying the

powers can get confused. These holy things are out in the open, nobody working them or caring for them the right way. Copper is sacred to the water beings. And look—an angry storm. Who knows what the copper is saying to the clouds?"

A chill sliced me. Had the copper hand brought the storm? I was caring for the Hand. I had rescued it. Wasn't it grateful?

"And what should Mrs. Dell do with these sacred things?" Miss Nadia said.

"Bury them where they were," said Mrs. Agosa. "Exactly how they were found."

"I want to help," Miss Nadia said. "But Mrs. Dell—no. She'll say this is an ordinary summer storm and you're talking superstition. She is only practical, this woman. The mysteries of life—she doesn't think of them."

"It doesn't matter what she thinks! Someone has to stop them. They think only of their own greed—her and that husband. Guy Dell. The thief. The murderer!"

Miss Nadia was frowning. "Maybe this is something Miss Blake shouldn't hear," she said.

"Why shouldn't she know? Everybody should know about this man. He stole my village. Burned it down!"

Miss Nadia was frowning. "Mrs. Agosa, I don't think—"

"You don't want to hear it? You don't want to know the man you work for, what he's done? I was there. I saw. I helped buy that land. You can see it yourself, twelve miles north of here, all flattened down, the trees all cut. Twenty families bought it. We grew our corn and potatoes, had our apple trees. But Dell, he wanted it."

Miss Nadia was listening. So was I. The big lake out the window was churning up.

"We had papers. Dell fixed up different papers. He got the sheriff to come with him. What kind of law burns up peoples' houses?"

Uncle Fowler—he was another one in the rich man's pocket, like my father always said. Laws were for the swindlers.

"All the men were at work," Mrs. Agosa went on. "Just the old men, the women, the babies were there. Guy Dell—his men—threw coal oil all around and lit it. Houses, orchards, fields. They burned it all. They'd have burned us if we tried to stop them."

Miss Nadia nodded faintly. "That's terrible, what happened to you."

"It didn't happen," Mrs. Agosa said. "It was done. He did it."

She swallowed hard and drew a long breath. "We had to walk all night in the rain carrying the children to where people had family to take us all in. My sister's grandson was sick. After that night he got sicker. Then he died. My sister's grandson, not even two years old."

Mrs. Agosa steadied herself on the back of the nearest chair. "So I know this man Dell," she said. "The robber. The killer of children. We went to lawyers. He paid everybody off and made it look legal. And now he steals what's sacred. You want to let him, you're as bad as he is. Those bones, they should be buried."

Miss Nadia turned to look out the window at the low, dim sky. Everything was restless—trees, wind, water. Lightning flashed from far across the lake. The vileness of what had been told hung in the room like smoke itself.

"You're right," Miss Nadia said. "It's evil to let evil continue. When I was a child, my family was robbed too. Not by one man. By many. Men, women, hundreds running in the street, breaking windows, doors. I can't forget the sound of them coming closer from the next street over. Seven years old I was. I carried my two little sisters to hide in the coal cellar. One was just a baby still. I kept them quiet while the mob upstairs was smashing our dishes on the walls, throwing our chairs in the street, cursing us, cursing all Jews. When they were gone, it was a blizzard of feathers all through the streets from cutting open every bed, every pillow from every Jewish house."

Miss Nadia turned away from the window. She looked as if she'd just seen a maggoty carcass and its rancid scent was permeating. "They didn't do it to get, to take. It was to destroy. Just for hate." Her chin lifted. She would never be vanquished by whoever might hate her.

"You can't stop hate," Mrs. Agosa said. "You can't stop greed. But you can't let them have it all."

"The next time the mob came through," Miss Nadia said, "my father stood at the door with an axe. We didn't have any trouble that time. Of course, there wasn't much left for anyone to break."

I could see them each from the side. I couldn't tell what their faces told each other.

"They're not ones for listening to anybody, the Dells," Miss Nadia said. "But I'll try."

Mrs. Agosa let go of the back of the chair and headed for the door. Her eyes caught mine. I was a rabbit in the fox's gaze. Miss Nadia came out from behind the table, caught up to Mrs. Agosa, and laid a hand on Mrs. Agosa's shoulder.

"I'll do my best," Miss Nadia said.

Mrs. Agosa was finally not looking at my guilty greedy eyes. She lifted her own hand to cover Miss Nadia's. Then she was grasping the doorknob before I could move to help her.

"Violet," Miss Nadia said when Mrs. Agosa was gone. "I wish you didn't have to hear such a terrible thing. I hate that the world is so ugly for you to grow up in."

She strode to the mirror, pulled out a hairpin, twisted a lock of hair. "I want to count on you not to speak about this tragedy of Mrs. Agosa's to anyone. She could suffer repercussions."

"But why did she talk about it then?" I said.

"I think she doesn't talk about it since it happened. Too much grief. But she feels kinship with the skeleton. And for the man who did the burning to be the owner of those bones, it makes her desperate."

"But what if it's not true? People make up things."

"This isn't something a person manufactures in her mind, Violet." The hairpin jabbed. "I have to know from Mr. Dell's own mouth. If he has some explanation, I want to hear it."

Her bravery shamed me. She would face up to Mr. Dell because he liked her and she could get him to see the light if anybody could. And if he yelled at her or fired her, she'd lift her chin at him. And she wanted Mrs. Dell to get her an exhibit at the Chicago Art Institute more than just about any-thing, but she wanted Isaac Duvall to be out of jail even more.

"You could please sort everything on the table," Miss Na-dia told me. "Make a pile for each subject and your favorite picture on the top. Let's see your taste." She straightened her-self and was out.

The table with the pictures on it seemed very far away. I felt wobbly, as if I'd just set foot on land after a long boat ride. I thought of little Nadia whispering her sisters a song as she piled coal on their little legs to hide them. How long would it take to get warm after walking all night in a cold fall rain? If Fry had died when he was just starting to say funny things from being new at talking, would I cry every day for the rest of my life?

I dragged over to the table. I couldn't have Miss Nadia mad at me on top of everything else. It was almost entirely dark outside. Wind rattled the windows. I dealt the photo-graphs like cards. Here was the serene little town, the row of tidy shops on Front Street, the butcher in his apron, Ingie Peterssen leaning on her broom. In my mind I saw the same picture, the same street, littered with broken chairs and shattered crockery in a blizzard of feathers.

I made many piles. Fishermen, nets on racks, boats on gleaming waves. Cabbies and their horses. Children in sand and water. Isaac Duvall. The hotel, windows glinting be-neath lofty angel clouds. A net full of fish was a bag of silver, a bellboy was a prince, a caddie was tree bark.

All I ever thought about was what I didn't have, and no-body had burned my house or smashed my favorite teacup.

I lived somewhere with chairs and pillows and bowls and tablecloths and books. I lived alongside raccoons and owls, not hateful destroyers. Nobody in my family was dead except the ones who got too old to be alive. The world indeed was ugly, but not every last bit of it.

The pictures I'd borrowed of Mrs. Agosa holding the Hand were still curled from being rolled up. They wouldn't flatten. Miss Nadia would surely notice, but I couldn't destroy them. I put them under a stack of other pictures. The whole pile buckled as the stolen ones coiled.

Miss Nadia was back before I was done picking my favorites. "I will not allow a photograph of mine to advertise this man's hotel!" she cried, hurling the room key at the table. The key bounced to the floor. She snatched up a white cloud beach picture from the top of my neat pile, ripped the hotel and clouds in two, and flung the halves overhead.

"Forgive me, Violet," she said. "I am leaving here. I can't take money from someone so unscrupulous. I wish we didn't have to part so suddenly, but I'll pay you an extra week because of this abruptness. You have been a great help to me."

"But Miss Nadia! You can't just leave!"

"I must. I did not tell him this. He will be angry, and Mrs. Dell will cry. I'll let them know after I'm organized. I don't want you to be part of any unpleasantness."

"I don't mind unpleasantness. I have to help you," I said. "Please. You haven't even had any tea yet. Here."

I poured shakily. The tea was stone cold. The sugar was grainy at the bottom of the cup. I handed it to her anyway.

Nothing was getting any better. Everybody was mad at everybody and the Hand was mad at me.

She downed the tea. "What did Mr. Dell say?" I asked her.

"He laughed! I am a sentimental woman to him, not able to understand with my small woman mind how business must be done. Mrs. Agosa and her relatives were trespassing, he said, and he has the right to burn buildings on his land if he doesn't want buildings there. I did my best to talk him into giving up the bones, but he was deaf to that. And while I'm at it, I appealed to him again for the sake of Isaac Duvall. In the hands of the authorities, he said."

"Well, you can't just leave if Isaac Duvall's still in jail. Nobody else cares what happens to him."

She put down her cup. "Well, there's no leaving today with no telephone to make arrangements. And packing all this up by myself—with two of us, it's faster."

We put the prints in boxes with tissue paper in between each one and made lists of the photographs and lists of things to do and get. Miss Nadia wrote letters and tried to use the telephone every five minutes or so and it was always dead.

Miss Nadia sent me to buy string and tape at Peterssen's store. Mrs. Peterssen was measuring cloth for an old lady, so Ingie was at the cash register. "Is the Russian driving you crazy?" she said, taking the five-dollar bill of Miss Nadia's I held out.

"Not at all," I said. "She's magnificent."

She made a sour face and pressed the keys on the register

in her maddening, deliberate way. "Aren't you scared, though, with all those blacks robbing everybody over there at the hotel?" The drawer clacked open.

"You don't know what you're talking about. Nobody got robbed!"

"Well, that's all *you* know. They've been stealing purses left and right, those blacks. You should quit that job. It's not safe over there. Now that one of them's caught, the rest of them are probably hopping mad, and they could—"

"They they they! They could *nothing*! You're an *idiot*!" I was shouting, not making sense, scrabbling at the change, breaking a fingernail on the counter. Mrs. Peterssen's scissors clattered on the cutting table.

"What a rude little girl," the old lady customer gasped.

"Out! Out!" Mrs. Peterssen flew at me with waving arms. "How dare you make a scene in my store?"

"How dare you spout your damn disgusting ignorance all over town!" I spat back. Clutching my parcel, I ran out before she hit me with a broom. I'd seen her do it to Ingie for much less.

She didn't come after me. The dank clouds were about to spit rain. I was trembling to the marrow. Isaac Duvall would spend his life in prison. I couldn't confess. If I was sent away and locked up, the powers would be more confused than ever with the Hand abandoned beneath the mattress. And if it was found, what would become of it?

I didn't tell Miss Nadia about Ingie. Ingie would hate me forever now, and she'd been the closest thing I had to a friend before Mercy came along. And Mercy would hate me if she found out that I'd lied to her about the real Hand. And Miss Nadia was leaving, and she'd be blackballed by Mr. Dell, whatever that entailed, and I would never see her again, and Isaac Duvall's life was ruined, and it was entirely my fault, and the Hand was getting madder every solitary minute.

We worked in the darkroom. Miss Nadia said that anything could happen when you travel, and packing undeveloped negatives was risky, so we had to do them all. There was no red light that we could see by, so everything took longer. At least Miss Nadia couldn't see how my fingers quavered as they stirred the prints in their smelly baths.

It was dark out when we were done with all the negatives. Miss Nadia lit the lamp and walked me to the door to light my way into the hall. She said to come at seven in the morning so that we could get everything done early. So she was planning on taking the afternoon train, then. I was sick at the very thought.

I was glad for the darkness. I didn't intend for anyone to see where I was going. The lake did its wild dance, leaping to meet the boiling roiling sky. I slipped around the side of the hotel, then got on the path that went along the edge of the harbor to the river road and ran my fastest—not to get ahead of the rain that still hadn't come down, but to get there before I talked myself out of it.

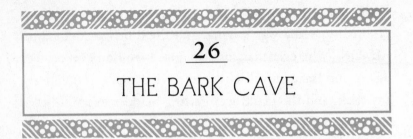

26
THE BARK CAVE

I found the house and Lucy Thornwood answered my knock.

"I need to see Mrs. Agosa," I managed to gasp. My heart was going too fast.

"What's wrong?" she said. "Are you all right? Do you need a drink of water?" My throat was so dry that swallowing hurt, but I shook my head no.

We went through the kitchen and out back of the house. I could hear the river rushing along. By Lucy Thornwood's lantern I could see a little birchbark hut on the riverbank, round like a cave. "Grandma," Lucy Thornwood said, "someone's here for you."

"It's late for a child to be out alone," Mrs. Agosa said. "Come inside." Her voice sounded hollow.

The bark cave smelled like grass and flowers. Mrs. Agosa's hand settled on my arm. I remembered how she knew things about people by touching them. I drew away, but her fingers tightened.

"Sit," she said, and pressed me down onto a low bench.

"Bad things are happening," I said. "It's the bones and—and all that. Everything's going bad. You have to do something. Please!"

"What's bad?" she said.

"I told you! Everything! Isaac's in jail for no reason—and Miss Nadia's leaving—and everybody hates everybody! Everything's worse—every day!"

"And what can I do about it?"

"You said the world could stop. You said the bones and everything—you said they had to be treated a certain way. And they're in the case, and—and they're mad at everybody!"

"Mad, you say. You feel anger from the bones."

"No," I said, because I didn't.

"What, then? Do the bones talk to you?"

"No! But you said they have to be buried! And they're not! And Mr. and Mrs. Dell won't! So isn't there something to make the bones and the copper hand and everything just calm down and stop getting revenge on people who didn't have anything to do with it?"

She said nothing for too long a time. My jaw clenched to keep from shouting at her.

"One thing about Georgia Blake," she finally said. "She's someone that bones would talk to. And maybe it wouldn't be the kind of talking that makes a sound. Sometimes a person hears something or they see something that they don't understand, and they can't forget it. Georgia can see and hear things like that. Maybe you can too."

Just hearing my mother's name made my heart into a sand dune, heavy, shifting, huge.

"It's not the bones," I said. Just saying that much made me feel better, not so hateful, but I wasn't used to telling things straight and clean.

"Say more," she said.

"I was the one who found—not the bones. The copper—" I stopped. Had I meant to tell her that much? I had to.

"The copper," she said.

"The Hand." Once I said it, a burden was off me.

"I only had it a day or two," I went on. "Willis Rankin stole it from me and said he dug it up. And I didn't say anything to anybody, because it's Mr. Dell's land, or he says it is. But it used to be ours. And I saw an old lady from a long time ago and the copper hand was hers, and it was just quick like a lightning flash. But I saw her."

"That copper hand's going to get weak," she said. "All these people grabbing it."

"Nobody's grabbing it," I said.

"You got hold of it, then some boy. He passed it around to whoever wanted to look at it. Your boss lady and her boss lady and the boss lady's husband, his friends, his workers, who knows who else? It'll get weak."

Weak! Sometimes the Hand seemed strong and sometimes not, like my mother when she was better from being sad and then worse again. If it was weakening, it was certainly my doing.

"Well, it's not my fault," I said. "I wouldn't have let anybody else even see it. But then Willis Rankin took it. I fought him and everything."

Yes, the Hand had been grabbed—grabbed and trampled and bent. Willis should be the one in jail. His teeth and hair and nails should fall out. He should fester with boils.

"This vision," Mrs. Agosa said. "How did she look, this lady from another time?"

I'd wanted to forget the feather lady. She hadn't seemed wicked or mean, but she had powers and wasn't from the regular world. But maybe Mrs. Agosa would summon her and get her to take the bad luck off me and throw it on Willis.

"She was wearing a cape of swan feathers," I said. "She had tattoos."

"Did she do anything?"

"She held the copper hand above her head and made snow cover the ground. Everything was white. And the air got really cold. Then she wasn't there."

"You saw what the copper remembered," Mrs. Agosa said.

"But how can it remember?" If it could remember, it would know my treacheries and show them to others, and the legacy of my lies would live forever.

"Everything remembers," Mrs. Agosa said. "Earth remembers battles. A house remembers sorrow in its walls. If someone beats you on the shoulder with a stick, that shoulder won't forget. You maybe saw a copper woman. The copper hand should have one now, to care for it, like before. Not a little girl. Someone who's been taught things."

"What's a copper woman?"

"Keepers of the waters. Protectors. Guardians. The water beings, they like copper, so copper women have their tools made out of it. Like that hand, maybe."

The Hand a tool? A shoulder holding grudges? She didn't know anything. Mrs. Agosa was like Grandmother Blake, addled and ancient. I couldn't believe a word she said, and I'd said too much.

"That's all I know about it," I said.

Even in the dark I could feel her eyes on me. I clutched my fists to stop the shaking of my fingers.

"The copper hand, it's used to being treated a certain way," she said. "It could get sick if it isn't respected. It could hurt people who are around it. It isn't good for it to be in that glass box."

"You mean the copper hand is bad?" I said.

"Not bad. Fire can keep you warm in winter, but it can burn a whole forest. Is it bad?"

"But what if it's sick already? Can it get well again?"

My eyes were used to the dark a little. She was a shrugging shadow. "There's not much I can know if it's locked up. When I was with it that one time I felt something from it, but nothing like you're talking about. It's behind all that glass now, out in the open. It's not how it should be." She turned away.

"Tell me about my mother," I said.

The moon had maybe risen high enough to shine through the trees and through the flap of bark that was her door. I couldn't see her eyes, but maybe she saw mine.

"You're mad at her for leaving," she said. "It's me you

should be mad at. I told her to leave. I told her where to go. I told her to take your brother and not you."

"What kind of busybody are you?" I said. "Who said you could go around telling people to abandon their own daughter!" I wanted to tell her to go to hell. She was a mother stealer, a surly selfish lunatic crone.

"I had reasons," she said. "Do you want to know about them, or do you want to say more about how mad you are?"

"*What* reasons?"

"Georgia didn't feel good," she said. "You know that. Visions can make you think you're crazy. Maybe that didn't happen to you, but it happened to her. Did she ever talk to you about when she was growing up?"

"Sometimes," I said. I'd hate myself forever if I cried. I chewed my lip so I wouldn't.

"I knew Georgia's mother, before she was married. Elizabeth. She was Odawa, like me. Elizabeth married a white man and they had Georgia. Then they both died when Georgia was younger than you. Do you know what happened then?"

Of course I knew. "She went to live with her grandmother," I said.

"That's right. Her white grandmother Charlotte. Everything about Charlotte was white as snow. Her house. Her china. White sheets, white dresses, white ribbons in little Georgia's dark Indian hair. Charlotte was going to make Georgia a white young lady and raise her to marry a rich white man, the kind of man who doesn't care what anybody thinks."

Like Mr. Dell, I thought. His children would have dresses from across the sea and voyages to islands.

"So what happened to Georgia when this Grandmother Charlotte died?" Mrs. Agosa said. "Do you know?"

"She lived with her other grandmother," I said. "The Indian one."

"Yes. But not for long. Georgia got sent off to Indian school, because the government said she's Indian and that's where they make Indian kids go to learn how to work for white people. Which Georgia was, in part of herself. And wherever she was, wherever she was living, with the white grandmother or anywhere, she was seeing what others don't. Indians don't consider that to be crazy, but she wasn't raised to be Indian. She didn't ever really have a home. She didn't know her Indian family. She was confused inside herself. Do you know what I'm talking about?"

"But then she got a home," I said. "Why did she leave it?"

"I'll tell you. Your father's mother, she wasn't right in the mind. You remember her, don't you?"

I nodded. Of course I remembered Grandmother Blake. It hadn't been a year yet since she died.

"Georgia was with that grandmother of yours every day," Mrs. Agosa went on. "Every night and every day when your father was gone all winter. And Georgia, she began to feel she'd caught that kind of sickness your grandmother had. If your soul is bruised and it travels outside this world, your soul can be borrowed. And sometimes when somebody borrows something, they don't bring it back. You understand me?"

"That doesn't make any sense," I said.

"Georgia needed help," she said. "I know someone up north who knows about these things, a healer. She lives nearby your relatives. Georgia had to go there. She couldn't take you, because you might have been afraid. Your brother, he's too small to know. He could stay with Georgia's people, maybe, while she got herself figured out. The healing might have made her sick for a while. But after you're sick, sometimes you come back stronger. You don't get the same sickness again."

"What kind of healer makes somebody sicker?" I said. All these dead and crazy grandmothers—how was it their fault that Mrs. Agosa made my mother go away? I didn't even want to understand.

"It's how it goes sometimes," Mrs. Agosa said.

"But where *is* she?"

"Way up north." Mrs. Agosa stood up. I heard her moving in the dark.

"*Where* north? Is it an island? How can we get there?"

"She'll be back when she's ready."

"It's not fair!" My fists tightened. I wanted to break something. "You're the one who made her go there! You said you'd tell me! You're not telling anything!"

"It's not for me to say. She has to decide, not me. You just have to wait."

"I've *been* waiting!"

"You can't understand it all," she said. "Later maybe you will. Go to Lucy. She'll take you home."

"But what about Isaac Duvall! I told you! Bad things are happening!"

"Get those bones buried," she said.

"How am I supposed to do that?"

"Don't ask me. Nobody listens to an old Indian woman."

"Well, they won't listen to *me*!"

She was through talking. Everything was up to me, as usual. Bury the bones. Free Isaac Duvall. Find Mama and Fry in some distant forest.

I pressed my mouth closed. Mrs. Agosa had tricked me into blabbing about the Hand so she could get it and use it for herself. I ducked through the low doorway of the bark cave and stalked into the woods so Lucy Thornwood wouldn't try to walk me home. Too much was churning—was my mother sick or not sick, and would the copper hand be satisfied with what I'd told to Mrs. Agosa, or had I said too much, and what did copper women do?

The river rushed along. I followed its banks. The trees loomed and drooped, and the river was hissing like it had it in for me, and the moon's cast was sickly orange, a color my aunt might have worn. Nobody ever did anything for anybody unless they got something out of it.

The wind strengthened as I made my way along the road home. At times it pushed me along when the road curved a certain way. At times I had to shoulder against it. I was cold, weary, mad at the operations of the world.

My father wouldn't notice if I stayed out all night, if I never came back. Maybe the Hand was like everybody else in the world—you had to say something over and over and over for it to sink in.

I bypassed the house and felt my way through the dark

woods to the rat root place. I took the Hand out and held it to the sky, just like the feather lady.

"I want to care for you the right way," I said. "I'm doing my best. And I know you can make good things happen. So don't be mad anymore. And please let Miss Nadia stay. She's the one who can get the bones buried if anybody can. And Isaac Duvall—clear his name, clear his name, clear his name."

I tried to talk to it in a magical way, like the feather lady would have. I talked to it and talked to it and held it to the dark sky until my arms went numb. It might have been five minutes, it might have been half the night. The dim moon lit me home.

The farmhouse creaked and clattered in the wind. My father's head was on the kitchen table with the lamp burning and a book fallen to the floor. He didn't wake and I didn't wake him. I didn't need questions, if he even had any.

What good were grown people? All they ever did was spout off and not do anything about the despicable. They allowed children to save the innocent and do all the dirty work.

I slid the copper hand under the pillow and tumbled into sleep, too mad to cry.

One of Greenstone's grandsons was the first to get sick. He came down with fever on the second morning of the sturgeon run. By afternoon he was covered with fiery bumps, and so were two of the little girls who had been keeping birds away from the fish as it smoked over the aromatic fire.

Everyone neglected the catch. The pregnant women stopped feasting on the roe. The women stopped boiling the bones to harvest them for needles. Every day, every hour, someone else was dizzy, felt hot, itched beneath the arms or at the back of the neck. Some died within days, others faded. How long ago had Greenstone been at the city of the sky-watchers? Her oldest grandchild had been a baby then, she remembered, just newly walking. Now he was a young man, almost ready for a wife.

She'd thought the diseases were done with. She'd thought her loved ones were protected. She'd thought they were far enough from the eastern shore, from the southern shore, from the desert where others had been stricken.

The burning rash wasn't the kind of thing that listened to anybody. It didn't require offerings or flattery. Those who weren't sick kept the kettles boiling, brewed the medicines, bathed the blisters, drummed and rattled and wailed and mourned. A few people fled. Nobody blamed them.

Greenstone's best apprentice succumbed. Fish rotted on the sand. The stench of blood and bloat was in her skin and hair. The last of the apprentices stopped breathing.

She made her preparations. She had her pick of canoes. She packed more food than she would ever need. Maybe she would come across someone who was hungry.

Those who were left were sleepless and bedraggled. There wasn't any way to catch up, to make anything clean. Wolves came to feast on the dead. Bones would be gnawed and splintered and strewn.

Greenstone could make wolves understand her. She asked them please to leave. They did so. She knew they would return once she was gone.

She pushed off from the beach. The water took the canoe. She didn't look back to shout at the wolves to stay away.

28

SUBJECTS

The day was clear and bright. I had the Hand with me. I couldn't leave it. I had told it of my pure intentions. It would reward me.

The roads would dry out and the telephone lines would be fixed. Most likely they were fixed already. Miss Nadia had found the best lawyer in the United States of America, but nobody even needed him because Mrs. Dell had been thinking all night about what a big mistake she'd made accusing Isaac Duvall and she'd already ordered him to be let out. Miss Nadia would decide to keep her job and stay all summer.

"Still no judge. Still no phones," Miss Nadia said as I came into the room. The room was clean and bare of the piles of pictures and papers and books that were Miss Nadia's work. I saw out the window that the big lake had gone from choppy to smooth overnight.

"So you can't leave today, right?" I said.

"Exactly right. This isn't a day for traveling. Especially

because today we're having the sky and clouds I've been waiting for. And no picture to make for anybody—no big square hotel, no happy babies on the beach. And there is someone I've been wanting to sit for me ever since I got here, a shy one who will want to say no. How can I convince someone like this?"

"That's easy," I said. "Just show them some of your pictures."

Without reply, she turned away and left the room. Outside, the day shone. She came back in with a stack of prints, ones we'd already packed away. She laid them out on the table.

"Some people aren't comfortable to sit," she said. "Some are too vain, and some don't like to be looked at. Either way, they turn out with nothing beneath the features."

She pointed at a picture of a chef downstairs in the kitchen, posing stiffly with his ladle. The picture next to it she'd taken when a pan caught fire. The chef was swinging an apron at the flames, a dragon slayer.

"You see?" she said. "The sitting's not so good, but in the other—certainly something. This girl sweeping. This man with his boat. This little boy watching the band. Just being alive, not keeping still like a bowl of fruit. This is the kind of picture I would want of Miss Violet Blake. Would you allow me?"

My insides clutched. This could be my very last day with Miss Nadia. Miss Nadia gone, never to return—I couldn't get used to the thought.

"But if I'm posing, I can't hand you what you need," I said.

She laughed. "You are so very responsible," she said. "Don't worry. I can hand things to myself quite well. Having you to help me is luxury. Most times I'm on my own."

There was a sharp rap at the door, and two envelopes slid beneath it, one with Miss Nadia's name, the other with *Miss Violet Marie Blake* in Mercy's handwriting, which I knew from her tree notes.

I pulled a piece of blue hotel stationery out of the envelope.

I am HERE! Please find me as soon as you can. My room is 307. Your friend, Mercy Rankin.

"Who are you hearing from?" Miss Nadia said, crumpling her note and pitching it into the wastebasket. "Nothing aggravating, I hope."

"My friend Mercy is here, but I don't know why. I hope nothing's wrong."

"I think you have to find her and see, then. Where is she?"

"Just one flight up. Could I really go? I won't stay. She knows I'm here to work."

"Why not have her picture too?" Miss Nadia said. "If all is well with her, of course. Two friends in summer. You both. Then maybe you're not so shy of the camera, to be talking, laughing with your friend."

My plea to the Hand was maybe working. Miss Nadia wasn't in a hurry to leave after all. Any minute now the Hand would settle the Isaac Duvall disaster.

The elevators were working again, but I took the stairs.

Men were fixing a broken window, one inside on the landing and the other on a tall ladder outside. The 307 door was opened by Mrs. Rankin.

"You mustn't think we've suddenly become grand," she said. "Our tents were ripped to shreds in that storm. Mr. Dell insisted that we stay here as his guests until they're repaired. What a wind, wasn't it?"

She showed me to the washroom, where Mercy was washing clothes in the sink. A wet white shirt dripped from the handles of the tub.

"I just got your note," I said. "Miss Nadia told me to run and find you the minute I told her you were here. She says I've been doing such a good job, she wants me to come to Chicago." It spilled from me, a ridiculous lie, easy to dismantle.

"You'll have to come and see us," Mrs. Rankin said. "What on earth are you doing, Mercy? There's water all over this floor. How did you get to be so clumsy?"

"The sink's too small," Mercy said.

"It's no such thing." Her mother tossed a towel over the puddle. "You girls get out of this room. I'll finish up here. I don't know why I bother, Mercy. You just make more work." She mopped up the floor with her foot.

"The hotel has a laundry service, Mrs. Rankin," I said. "You just put your clothes in a bag outside the door and they're ready in the morning."

"That's very nice for some," she said. "We don't want to take advantage of Mr. Dell's generosity, I'm sure."

"Miss Zalzman wants to use Mercy and me for subjects," I said. "I think she wants to put us on the beach."

"Well, that will be exciting," said Mrs. Rankin. "It's quite a day for a photograph."

"Thank you, Mrs. Rankin," I said. She's not so terrible, I thought. Maybe not a busybody squirrel so much as a herding kind of dog, all bark and briskness.

"Wasn't that storm marvelous!" Mercy said when we were out in the hall. "Guess who was inside one of the tents that blew over?"

Had Willis been flattened, squashed and lifeless as a fly? I couldn't help but think it. Once I had, I tried to put it back, but thoughts are like eggs—once out, they're out. I didn't really want him hurt. Not badly, anyway. To not have something that he really wanted—that's all I was after. Just a measure of deprivation, disappointment, dismay, maybe lasting a year or two. I would have wished for that.

"Willis thought a panther had jumped on the tent," Mercy said. "He slashed the whole tent up with his pocketknife, he was so hysterical with fright. And meanwhile *my* tent was leaking. And the wind was completely fierce. So everybody had to spend the night in the big church tent, and everything was soggy and smelled bad. So then yesterday everybody worked like crazy trying to get everything fixed, but nothing was getting dry and it seemed like it was going to rain again, so we came to the hotel. Mr. Dell's letting us stay for free."

We descended the staircase to the second floor. Mercy leaned close. "I guess you didn't get the you-know-what yet. But I'm here now and I can help."

Would she recognize the false hand, the very one she'd

made, in the glass case? I'd made it look old. She'd only seen it shiny, and she had no reason not to believe me. I couldn't share the Hand with her. It would get weak, everybody fooling with it. Mrs. Agosa had said so.

"It was a travesty," I whispered. "I was practically arrested by my own uncle."

"What! No!'

"Well, I thought I would be. Getting the keys from Mrs. Dell's bag was easy. But I was just about to open the case when all of a sudden there were people swarming all over the lobby that two minutes before was completely deserted. It was raining and people were running back inside. And I almost got caught, because people were crowding around and pointing at the skeleton. Even Mr. Dell came along to show some of his rich friends. So I had to scurry out of there. And I was so rattled and scared and everything that I threw your hand in the lake."

"Not mine," she said. "Ours."

"Everybody came out of nowhere. It was uncanny. And so I thought maybe it was a warning from the real Hand. It's mad that we copied it, maybe."

"Maybe," she said. "But maybe it was just an accident, and the Hand wants us to get it out of that prison it's in. I could make another one. We could get more copper."

"Except they hired Pinkertons to guard the case. They're disguised as regular people, like old men who pretend they're sleeping. It's supposed to be a secret, except Miss Nadia told me. But the worst thing is that one of the bellboys got accused of taking Mrs. Dell's keys, when really it was me. And he's in jail right now. And Miss Nadia's quitting her job because of it. The Hand's bad luck. It's not to play with."

"That's terrible!" she said. "Can't your uncle the sheriff get the bellboy out?"

"He won't. Miss Nadia's doing everything she can. Don't say anything to her. I'm not supposed to tell anybody. And today might be her last day. That's why she wants to take pictures of us being happy and carefree. We have to pretend we are."

"Well, maybe it'll cheer us up," she said. "And it's a good thing I'm here. Maybe we can rescue the bellboy. Can't you get the jailhouse key from your uncle somehow? All you have to do is stick it in some wax and then we'll make a new one and let him out."

"No! My uncle guards the jail every hour of the day and night. Or the deputy does. They've got guns. Don't you think I've been wracking my brain about this? It's not a game, you know."

We were almost to Miss Nadia's door. Mercy put a hand on my arm and stopped us both. "I'm so sorry, Violet," she said. "It's my fault this all happened. I had a bad feeling all along, but it was so exciting that I didn't want to not do it. I'm sorry."

"Don't say that," I said. "It's not your fault." Why did everybody always make me feel worse all the time?

"Well, can Miss Nadia get the bellboy out or not? We can't just wait around hoping. An innocent man's in jail for something we did. I mean, you did the part that was dangerous, but if I hadn't made the you-know-what, then you couldn't have done it. We might have to confess. They might send us to reform school, but maybe at least we'd be together."

Two young men in matching boaters emerged from the elevator. We couldn't just stand in the hallway being overheard by everyone. I motioned for her to follow me into Miss Nadia's studio.

Miss Nadia shook Mercy's hand and looked her over. Mercy smiled bravely, showing her big teeth.

"Well, look at this day," Miss Nadia said. "Do you girls swim?"

"I do," Mercy said. "I can swim almost as fast as my brother, and he's older by a year and a half."

"I could swim before I could walk," I said. It sounded like a lie, but wasn't.

"Perfect," Miss Nadia said. "Two summer friends and a glorious beach day. Violet will call down and have them make up a basket. Is there anything especially you'd like, Miss Rankin?"

Mercy grinned. "Oh, anything! I'm famished."

She would make an excellent actress, I thought, if she decided to go that route instead of marrying into money.

As the telephones were still out from the storm, I went down to the kitchen to order our provisions while Miss Nadia and Mercy went to talk to Mrs. Rankin.

"You really don't have to bother, Miss Zalzman," Mercy said. "I always follow the rules. I'm allowed to go in water up to my collarbone as long as I'm not by myself and there are grown-ups on the beach."

But Miss Nadia said she'd be more comfortable if she talked to Mrs. Rankin first. We reconvened upstairs. Mercy had on a bathing dress and had borrowed one for me. I went into Miss Nadia's washroom to put mine on. I would stow the Hand behind the mirror. I took it out from hiding and traced the swirls on it with a finger. It seemed lighter, as if some essence had drained away. I'd thought before that wishes would deplete it, and it did seem wizened as a leaf so old that it's mostly only veins and stem.

I remembered how I'd found it crusted with dirt and rotting leaves, and how I'd rinsed it in the lake and felt its warmth and pulsings. If it's worn out, I thought, the lake will revive it. It's sacred to the water beings—hadn't Mrs. Agosa said so? And anyway, it doesn't like to be left behind. It makes it feel slighted.

So I put the Hand back into its secret pouch and fastened its ribbon around me and buttoned myself into the bathing dress with the Hand beneath. When I emerged, the day outside the window was sunnier than ever.

"Let's go, let's go!" Mercy urged. "What took you so long?"

"No hurry," Miss Nadia said. "The light is harsh for another hour or two. Then it will get better and better."

I doubted that very much. Everything always got worse, no matter what you did.

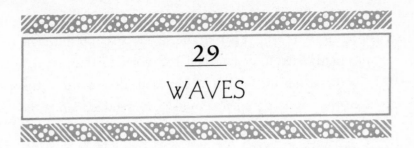

29
WAVES

It was strange to have to pretend to have a perfect beach day, when it could have been one if I'd deserved to rollick around being happy when others were in the gray chill of prison. Mercy and I dove beneath the waves and let them take us to shore. When we were chilled we came out of the water and stretched ourselves on the sand until we were almost dry, then went in the water again. Miss Nadia wouldn't hear of me helping her with the plates or keeping sand off the camera or moving the tripod. She didn't tell us where to look or not look or what to do with our arms or chins or hair, and after a while I forgot that I was in the pictures she was taking.

I showed Mercy how to find petoskey stones, and we strolled along the beach hunched over, eyes on the spread of wet rocks that shifted with each ebb. We ate cucumbers on white bread and yellow cheese on dark bread and butter cookies and jam tarts and grapes. We built a fairy palace with leafy flags and a woven grass carpet and tiny rock dishes on stone tables. The moat soon collapsed from too much water rushing in. We made repairs. The sun wasn't too hot. The white clouds surrounded it, then let it come forth.

"I'll be exploring," Miss Nadia said after a time, and hoisted the tripod over her shoulder and trudged along the sand away from everyone. The hotel, it seemed, had emptied onto the beach, and so had the entire town. The sand was scattered with chairs and umbrellas and ladies in their white dresses and straw hats. Men, dogs, and children yelped and splashed in the water that was strangely still. Horses stood in the shallows and gazed at the blue. Out deep it was green where the cloud shadows cast a chill.

I saw him first, striding along the beach, thrusting a long stick into the sand and vaulting himself, then whapping at the waves with it.

"Here comes your brother," I said. "Armed."

I felt among the folds of the bathing dress for the Hand. He doesn't know I have it, I thought. Even Mercy doesn't. If he wants to fight, don't.

He came up to us. The tip of the stick stirred the water in the moat, making waves. "Where'd you get that? Who said you could have it? Did Mother say so?" he said to Mercy. She was eating a leg of chicken, salting it with the doll-sized salt shaker the hotel had tucked into the basket.

"Where's Emmet?" she said.

"Playing tennis with some sissy kids." He looked pale around the lips, like he was thirsty, and was dripping water and was trying not to shiver. He'd been in the lake a long time. The tips of his fingers were wrinkled and white.

I pressed the Hand in its pouch against my ribs. *Begone,* I said inside myself. *Disappear. I never want to see that nasty grasping face again.*

I wanted to blind him with sand and scratch all his skin off, but I wouldn't subject the Hand to such indignities. I had the Hand and he didn't, after all.

"You must be starving, as usual," Mercy said. "Have a worm sandwich. Your favorite."

I didn't blame her. She'd had a lifetime of his sneering and strong-arming. But of course he was inflamed then, and wasn't one to let someone get away with anything. He bent down, took up a hearty fist of sand, and flung it her way, aiming for the chicken. Sand crusted it.

"You're a stinking beast!" she cried, brushing sand from her eyes.

"It needed salt!" he said. "Taste it! It'll be delicious."

"Never mind," I said. "Just throw it away. The panthers will be glad to have it. They don't mind a little sand."

"Go bother someone else," Mercy said.

"Who's bothering anybody?" he said. "You're such a baby."

I took the leg of chicken from her and tossed it into the beach grass. "Chicken is a panther's favorite food," I said. "Maybe we'll get to see one, once they smell it. The young ones are hungry this time of year. They don't hunt that well yet, and the mothers are tired of doing it for them."

"You're crazy," he said. "The panthers all died off."

"That's what you think. I saw tracks just yesterday, big as my hand, right up the beach there. Let's put out the rest of that chicken. I adore panthers." I opened the lid of the basket and rooted around inside.

"You're deranged," he said.

"I guess this is all that's left," I said, tossing bones. "The panthers won't mind. Chicken's chicken as far as they're concerned."

"Do you think we might really see one?" Mercy said. "Here, kitty kitty. Here, kitty."

"If you're late for supper, I'll tell Mother you got eaten up," he said.

"You do that," she said.

"I will." He turned from us, spraying sand on us on purpose as he ran.

She made a face at his back. His stick made a furrow in the wet sand that the waves smoothed away. The water had gone gray now instead of the blue and green it had just been. Everything was pale and dull. The lake hovered and quivered.

Mercy went to work again on the moat. Water came back up and made a pool. I kept Willis in the corner of my eye, in case he were to return. Almost everybody else on the beach was close to the hotel, while we had our own domain, a little bit away from the throngs.

The walls of the moat were crumbling again. I gathered stones to shore them up. A fossil showed itself as the water came over.

"This moat is hopeless," Mercy said. "Want to swim some more?"

I waded in slowly. I felt the Hand at my ribs, then it was floating behind me on its cord. The cord bit into my neck but wouldn't break. The Hand would never leave me. It needed me to take care of it the right way.

Mercy swam, face in, face out, her mouth round and gasping. The water was silver and felt heavy to wade through. Nothing seemed to have the right color to it.

The waves were almost too still. Far from shore, a shadowy ripple snaked beneath the waves, a sturgeon maybe, or cloud shadow, and then it felt as if the whole lake tipped, and the water where I stood was drawing away from shore and tugging me as hard as a big wave could have done. But there was no big wave.

I was pulled off my feet and then I was beneath the water, swept along, pressed down, flailing and struggling to be out in the above, hurled into a wall of rock and sand. I clutched at rocks for something solid. They came away. There was no holding. Sun and earth were gone. Then I was in the bright. I saw it then, a wave that shouldn't have been so big. Again I was under. The heavy water forced me from rising.

Between waves I fought my way up, and then I was in them. Wave after wave came over me. The shore kept getting farther away. Something grabbed my arm.

"Don't struggle!" said a voice. That's what it wanted, the watery deep, to take you as a prisoner, away from air and food and time and all you'd ever known. You had to kick against it, use every mite of strength you had, not listen to its lies.

My face met air. I gasped and choked. One arm was no longer mine, but in somebody's clutches. I kicked myself away. Again I went under. It had me by the hair then. It hurt like anything. Again I gulped breath. My captor yanked me along. I twisted around to pummel him, if one could fight a watery being. My fists met flesh.

No underwater demon had me, just a man. He had Mercy too, who wasn't struggling, but trailed along beside him, limbs limp. Another wave went over. The man kept hold. I let him.

We got to shore somehow, where people were massed along the waterline. Arms helped pull us out. Someone dragged Mercy up the beach. She didn't move. Her eyes were open just a slit. The man was rolling her on the sand and pressing on her and shaking her and still the eyes weren't all the way open. People came around us, hands over their mouths. Someone put a heavy wool red and blue blanket around me.

"She's a goner," someone said.

"Keep the children away," said someone else. A lady picked up a little boy and took him elsewhere.

I crawled to Mercy. "Wake up," I said. "Wake up. You're not dead." I shook and shook her.

"Stop! You'll break the poor girl's neck," the man said. He put his ear to her mouth, his hand on her chest. "She's breathing," he said, "but barely. And she's still out. Some-one get a doctor!"

"Right here!" someone called, and it was Dr. Larson, who came to see about my mother when Aunt Phyllis was worried. His medicine brought color to my mother's face again and got her out of bed, but then she threw away the rest.

"Hurry! My friend won't wake up!" I shouted.

A faraway arm reached out of the water and was gone. "He's way the hell out there!" someone said. A man who'd run into the waves returned, battered and shivering, to shore.

The doctor dropped to his knees in the sand, put a hand on Mercy's neck, felt her wrist, opened one of her eyes with two fingers. "Somebody fold up that blanket and put it under her feet," he said. "Higher. Good. Young lady! Can you hear me?"

The life-saving men were arriving in their crisp caps, with lifeboats on a rig. Mr. Dell was with them, waving his arms and shouting. "Step it up, men! Get in the water! *Move!*"

Mercy let out a deep sigh and opened her eyes. "Do you know where you are?" the doctor said.

"Beach," she said. "Violet! There you are! I didn't know if—" She started to sit up and tried to kick the blanket away, but the doctor shushed her and eased her head back down.

"Don't get up yet," he said. "Are you dizzy?"

She wasn't dizzy, she knew her name, she knew what year it was. The doctor was called over by a lady whose elderly companion was weakly fanning herself with a hanky.

"You two just stay put," Doctor Larson told us. "Let your people find you—don't go running around getting in the way."

Mercy and I huddled in the blanket. She was pale and shuddering. Men bounded into the surf with ropes. The boats bounced and careened. One of the rescue crew fell in the water and lost his cap. And there was Miss Nadia with her tripod, setting up to photograph the launch. She saw me, rushed over, leaving the camera and everything else, and gathered me in a tight embrace.

"I was scared out of my wits!" she said. "I thought you were in the water. I thought—"

And there was Mrs. Rankin, running up behind her. "I'd like to know how my daughter almost drowned!" Mrs. Rankin snapped at Miss Nadia. "Why were these girls swimming unsupervised?"

"I-I wasn't far away," Miss Nadia stammered. She wasn't often taken aback by anybody.

"Careless! I should have known you'd be careless! A woman with no children—"

"Please. The waves came suddenly from nowhere," Miss Nadia said.

"I wasn't even swimming, Mrs. Rankin," I said. "I was just standing in the water and I got knocked over. I didn't even see the waves and I was right in the water."

"They're saying it's a rare kind of tide," Miss Nadia said. "It comes after a storm once in a long while. It couldn't be anticipated."

"Where's Willis?" Mercy said.

"The boys were at the tennis courts when this all happened, thank goodness," Mrs. Rankin said. "Worrying over one child is all I can take for today."

"But Mother—"

I hadn't seen him in the water, but he might have dived in when I was looking elsewhere. He could have left the beach and gone to the tennis courts or to the stables or the golf course or the bowling alley or the billiard room. Maybe he'd gone somewhere to make his plots, or read about old bones, or be lonely in his superior knowledge, strength, cunning.

"I can't be sure," I said. "He was *by* the water when I last saw him. I don't know about *in* it. He probably wasn't."

"Keep your eyes open," Mrs. Rankin said. "Don't move from this spot." She ran across the sand.

"The camera!" Miss Nadia realized she'd left it where everyone was running. "You're all right?" She too was gone. The camera had been knocked over and lay in the sand. Mercy and I watched the rescue boats. We were shivering in every particle, despite the blanket. Some of those who had been rescued began to leave the beach. Mr. Dell strode along the shore, having a word with everyone he passed. The sun was lowering.

Mrs. Rankin returned. She had Emmet with her, and no Willis.

"He probably went to get changed," I said. "He was cold. He wouldn't have gone back in the water. His lips were blue. Remember, Mercy?"

"I asked everywhere," Mrs. Rankin said. "Not in the room. Not in the bowling alley. Not—" Her face was in her hands.

Dread froze me. The copper hand, would it do such a thing? Beneath the blanket, I maneuvered the secret pouch so I could get my fingers in. The metal was so cold it burned me. *No*, I begged it. *Find him, find him, find him. He's Mercy's brother.*

"Children," said Mercy's mother. "We're going to pray."

We stood and everyone else closed their eyes. I kept mine open, staring at the waves and pressing on the copper with my fingers.

He's got to be all right, I told the Hand. *Please let Willis Rankin be all right. Please please please please please.*

Willis wasn't the only one missing. A rich lady's maid who couldn't swim a stroke was nowhere to be found, and so was the man who had gone back in after pulling me and Mercy out. Someone had seen him get taken by one of the big waves and not come up. Moments before, the water had been filled with flailing arms, ropes being cast, people being dragged to shore. Now all who had a hope of being saved were on the sand, surrounded by those who had thought they surely had been lost.

"He's always been a strong swimmer," Mrs. Rankin kept saying. "He might be far from shore, but he'll make it back. He's a strong swimmer."

Someone went for Reverend Rankin—he was over by Blue Lake, drying out the tents—and Miss Nadia said she'd take Mercy and me inside to warm up. We were both still shivering. The bathing dress clung damply to me and smelled like a wet horse. Nothing in me didn't hurt—inside the head, the passage of the throat down to the belly, heart, behind the eyes. Breathing made my blood ache.

Walking wasn't easy. I was scraped and chilled and horrified to the depths. Mercy must have felt the same, but more so. Miss Nadia was between us, arms around our shoulders, helping us to move on forward. A bellboy who wasn't Isaac Duvall opened the door. Miss Nadia led us past the glass case to the elevator.

Miss Nadia ran us each a hot bath. Mine was in the washroom that was the darkroom, which smelled faintly of the solution that stained Miss Nadia's hands. She stacked up the empty trays and shoved them in a corner and wouldn't let me help clear away the gloves and bottles and tongs. She had to pack them anyhow, she said. My eyes stung when she said that, but I wouldn't cry. There was too much to cry over, but maybe it could still come right. Willis was a strong swimmer, and so was the other missing man. The maid— maybe she'd been rescued all along, but had wandered off, and had been found by now, having tea at the café.

Miss Nadia had a flask of brandy, and gave me a finger of it. Mercy said she wasn't allowed if it was spirits. Miss Nadia said it was medicine, and any medicine you'd buy would have alcohol as an ingredient, but this was more pure. The brandy made me feel better right away, warmer and not so scared, but even when I was immersed in the warm tub, my heart wouldn't slow down. Of all things, I longed to see Willis, solid and real.

I didn't wish it. I was afraid of the Hand now, afraid of what it did to wishes, ignoring them or twisting them all around at its whim. My shift lay crumpled on the floor, covering the Hand in its secret pouch with the ribbon that had my blood on it from sewing it so tight. I contemplated tossing the Hand out the window. It would have landed on the veranda below, or on the sand, only to be found by someone else who didn't know what it could do. As soon as I was out of the tub I was chilled again.

Miss Nadia said we should go back to find Mrs. Rankin. Mercy was pale and wordless. We went out into the corridor and were waylaid by Mrs. Dell in a huge veiled hat. "Nadia," she breathed, "I must have a word with you. What is the meaning of this slanderous accusation? Why, my husband would never in a hundred—"

"Do you know what's happened?" Miss Nadia said. "There was a huge tide that came all the way—"

"A *tide*? This is a lake, Nadia, not the Bay of Fundy."

"A seiche, it's called. It happens in lakes. This young lady's brother is missing." She started for the stairs, guiding Mercy and me along, Mrs. Dell right behind.

"Where are you going?" Mrs. Dell said. "I need to talk to you, Nadia. Who else has been spreading these hateful rumors? There's absolutely no substance."

"I'm taking Mercy to her mother." Miss Nadia was annoyed. "The family's on the beach waiting for the life-saving men."

"It's serious then! I thought you were talking about a boyish prank."

"What prank? There were dozens of people overcome by this seiche—big waves, strong tide, all of a sudden out of nowhere. These two girls almost drowned."

"How terrifying! When was this?"

"It doesn't matter when. An hour ago or two. Why did nobody tell you?"

"For heaven's sake! What's this tide called again?"

"*Saysh*." Miss Nadia said it through her teeth.

Outside, those who hadn't left the beach were leaving. Mothers had their children tightly by the hands, or carried even the ones who were too big for carrying. Some seemed to whisper as we went by. Seagulls screeched above.

Mrs. Rankin and Emmet weren't where we'd left them. The whole stretch of beach was empty but for men loading up the life-saving rig and a couple of boys with fishing poles staring at something down the beach. A lean man was walking toward them from the place where they were staring. It seemed to me it was Uncle Fowler, though he was far enough away that it could have been a lot of people.

"It's getting cold," said Mercy, rubbing her arms. Beneath her eyes were crescents, dark as bruises.

"Isn't that Fowler Wilmot?" Mrs. Dell said. "Maybe he knows something."

We approached each other. "Afternoon, Mrs. Dell," he said, touching the brim of his hat. "Miss Zalzman. We're asking for people to stay off the beach for a while. We've had an unfortunate situation."

"This is Mercy Rankin. She's looking for her mother," Miss Nadia said.

Beneath his hat, his eyes said it. "The family's down the beach there," he said.

"Has the boy been found?" Mrs. Dell said.

"Yes. He was," he said. Mercy was white, as if she was about to be sick. "I'll take her over," he said. "Her mother's been asking for her."

Her feet were planted in the sand and she had me by the arm. "Come too," she said.

Mrs. Dell put an arm around Mercy's shoulders. "We'll all go with you," she said. "Hold your friend's hand, Violet." Mercy's hand trembled. Me holding it helped her.

We made our way across the empty beach. The gulls took off when we were too close. When we were almost to the waterline we could see people kneeling in the sand, singing a thin hymn. In their midst was a still, still boy, pale as the sand he lay on. His mother had her face against his. We had to keep on walking. It seemed our steps took us no closer, until we were almost on them, and it was then I wished I'd fled at the beginning.

Mercy's mother couldn't see her daughter, only the lifeless cheek of her oldest boy. Mercy's father drew her to him and welcomed the rest of us with his shocked sad eyes. A life-saving man was there with his wet cap in his hand, and some people from the Association, and Emmet. Nobody was crying, but for one lady who gulped her sobs to quiet them. The waves hissed and slid toward us and went back as they would do when all of us were gone and thereafter always.

"When you're ready, Mrs. Rankin," Uncle Fowler said, "the men are here to take him."

She wasn't ready, never would be, but had to let them. They had a stretcher. Miss Nadia and Mrs. Dell told Mrs.

Rankin and the reverend that they were sorry. What were *they* sorry for? I was the one who'd done it.

Miss Nadia steered me away. Mercy didn't need me now, or anyone. There wasn't anything to be done for anybody. Nobody was believing that they could maybe wake up to a new unsullied day, not this one that was sinking into the big lake and leaving pink sky behind for a while, the wrong color for the pale stiff stillness that was before us.

Mrs. Dell's shoes clacked along the boardwalk. "That poor woman," she said. "You don't get over losing a child. Never. It's a fracture of the soul."

She stopped. She laid a hand on Miss Nadia's arm. "That skeleton," she said. "It has to go. Before the day's out, Nadia."

"Go where?" Miss Nadia said.

"It doesn't matter where. I'm not superstitious in the slightest, but—all this. Bad luck indeed. Just like you tried to tell me. But let's get Violet home. We'll go with her. She's had an awful shock." She waved to a buggy standing on the road by the hotel.

"I'm all right," I said. "I can go alone."

"You brave, brave girl," Mrs. Dell said. "Maybe you should have something to eat first. You shouldn't go on an empty stomach."

I shook my head. I didn't deserve food.

"I couldn't," I said.

She smoothed my hair. "You're quite sure?" she said.

"Yes, thank you," I said. The buggy had pulled up. Miss Nadia squeezed my hand in her stained ones and told the driver where to go. Mrs. Dell took my arm and helped me in, then turned to speak to Miss Nadia.

There were still rosy streaks over the big lake, and stars above beginning to emerge. I had the driver let me out at our road. I didn't want to contend with my father's questions— where had the buggy come from, who would pay.

"Is it you?" he said, a voice in the gloam. I could only see edges—table, door frame, chair leg. Outside it was close to dark and inside it was darker. He was nothing but a voice— fleeting and out of nowhere, like the rare tide. Inside were lurking shadows, my grandmother's ghost, the empty house without my mother in it. I had nothing and never would. There was nothing anywhere but shadowy dust and the fingers of death that would grab you without warning, which-ever way you turned.

"You coming in?" he said. I was rooted. Any direction I went, terror would enclose. I stood in the doorway, where I could still see the little light the sky still held. Half inside, the wildness couldn't take me.

I heard his chair scrape against the floor. A match flared. The wick of the lamp ignited. I could see his face. He held the lamp up, casting light on where I stood.

"Little one," he said. He hadn't called me that since I was small. "Come on inside. You live here, remember?"

But it seemed an unknown, unfamiliar place, and once the sky was dark, how could you know where sky was, and once sky was gone, wouldn't air disappear? How would you know which way was up toward breath, which way was to the darkest deep? If arms took hold, how could you tell if they were bent on dragging you under, or would take you to shore?

I'd seen him once approach a baby hawk that had fallen from the nest. He came toward it slowly in the same way he was nearing me, one step, a pause, another. He crouched down by me. I could hear his breathing.

"What is it, little one?" he whispered. His hands gently cupped my arms, as if to scoop me up, return me to my branch. "Did something frighten you?" he said. "Tell me."

I shook my head. What could I tell? More than anything I wished to say that nothing was amiss, what did he want for supper and were the chickens fed? Why had he kept the house so dark? My mother—she made sure the lamps were filled and ready to be lit, made sure we had berries most mornings, kept our clothes from moldering into rags. Why feed the chickens, anyhow? Why not set them free and let the hawks have them?

He touched my cheek. The skin of his fingers was rough and worn, but he tried to make them tender to soothe me, and never would they be soft from all the work that tore and tired him. My mother's hands were always soft and smelled of cream that she rubbed on at night from Peterssen's store and gave to me for my hands, until she took it with her. . . .

"I didn't mean to," I said. "All I wanted—just—for Mama!—for Mama and Fry—" Then I was gulping, as if there would never be enough air, and floods came out of me, words that didn't tell and water that didn't wash anything away, and his arms were around me, my head against his chest, and I could hear his heart.

"We all do things we didn't mean to," he said. "Maybe I can help you straighten it out."

"It's too late! The powers got stirred up!—wind, and lightning, and a huge wave, but invisible! And Willis—"

I thought I would fly apart. His arms encircled. We were on the floor. My feet had given out and were beneath me. The rest poured out—digging at the rat root place to bury Mama's moldy clothes and wishing on the Hand and getting two dresses, not just one, and Mercy's replica, Mrs. Dell's keys, Isaac Duvall. He smoothed my hair and held me up and let me cry into his chest until I was out of tears.

"I'm sorry," was all he said. "I'm so sorry." Out the door I could see nothing, as night had fully fallen. Foxes roamed, and the owls, and they would find what they could. Inside, the lamplight reached the corners. Even the spiderwebs shone. Fairy nets, Mama called them.

I sat up. Tears streaked his face. He didn't try to hide them from me or wipe them away. He stood and shook out his bad leg. "Foot's asleep," he said, holding out his hand to help me off the floor. He led me to a chair, hobbling, and pointed for me to sit. He opened the stove door and threw in the handful of twigs and leaves that were left in the kindling box and blew on the embers. Something caught.

"Nothing you did made that boy drown," he said, putting fresh water in the kettle. "You hear me?" The kettle clanged against the stove. He measured tea into the pot—the mint my mother gathered from the banks of the stream, not the black store kind.

It wasn't that I believed him, but I wanted to. He didn't

believe in anything that he couldn't exactly see—not Jesus, not animals inside of people, not magic. He said no more about anything until I'd had a cup of tea and bread with jam he coaxed me to eat. I thought I wasn't hungry, but I wolfed it. He himself had nothing.

"I should have realized," he said. "I haven't seen things right. You've got to have your mother back." More tears came down, but he was almost smiling. "It's just—I don't know what her plans are. But you and I, we'll just go on up there and see." His mouth quivered.

"But you don't know where," I said.

"Well, I don't want you worrying about it. I'll figure it all out. You with me?"

How could I not be? I would have gone with him anywhere, especially there—wherever it was. Of course, he often had his brainstorms. He'd draw a new chicken coop on a paper bag, mark the ground out, get the wood, and then he wouldn't build it, but would try and shore up the old one's sagging walls instead. He often made plans that never got past talk—land he would clear for the raspberries, books he would read to me, fish he'd catch once he fixed the skiff that rotted in the shed—and a trip to the unknown north might be forgotten in the light of day.

I went up to bed. I didn't take out the copper hand or wonder what it would do for me or to me. My room smelled damp from rain leaking in. I opened up the window and heard the lake like a breathing creature. I left the window open. Let whatever would come for me come.

It wasn't that I was happy. It didn't seem I ever could be,

even for a fleeting moment, after all I'd done. But he had of-fered something, anyway, and there was nothing more I would have asked for if I was doing any asking.

Most likely he'd remember nothing in the morning, or there would be a dozen reasons why he couldn't leave, or he would go without me, never again to return. But I wanted to believe him, and just before I fell into oblivion, I let myself.

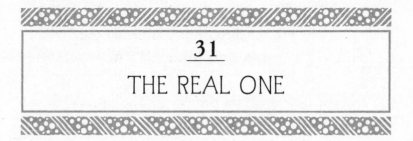

31
THE REAL ONE

If I'd had an endless wish supply I would have wished to walk into town instead of being taken by plodding old Bonny in the cart, because at least with walking you don't have to think about being locked away for decades and instead you'd be noticing that there's more beach pea blooming this year than ever before, or looking into the stands of maples for the shy, elusive woodchuck, or hearing woodpeckers.

The Hand was docile in its secret pocket. I couldn't just leave it unattended while I was being herded from jail cell to reform school. Maybe the Hand would finally pity me and get me a short sentence before being discovered on my person by the warden. Then it could have a restful life in a museum. Its powers would be over with. Maybe that would be best.

My father had us go to Aunt Phyllis first. She'd have been madder if we didn't. The front door was locked, which it never was, and we had to stand on the porch with my father looking grim. Finally she let us in.

"What a night." She locked the door behind us. "Violet, you may go into the kitchen while your father and I talk."

"She's why we're here," my father said. "We've got something to sort out."

"Did you hear about the drowning? The boy who found the skeleton in the woods? Unthinkable. The poor mother."

"Yes," he said. "Terrible. Nothing anybody can do about that. But Violet's got something to say about the bellboy who's locked up out there. Isaac Duvall."

"That's what I was about to tell you," she said. "It's shameful, the ugly things people have been saying. Disgusting epithets, Henry, and wild accusations. I refuse to—"

"Phyllis!" my father said. "Let Violet talk."

I swallowed. "Isaac Duvall didn't take Mrs. Dell's keys out of her purse. I did. And I know it wasn't right, but I had to—I mean, I *wanted*, I wanted to get the copper hand back, because I was the one who dug it up, and it was taken away from me by force by—by Willis Rankin, and the summer people said it was their land where I found it. But it was ours, or I thought it was. And it really might be. And I'm sorry I didn't speak up before, but I thought the judge would come and there wouldn't be a case."

Aunt Phyllis looked at me, and not in a mean way. "Where are we talking about?" she said.

"Just west of the stream," my father said. "South of the road."

"I've got the deed map somewhere," my aunt said. "The piece was part of that strip that got cut in half. I was about

Violet's age. I remember how upset Mother was about selling it. Go see Fowler."

We went around the side of the house to the jailhouse. My father led me by the shoulder, possibly to keep me from bolting, possibly to sustain me. Uncle Fowler let us in the office. I told my sorry tale. I couldn't see Isaac Duvall in his cell, but surely he heard all that I said.

"You've caused a lot of people a lot of trouble, Violet," Uncle Fowler said.

"I know," I said. "And I'll do whatever you say to make up for it. He can go free now, can't he?"

"What about the money?" Uncle Fowler said.

"What money?" I said.

"The money you took from Mrs. Dell's purse."

"I didn't take any money."

"Well, Violet, someone did. You admitted you took the keys. What's the use of lying about the rest of it?"

"I'm not lying! *She's* lying! Nobody took any money! She's always losing and forgetting. Ask anybody who's ever been around her!"

Uncle Fowler turned to my father. "I don't know what to believe," he said.

"If my daughter says she didn't take money, then she didn't," my father said. "Tell that purse woman what really happened, and get Mr. Duvall out of here."

Uncle Fowler clanked the keys on a ring on his belt and frowned at me. "You could have ruined a man's life. Go make your peace with him."

He unlocked the barred door and pushed me, not hard but with purpose, into the corridor between the two cells. Isaac Duvall sat on his cot, neatly made up with a blue blanket and a pillow with a white case. The hamper that Miss Nadia and I had packed for him served as a table with a half-eaten apple on it.

My uncle stood at the desk with the telephone at his ear. His mouth was moving. I couldn't hear his words. My father watched him talk. It seemed that the telephones were working again. Maybe everything would stop getting worse now.

"Mr. Duvall," I said. "I was the one who took Mrs. Dell's keys. I should have said so right at the beginning, and I didn't. I wanted the copper hand that was in the glass case. I thought I had a right to have it. So it's my fault you had to be in jail, and I'm very, very sorry. I wish none of this had ever happened."

"It didn't just happen," he said. "You did things. Or didn't do them."

"I know," I said. A long silence passed.

"I tried to tell Mrs. Dell," I said. "And then I thought that Uncle Fowler would let you go because there wasn't any evidence. And then I thought the judge would. And I'm really, really, really sorry. And I wish I could make it up to you. I wish I could."

I could feel the small weight of the Hand below my shoulder blade. Maybe it would hear me. It was a true and fervent wish.

"You can't," Isaac Duvall said.

When you say you're sorry to somebody, they're supposed to tell you it's fine, but nothing would ever be fine again, if anything had ever been fine in the first place.

"I wish it anyway," I said.

"Wish your head off," he said. "Bad things don't get wished away. You can wish for years on end for your gangrene to disappear, but if you want to stay alive you'd better get your leg amputated. You don't just go around wishing."

I didn't want that to be true. It was probably so, but maybe not. I nodded anyway, so he'd know I was listening.

"What was going through your mind?" he said. "Why did you want that copper thing so bad that you had to steal and lie and let somebody else take the blame?"

Explaining wouldn't make up for anything, but I couldn't deny what he asked of me. There was nothing else to offer.

"The Hand . . ." My chest was empty. I couldn't breathe all the way in. "When I found it, it was—I saw—it made things happen. It really did, I wasn't imagining. So I made a stupid little wish just to try it, and the wish came true."

He was looking at me. I was a ridiculous child to him, selfish and deluded.

"I wasn't after money or anything like that, even though we don't have any," I said. "Just—all I wanted was—just for everybody to be together. And get along."

"Everybody who?"

The truth, I realized, would sound like I was after sympathy. But I wasn't. I hated sympathy more than just about anything.

"My mother went away," I said, "and she took my little brother, and nobody ever told me where they were or why they went there. I thought the Hand might bring them back. I know it was crazy and selfish and wrong, but that's the reason. And I know it sounds like a big fat lie. But it isn't."

I took in air. My lungs filled. I looked right at him and didn't give him my innocent not-lying face, but just let my face do what it would.

"What made you speak up, then?" He still looked mad, but at least he wasn't feeling sorry for me.

I didn't turn or look away. "Everything was wrong," I whispered. Tears gathered and ran.

He nodded, as if any of it made sense. He was less mad, but maybe always would be, at least a little. I'd have stayed mad forever if I were in his shoes.

"Anyway, you finally did right," he said. "It just took you too long. Being locked up is no picnic, even for five minutes. But the books you brought helped a little."

Uncle Fowler put down the telephone and strode over to us, keys in hand. My father waited by the desk.

"Mrs. Dell found the money she thought was missing," Uncle Fowler said. "Seems she forgot that she put it in the hotel safe. She was just about to let me know, or so she said. Just about to! If it didn't slip her mind first. A careless woman, I have to say."

He unlocked the cell. "You're free to go, Mr. Duvall. If you'll come in the house, my wife will give us some breakfast while we're waiting for arrangements to get made. Violet, go tell Miss Zalzman what you did, and don't be surprised if she fires you. Go on."

My father gave me a nod and waited until I started off.

Then he followed my uncle and Isaac Duvall into the herringbone brick house.

I felt the Hand's small weight in its pouch. Miss Nadia would hate me. I couldn't exactly blame her.

She opened to my knock. "Oh, but Violet," she said. "I wasn't expecting you. We didn't say a time for today, did we? I'm just—"

"It's about Isaac Duvall," I said. "Him being in jail—it was all my fault, Miss Nadia. I took Mrs. Dell's keys. And he's getting out now, and Mrs. Dell's going over there to get him restored, and she remembered that she put her money in the safe and it wasn't in her bag like she thought it was. It was stupid and terrible, what I did. Everybody's mad, and they should be. I'm sorry."

She frowned. "Oh, Violet. Why did you do such a stupid and terrible thing?"

My chest hurt. My throat hurt. I took a breath and swallowed.

"I thought the copper hand should be mine, because I found it. And where I found it was on land that used to belong to my family and I thought it still did. And it was taken from me, so I tried to get it back. And I didn't know how bad jail was, and I thought he'd get out a long time ago, so I kept not saying anything so I wouldn't get sent to reform school. So that's why, but I know those aren't good reasons."

Her arms were folded. "And all this time you pretended to me," she said. "I don't like being lied to. At all."

I swallowed again. "I didn't want to lie to you. I tried not to. It was selfish and—and babyish and everything."

"But why did you want this copper hand so badly?"

I couldn't really tell her, but not telling can be a lie. "It just—I wanted it to help me, and it seemed like it could."

"And what did you need help with?"

"Just—just everything! The cherry trees that might be dying, and people who were being sad all the time. Things like that."

She unfolded her arms and looked me over. "I'm disappointed what happened," she said. "But you did speak after all. And that was brave."

"It wasn't," I said. "I really only told because the bones brought bad luck, just like Mrs. Agosa said they would."

"Well, that's honest of you to admit. I think you were pretending to yourself too, not just the rest of us, yes? So Isaac Duvall—Mrs. Dell is dropping charges? Do you know this absolutely?"

"My uncle let him out. He said there isn't any case against him because I took the keys and the money isn't missing. And she said she was going over there to make arrangements for Isaac Duvall."

"Well, it's quite a day for Alice Dell, then. I just left her. She's quite upset with me, not a surprise. I am arranging to pay everything back to her husband, everything—hotel room, the film he paid for, tickets, all of it. Since you're here, you can help me if you like."

"Only if you don't pay me," I said.

"No," she said. "That would be against the law." She didn't smile. She'd never like me again, if she ever had.

It was an awful day. We cleaned the insides of the camera

cases and packed the cameras and recorded every last photograph in her notebook. We emptied out the darkroom and took down the dark curtain and the red lightbulb and folded her clothes in tissue paper. Miss Nadia barely spoke or smiled.

Finally she said I could go. The room was stark and bare, the tables empty, the cases lined up by the door.

"Thank you, Violet Blake," she said, handing me a scrap from her notebook with the figures for my work days added up. "Tell me if this is right."

I examined it, but only because she'd made mistakes in my favor before and I didn't want to let her get away with that if there were any, but there weren't. "It's exactly perfect, Miss Nadia," I said.

"If you won't mind," she said. "I expect my money to be wired in the morning. If you will come at twelve o'clock, I could pay you then."

I let myself out. She would never forgive me. I was empty inside. I would never be sad or happy or worried or excited again. I would waft through the days like a dry leaf on the breeze. Better that than having hopes dashed at every turn. Hope was like pink ripples on water—the water seems to be a color that it isn't, then turns another hue.

The sun was half consumed by the big lake. The Hand moved against my shoulder blade, hidden from the world. The water looked full of rust.

I yanked the ribbon that held its secret pouch. The ribbon didn't break. I'd sewed it tight with my very blood. I shrugged the secret pocket off me, brought the Hand out into the last of the day, held it between my palms, lifted it to the darkening sky. The touch I felt was like the remnants of a spiderweb. Fingers brushed my face, and reaching to whisk away whatever stray strand or lost moth, I felt the touch of fingers with my own. They were hers. My mother's.

Those fingers had touched my face since I was born, soothing away a disappointment, reminding me of what I'd forgotten, how pretty a girl, how good I'd been, how lucky she was to have me. Never had they slapped or pinched or grabbed my chin to glare into my eyes. Aunt Phyllis did all those things. Her touch was that of a conqueror, while my mother always touched my skin like it was precious and perfect. When her moods went dark and darker, I began to forget her fingers gentle on my face, as if I'd never known them.

And so much had been forgotten, and there was the copper hand in my palm. And there was nothing else to wish but the whole big complicated one, the only one there truly was, the four of us together again, nobody quarreling or struck down with mysterious ailments, and Aunt Phyllis not meddling.

It can be the last wish, I told the Hand, if that's how you want it. And I made it an entreaty, not an order. *I want her back*, I told it. *Both of them. My mother. My brother. The real them, in the flesh. You can do it. I know you can. Bring them home, oh please. I beg you, entreat you. Take pity on a foolish girl.*

I headed for the river road. I passed the mill, closed for the day. Fishing boats were coming in. It was dark beneath the willows. I got to Mrs. Agosa's house. Lucy Thornwood opened the door before I even knocked.

"My grandmother's out by the river," she said.

"I can find her," I said. I somehow knew where she'd be, even before I was told how to get there.

"Down that way." Lucy Thornwood pointed. The slope was slick with mud.

"Mrs. Agosa," I said softly. My voice seemed to come from deep inside a cave of stone.

"Violet," she said.

I went up to where she was. "Take it," I said. "It's the real one."

There was no other way. I couldn't lie. I stood with my hand out with the Hand in it. She didn't reach for it. The river rushed along. The dome of her bark house was a shape in the near dark. The Hand was light in mine.

"It's the real one," I said again. "The one that's in the case—I made a fake. This is the copper woman's. It's just like you said. I never should have fooled with it. Everything I did was wrong. Please make it stop."

Still she wouldn't take it. "Put it down," she said.

I did so and backed away, as if it was a snake that might wake up and slither and strike. "What makes you think I can stop anything?" she said.

"You said the Hand—it wasn't just for one person. You know things."

"Things? You don't know what I know."

I didn't. I didn't even know what *I* knew. She reached into a pocket in her apron and took out a pinch of dry crumbled leaf and scattered it around the copper hand. She motioned for me to come near her. She put her hand on top of my head and left it there. She wasn't trying to make it better for me, but things didn't seem as bad somehow with her hand like that.

"You're still a child," she said. "You didn't want for anyone to be hurt. You only wanted what you wanted. Something about this copper hand—it helped you through your days." She took her hand away.

"Make it stop," I said. "It isn't helping anybody."

Hummingbird wings were inside my heart. I wanted to be gone from there, to leave the Hand behind, to sleep and sleep . . .

"Nobody can make it do anything," she said. "It's got to be listened to. It has its ways."

"But people are dying," I said.

If there's magic anywhere, can't it make miracles, can't it undo? Or is magic just what children hope for when there's no use in even hoping?

"People die," she said. "Everything dies some time or another. It's part of everything."

"But the Hand—water—" I couldn't talk sense.

"There's a lot to find out," she said. "We'll need as much help as we can get."

"We?" I said. "I don't want to ever see it again." I'd been hoping she'd just bury it, or melt it in a fire. "I'm giving it to you," I said.

"It isn't yours to give," she said. "You know that."

She still hadn't touched the Hand. The dry leaves moved around it in the breeze off the river. It was the time of the evening when quiet hunters start to come around—owls and foxes, panthers, wolves. She was a hunter herself—one who bides her time, who can starve for many nights until the right thing comes along.

"This river," she said. "It's tired of carrying logs. It's tired of being dirty from sawdust and oil. Do you hear it say so?"

I knew what she was talking about. Sadness was in everything. It wasn't fair that even a river couldn't be glad. The moon was impaled on a branch, stabbed through the heart. Leaves blew over the copper hand as if to bury it. "Tell it that you're grateful," she said.

"For what?" I said.

"For what it brought you," she said.

I'd talked to it so many times, and hadn't ever known how to address it. I crouched down. I didn't take it up, but left it on the earth with leaves around it and the river nearby. With one unsteady finger I traced the swirls on its palm. "Thank you," I whispered.

The tears came down. The river had its songs and smoothed the stones. I'd never be able to fathom it all—what had been, what could have been, what still could be. I couldn't know what was to be done or not done. It wasn't for me to know. The river sang its regrets and also its anticipations and joys, all mingled. I stood. The moon was just above the trees, the shape of half a pie.

The copper hand lay in the leaves. It was a small hand, the hand of someone needing notice, its graceful tapering fingers deserving of it. Mrs. Agosa bent to pick it up. Her knees cracked. She held it to the sky.

"We thank you," Mrs. Agosa said. Fingers reached—the wizened ones, the copper ones that someone had pounded and cut and polished with sand and bone and stone.

The copper shone in the light from above.

32

THE FEATHER LADY

"Now," said Mrs. Agosa. "It's time for you to go home. I'll take you."

"You don't have to do that," I said.

"I think I do," she said.

We walked. She wasn't slow. She didn't speak, and I was out of questions. We took the back road. From her house it was the straightest way. Most likely she would tell my father about the copper hand. It was hers now. She could talk about it all she wanted.

We came to the path that went from the road to the cherry trees. "My house is this way," I said.

"Keep going straight," she said. She meant for us to go to the rat root place. She led me to the grave. The canvas lay crumpled in a soggy tangle. Her hand was on my cheek.

"Sorrow," she said. "Anger. Everything you feel is deep. Maybe sometime you'll see it's a gift." What kind of gift was that, to be mad and sad every minute? She took her hand away, but I still felt its warmth.

She wasn't so mean. She wasn't like Aunt Phyllis, who simpered up to important people and wasn't nice unless she had to be. The path into the strip of woods was narrow. I stood aside so she would go first. She wasn't wolf at all, but some kind of bird. I would have said a crow, but she wasn't so ponderous and bossy. But she was canny as a crow, not fluttery like some birds are. Owl, maybe, or hawk, but no.

"You're a brave girl," she said.

She fumbled in a pouch she wore around her neck, shook some dry leaves into her palm, and let the wind take them while she said something that sounded like my mother when she was deep asleep or in a fever. She raised her arms, the palms pressed together with the copper hand in between, and threw her head back to face the sky. She stayed that way a long time, so that the blood must have left her arms.

Mrs. Agosa's arms came slowly down. "She came from the north," she said. "She was looking for people who were no longer here. She had teachings to pass along. Her own clan died—everybody. She was alone."

Tears spilled and ran. She didn't blink them back or wipe them off or smile them away, but let them course. I looked elsewhere.

"The copper hand was made a long time before her time," she said. "It was to help women pray, to honor the water be-ings. Women are the guardians of water. Or we used to be, sometime way back. In those days, women were respected. We went after wisdom. We were leaders. Priestesses. A man who struck his wife was punished. Men didn't go to war without the women's say-so."

Streams ran down her cheeks and made a pool in the bones at the base of her throat. And whether it was what she told, or whether it was water calling forth more water, or whether it was just the hideous stabbing beauty of the clear lake rosy from the coming day, I'll never know, but all the sadness I had ever known was but a drop in the boundless grief of ages, and I was a basin overfull and spilling over. And yet I strangely didn't feel exactly desolate, but was welcomed into a much greater sadness than my own, and the hugeness of it made me feel less lonesome.

She looked at me and almost smiled, stretching her wet cheeks. "The copper woman wanted for the Hand to be found when it was needed more than ever," she said. "Copper brings things together. Makes people understand better, or that's what I've been told."

She put the Hand back in her apron pocket. It was just the right size. "Now your father," she said.

He was in the house, tearing up a warped and rotten windowsill.

"This is Mrs. Agosa," I told him. "She and Mama know each other."

"I told Georgia to go away," she said. "I could have talked to you before. It was wrong of me."

"She never liked this place," he said.

"It wasn't the place," Mrs. Agosa said. "I know what I'm talking about. It wasn't this house, this town, this lake, this orchard. It wasn't even your sister. All that's just trappings."

He stood with the splintered sill in his hand. "My sister looked down on Georgia," he said. "And my mother treated Georgia like a daughter. That burned Phyllis right up. Georgia was nothing but sweet as pie to her, but she wasn't having any."

"Your sister didn't drive her away," Mrs. Agosa said. "It was trying to be white, but she's not all white. That's why she'd come and talk to me, to remember her mother and that side of her life. But all that did was make her soul more hungry."

He was looking at her. He wanted to believe her, but he didn't believe things easily. I wanted to say that Mrs. Agosa wasn't the kind who would say something just to make a person feel better.

"The way I was taught to believe," she said, "a soul disease needs a certain type of treatment. That's why I sent her up north to see a certain healer, and to be around her cousins and the other people there, the part of her she doesn't know. Stop thinking it was because of you or your sister or how she was treated in town. You too, Violet. It wasn't anything either of you did. Stop thinking that way."

"A person can't help how they think," he said.

"You don't believe that either," she said.

When someone comes to visit, you're supposed to offer them coffee, or at least a glass of water. My father was a foreigner to life. I went to make the coffee. Maybe the Hand would fix what it could. My father would remember how to dance. Cherries would overflow our buckets. Fry's mouth would be stained with their sweet juice.

It didn't seem impossible, at least.

Greenstone stood at the edge of the stream that fed the blue lake clear as tears. She pressed the copper hand between her palms. Each of the Hand's keepers had left her print. Storms had been appeased, feuds mended, battles prevented, starvation averted, floods diverted. Meetings, visitations, conversations, agreements, compromises had taken place. Requests, petitions, pleas, entreaties, prayers had been put forth.

The prophecies would continue to manifest. Undrinkable waters. Exile and disillusionment. But she could see a time when copper women would again heal rivers. Languages almost lost would be spoken by many. Robbed and broken people would be restored. The scattered would draw together. There would again be beauty where there had been desolation and ruin and stink.

The sky darkened. Sky beings listen when copper has something to ask.

"Thank you," Greenstone said. "Thank you, earth, for

your hospitality. May the water in you make me a bed of ice."

She lay on the dry leaves. The ground was good and cold. Her dress froze around her. Her hand covered the copper hand. Snow covered them over. White dress, white swan feathers in white hair, white snow.

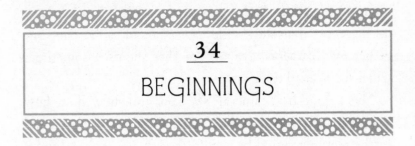

34
BEGINNINGS

So much that happened would sound just like a pack of lies if someone told it, even if whoever was doing the telling was a preacher who was never known to stretch the truth. Maybe if you believe enough in something, it will grant you boons. If magic wasn't on the job, I don't know what was.

That next morning after I gave over the copper hand, my father took me out to the orchard and showed me the trees. Where he'd cut off the black knot, new baby shoots were bursting forth. Under other circumstances, he might have danced. I'm sure he wanted to, but it wouldn't have been fitting on that day. He did smile. His eyes did shine, and not with rage.

I missed the copper hand. I remembered how just knowing that I had it made it seem that there were possibilities in the sorry barren world. I missed Miss Nadia. I didn't intend to collect the money from her. She had only offered it from obligation, and she'd never think of me a single moment in the rest of her life. And then she came. She had my money for me, more than she should have paid, and a present—one of her own cameras, a small one that she used sometimes when she needed to be fast.

"It's a good first camera," she said, and showed me how to load it and what to push. It took roll film, not plates, and so the pictures would be small when they came out, and it was no bigger than a book, so it was easy to carry places. "Put the film in here when you've shot the roll," she said, handing me an envelope, which had her name on it and a Chicago address and some stamps. "I can send your prints back to you. Promise to take some pictures, so I can know what you've been looking at. All right?"

She wanted to meet my father, and I didn't lie and say I didn't know where he might be. He was out by the rickety barn, building a cover for the cart out of wood that once had been a hayloft. He wasn't rude to her, but stopped his work and asked if she would like some coffee.

"I regret," she said, "my time is not my own today. I leave here in two hours and still have a hundred things to do."

"I could help you," I said.

"I wouldn't impose that on you," she said. "Mr. Blake, your daughter is a hard worker and has a sharp eye. I've enjoyed her very much." She held her hand out for him to shake, then presented it to me.

"Miss Blake," she said. "I look forward to seeing you in the future." I felt like a dignitary. I took her hand. It was a small strong hand with a sure grip, stained brown at the tips.

"Oh!" I said. "Can't I take your picture?"

"The light is bad," she said, looking up at the sun that was overhead. "I'll look ancient."

"Maybe over here by the shed," I said. Light streaked the ground there. A spider hovered in her web. The web shone if you looked at it a certain way. Miss Nadia went where I pointed and looked where I told her to look. A stripe of light went across her shoulder like the band of a quiver. The shutter snapped. It might be a good picture, I thought.

I went inside as soon as the buggy began to turn around, instead of standing and watching her go, and took the camera and the money and the envelope upstairs. The copper hand, I thought, is giving me my wish. My father's fixing up the cart so we can travel in it, and I've got cash so we can eat along the way.

But it didn't feel right, the sudden having. Others had lost. My father said he was going into town, and while he was gone I was to pick every last bean and tomato and ear of corn from the garden that was anywhere close to ready. There was a lot to pick. But instead of even starting, I went to see about Mercy.

The preacher camp was in disarray. Two men shook dirt and sand from a dismantled tent. None of the Rankins were in evidence. Someone thought they might return later that day. Nobody knew for sure.

I took the way home that went by the tree house. In her meticulous beaver way, Mercy had installed a pad of paper and a pencil there for the leaving of missives. Hers said:

It's my 13th day here. Only 11 to go. Doom and despair! I'm going to be desolate. I hope you get a day off soon. I made friends with a raccoon mother and her four babies. I hope your endeavor with the you-know-what was successful. Always, your friend.

There was no initial, because we'd been spies in an ancient time when girls pretended. It seemed that centuries had passed since I'd last climbed the ladder she'd made and found the copper replica she'd fashioned. The Hand had brought me its memories, caused Mrs. Agosa to spill her tragic tale, stirred up the skies and tides, maybe brought some green to my father's trees. I couldn't know what it had done or what would have happened if the Hand had stayed buried.

There was too much to say to Mercy and nothing to write. Instead I made myself small and still and listened to the leaves above and the waves on Blue Lake.

She came rustling through the woods. I knew it was no deer or fox. I handed down the ladder to her. She ascended as if she didn't trust each step not to snap in half. I couldn't not tell her some of what clutched me.

"You might not want to ever talk to me again," I said. "I wouldn't if I were you."

"It can't be that bad," she said.

"It is. It's worse than anything." I wiped the tears away, but more came down. "I didn't really lose the hand you made. I got the real one, and I kept it. I should have told you, and then everything wouldn't have happened. The waves, and—and Willis."

I covered my face and gulped for air. She didn't say anything. She would forever despise me. I could have had a friend, but I didn't deserve one.

"I don't believe it," she finally said. "Magic wouldn't do that."

"It could," I said.

"It could," she said, "but it wouldn't. It's not that kind of magic. Remember when you let me hold it? It was—I don't know what it was, but—" She took my hand and squeezed it hard. It hurt. She was strong. She could build things with those hands. "Anyhow," she said. "I'd have probably done the same thing."

Breathing hurt. My eyes stung. "We're going to where my mother is," I said. "My father and me. We don't know when yet, but it might even be tomorrow."

"When will you come back?"

"We don't know. It's far."

"Oh," she said. "It's good you'll be able to be with her, isn't it? You've wanted it for a long time."

I could only nod. We listened to the trees. Clouds moved fast over the water.

"Willis used to be nice when we were little," she said. "Mother used to say he had growing pains. He would have been nice again someday if he ever—if he—" She couldn't finish. I held her hand while she cried into her knees. After a time she dried her face with her dress and sat up.

"Father and I had a long talk," she said. "He knows a lot about death, because just about everybody in his family died when he was just a little older than Emmet. He says it's extra hard to lose someone you've been mad at. And sometimes

people think they made it happen because they wished bad-
ness on the person. But people just die. We all will, sometime."

"But the copper hand," I said. "I think it made those
waves. I shouldn't have played with it. I didn't know what it
could do."

"How do you know what it can do? Did it tell you?"

"No. But it showed things—or I saw them." I struggled
to remember. What had I really seen and what did I really
know? I thought there might be underwater beings who required appeasement that I hadn't known to offer. But I
thought they wouldn't know or care if someone wasn't a nice
boy or was a boy who was afraid of panthers. They'd take
whoever was out in the depths—a criminal, a saint, they
didn't weigh souls.

I tried to say this. It sounded made up but could have
been true. Proven liar that I was, she still believed it.

So we were still friends, and when I said I had to go and
dig onions she said she'd help me, but Mrs. Rankin needed
her for something else. When my father came back from
town I was hot and had mosquito bites all up and down my
arms and still had a row of tomatoes to pick.

"Look," he said, and he was more than smiling, he was
grinning. I hadn't seen his teeth in a thousand years. He took
an envelope from his pocket and handed me the whole thing,
not just one page.

"I was on my way to the telegraph office," he said. "I had
the telegram all written out—*Violet Henry arriving Sugar*

Island 3:00 PM August 1—but something told me to check the mail first. So I did."

"What's Sugar Island?"

"Sugar Island! Doesn't that sound like a made-up place? But it isn't. Mrs. Agosa spilled the beans. It's where your mama is, and big man Fryman Blake, king of the forest."

Dear Both of You, I wish there was a way for you to come up here. I know you'd both love it. Write me and tell me if it's possible. If we can't spare the money, Fry and I will get on the next train. Please let me know soon. Love forever.

My father had everything figured out. He took a stick and drew curved lines in the dirt. "Here's us," he said, "right on the shore of the big lake. First we'll take a steamer all the way up north to here. Then a train to here. And then—" He drew a line, a circle. The stick prodded the ground. "A ferry to Sugar Island. Mrs. Agosa is going with us. I bought the tickets. She knows her way around up there."

She wasn't going completely out of the goodness of her heart, I knew. She was hoping that somebody up there would know something about the Hand. It wasn't for me to worry about where the money would come from, and Lucy Thornwood and her husband would be glad to stay at our house while we were gone and take care of the animals and the garden and orchard until we got back.

But first there was the funeral. I was surprised my father wanted to go—not that he wanted to, but he said it wasn't a choice. I brushed his suit for him and trimmed his hair. I'd only been to one other funeral, and that was for Grandmother Blake. The one for Willis was worse by far. A lot of people came, but not the Dells or Miss Nadia, as Miss Nadia was already gone and so were the Dells, who had left that morning because everyone in town knew how Mr. Dell had swindled the preachers into buying the rat root place when it wasn't his to sell. Aunt Phyllis had found the deed map and proved it.

The Dells sent a massive arrangement that my aunt said was gaudy. Its scent permeated the church. Reverend Rankin began to speak, but couldn't for weeping and had to sit down, while Mrs. Rankin was grimly dry-eyed.

Aunt Phyllis came to see us later that day. Mr. Dell had decided that he didn't have the money to pay for Uncle Fowler to run for Congress, not that Uncle Fowler would have taken Mr. Dell's money anyway, now that he knew what a swindler he was, and Mr. Dell was going to sell the Voyageur Hotel and wouldn't be coming to Pigeon Harbor ever again probably, so Aunt Phyllis wouldn't get to go live in the state capital in a big house on the hill.

"Don't you dare gloat," she said to my father. "And what did you say to Fowler that made him so mad?"

"It's between him and me," my father said. "Or him and his conscience, if he's got one. You're still my sister, no matter who you're married to, and he doesn't have to like me."

I knew what my father had said, because he told me. It was about the burning of the village. My uncle said it was legal and all he was doing was executing the law, and my father said my uncle was in the rich man's pocket. But maybe he wasn't, anymore.

The next morning I went to see Mercy one last time. I brought Mrs. Rankin three jars of the soup my father made from our tomatoes and beans and other things. She cried and held me tight in her arms, and I cried too. I was getting tired of crying every minute, but Mercy said it was good for me because I hadn't ever been a crier before.

Mercy and Emmet weren't allowed to swim, of course, even in Blue Lake, which hadn't ever had a freak tide or an undertow, but Mrs. Rankin wouldn't listen to reason, and nobody in her shoes would have either. We could wade up to our ankles, but no deeper, and so we walked in the shallows and let crayfish scuttle over our pale cold feet as we chewed on mint leaves. We took Emmet to the tree house. Mercy held the ladder for him. He wasn't afraid to scramble up it. He said he could see almost the whole world.

Mrs. Agosa and Lucy Thornwood and her husband came that afternoon. Papa went to fetch them in the cart. Mr. Thornwood said he'd take a look at our skiff and maybe he could fix it, and then he could fish on Blue Lake while he was staying at our house. Lucy Thornwood brought her birch boxes and a freshly killed porcupine that she took the quills from and then roasted in the oven. I thought it would be vile, but she put carrots and apples in with it and it tasted wild and rich.

That night the feather lady's bones went back beneath the dirt. Mrs. Dell had told Miss Nadia to take them off her hands, and Miss Nadia had given everything to Mrs.

Agosa—the copper woman's beads and copper knife and the false copper hand. Mrs. Agosa arranged the bones on flat dirt and sang to them. Lucy Thornwood and her husband sang with her, and so did my father and I. You didn't need to know words.

On Sugar Island, Mrs. Agosa told me, there were people whose aim it was to consider the mysteries. Maybe, I thought, they would foster the copper hand, pass it around among themselves, give it what it needed, let it bring what it would. They wouldn't let it be captured by those who would scratch a label on it with ink that would never wash off. I didn't think Mrs. Agosa would keep it for herself. She knew, I figured, that the copper hand had a purpose greater than a single mind could know. But maybe she had desires she thought it would bring her, or revenge she thought it could exact. It wasn't my business what she did.

That night the house was glad again. It had been lonely, and ghosts prefer a lonely house. Grandmother Blake had maybe found her rest. I opened up the window in my room and listened to the lake and trees and wind having their conversations. I knew I'd better sleep. The next day we'd be up before light. Mr. Thornwood would drive us into town. We'd line up at the dock and wait to get on the steamer. Of all the times I'd thought of going on a boat, I'd never thought of heading north before. I'd always wanted to go south to where the cities were—Chicago and St. Louis and New Orleans and New York.

But that's the way of magic, maybe.

AFTERWORD

Long ago, when I was eleven, my friends and family found scattered human bones in a Michigan sand dune near our summer cottage. Some kind of expert said the bones were most likely American Indian, but not old enough to be archaeologically interesting. Therefore, we could keep them. My grandfather pieced together a skeleton and mounted it on plywood. He showed the skeleton to whoever wanted to see it, until my sentimental, superstitious grandmother insisted that the bones be buried in the woods and prayed over.

My grandfather was a good and fair man, a liberal pacifist minister who preached for racial integration and world peace, but it didn't occur to him that treating someone's ancestor's bones that way might be disrespectful to living people. Would he have assembled and displayed the bones of a white boy killed by a Civil War musket? Probably not. He believed in justice for all, but an Indian skeleton was a curiosity to him, a scientific puzzle, a relic of days gone by.

Thanks to the courage and diligence of indigenous activists, there are now laws that require tribes to be consulted when human remains are found. I believe that my grandfather would have tried to make things right if a living, breathing Native American had objected or explained. He didn't know better, but I hope he would have wanted to.

I remember how the bones felt in my hand, light in weight, heavy with significance. They creeped me out, even to look at, and I avoided them after the buzz of discovery wore off. But I didn't forget them.

Pigeon Harbor and Blue Lake are fictional versions of the real harbor town and clear blue lake near the sandy bluff where we found the bones. In the actual town, a sand dune was really flattened to build a hotel, and that hotel really did have to be rebuilt when the roof caved in after a snowstorm. A channel was dug between the lake and the harbor, and the lake gushed out. The real people of the Chaboiganing Band were yanked from their houses by a crooked land grabber and the local sheriff, who flung kerosene over homes and orchards and burned down the whole village, just as Mrs. Agosa tells it. For generations, many thousands of Native American children were forced to attend government residential schools, as Georgia was, and punished for speaking their native languages. Real communities, like Greenstone's, were decimated by white peoples' diseases. Not long ago, it was against the law to practice certain Native religions and ceremonies in the United States of America. The fictional Greenstone—and real seers—foresaw this.

Copper was mined in the Lake Superior basin thousands

of years ago, traded downriver all the way to Florida, fashioned into exquisite sacred art. Copper accompanied the esteemed dead, those with spiritual and political clout. I made up the copper women, but there could have been a female association of wisdom keepers and water protectors back then, as there is today.

The memory of the bones from the bluff gave me a way to tell something of the place that's in my marrow, a place that's always felt magical to me. When I was young, I was sure I saw fairies in the ferns by the clear blue lake. In its waters I felt the presence of invisible, powerful water beings. Once I saw a meteor shower and the northern lights, both at once. Often I've seen deep red dawn in clouds and water.

If that's not magic, nothing is.

ACKNOWLEDGMENTS

Heartful gratitude to the legions of light bearers.

Thank you to the indigenous copper artists of fifteen hundred years ago, whose work was so exquisitely crafted that white people refused to believe that white people didn't make it.

Thank you, ancestors, who made it possible for me to live among trees.

Thank you, beautiful outlaw family of sublimely conscious beings. You are my sustenance and juice.

So many on the hilly muddy road shared their wisdom, especially: Cathy Carter of the Benzie Shores Library, ace archaeologists Brad Lepper and Jarrod Burks, genius of light and lens Dennis Skotak, spirit worker Erica Swadley, and Anishinaabe waterwalker Josephine Mandamin.

I'd be protoplasm without the brain trust: Erich Anderson, Jacqueline DeAngelis, Kathleen Dowdey, Lucy Gibson, Heather King, Matt Knight, Paula Lumbard, Tamara

Major, Penelope Moffat, Michele Montgomery, Elizabeth Norment, Dan Pyne, Lenore Rinder, Linda Sandoval, Noelle Sickels, Saxon Trainor, Terry Wolverton, Natalie Zoe, and many others.

Thank you forever, those who brought my work to light: Kate McCallum, Robert Gould, Ellen Steiber, Susan Chang, and Ginger Clark.

And Aaron, my chosen one, who knows all.

I'm too lucky for words.

ABOUT THE AUTHOR

JULIA MARY GIBSON was raised by radical activist poets and grew up to be a communard, welfare mother, garage animator, visual effects producer, and mentor to unwed teens. She lives in sight of the Hollywood sign and spends time in the mountains of New Mexico and the lake country of the Midwest.